# THE 9:45 TO BLETCHLEY

*Also by Madalyn Morgan*

Foxden Acres

Applause

China Blue

# THE 9:45 TO BLETCHLEY

Madalyn Morgan

The 9.45 to Bletchley @ 2016 by Madalyn Morgan
Published worldwide 2016 @ Madalyn Morgan

All rights reserved in all media. No part of this book may be reproduced or transmitted in any form by any means, electronic or mechanical (including but not limited to: the Internet, photocopying, recording or by any information storage and retrieval system), without prior permission in writing from the author.

The moral right of Madalyn Morgan as the author of the work has been asserted by her in accordance with the Copyright, Designs and Patents Act 1988.

All characters in this publication are fictitious and any resemblance to real persons, living or dead, is purely coincidental.

British Library Cataloguing in Publication Data.
A catalogue record for this book is available from the British Library.

ISBN: 978-1533317483

# ACKNOWLEDGEMENTS

Edited by Morgen Bailey.
https://morgenbailey.wordpress.com/editing-and-critique/

Formatted by Rebecca Emin
www.rebeccaemin.co.uk

Book Jacket Designed by Cathy Helms
www.avalongraphics.org

Photograph of the woman and the policeman on the station:
Toni Frissell / Universal Images Group/Getty Images

The photograph of Bletchley Station:
Image courtesy of Living Archive Milton Keynes

Author photograph: Dr Roger Wood.

Thanks to author and friend, Debbie Viggiano, my beta reader, my mentor, Dr Roger Wood, for his brilliant critique, Christopher Hunter, an expert on the machines at Bletchley Park, for sharing his vast knowledge with me, and Jean Cheshire, nee Budd, who lived at Bletchley Park from 1938.

Thanks also to my friends, Jean Martin, Geraldine Tew and Kitty Jacklin, author friends, Theresa Le Flem and Jayne Curtis, and the LRNA - the Belmont Belles - for their support and encouragement. To Pauline Barclay at Chill With A Book, Gary Walker at Look 4 Books, Sarah Houldcroft at Authors Uncovered, Amy McBean Dennis at Oh Lovely in Lutterworth, W.H.Smith and Hunts Independent Bookshop in Rugby, and the Lutterworth and Rugby Libraries.

This book is dedicated to my mother and father,
Ena and Jack Smith,
and my cousins, Sally Glithro and Jules Bottrill.


I also dedicate The 9:45 To Bletchley to the estimated ten thousand men and woman who worked at Bletchley Park and its associated outstations. In twenty-four hour shifts, they worked on the complex tasks of intercepting, deciphering, analysing, and distributing intelligence received from enemy radio signals. Because of the Codebreakers' efforts, the Second World War was shortened by two years, saving tens of thousands of lives.

Last, but by no means least, I dedicate this book to the wartime factory workers, the majority of them were wives and mothers bringing up families while keeping the home fires burning, so the men and women of our armed forces had a home to come back to.

# NOVEMBER 14, 1940

## CHAPTER ONE

Ena heard the air raid siren start up. Some minutes later, she heard the planes. A distant hum at first, growing louder as they drew near. She panicked. Time was running out.

'Ena…?' her father called, his words drowned out by the siren's penetrating wail.

She glanced up. Thomas Dudley stood in the doorway of the annexe where she worked. Behind him, most of Lowarth's ARP wardens were evacuating the factory. 'Two minutes!' she shouted, and returned to her work. It was vital that she finished the job before she left. The following morning, her boss was taking it to somewhere called Station X. Ena didn't know where Station X was; the address was classified.

'Now!' Thomas Dudley ordered, ushering the factory's owner, Herbert Silcott, and his assistant, Freda King, out of the room.

'I'm coming!' Ena held the last of the wires between her thumb and index finger as enemy aircraft thundered overhead. Her pulse quickened but she remained focused. Gently, slowly, she massaged the fine wires until they were touching. She took several breaths to calm herself and, willing her hands not to tremble, lifted the soldering iron. It was crucial that she fused the wires and pulled them through the hole in the centre of a disc on what was called an X-board. Only then could she put the work in the safe. She took a final calming breath. 'One… two… done!'

As she slumped back in her chair, exhausted,

Ena heard an explosion. It was close. She ducked instinctively and looked up. Asbestos floated down from the prefabricated ceiling panels. She glared at them, daring them to fall. When she was sure the roof wasn't going to collapse on top of her, Ena leant forward, head down and arms outstretched, to shield her work.

Fine dust, like talcum powder, filled the air. Hunched over the X-board, Ena stood up and placed it in its box. Pulling on the lid, she felt the locking mechanism thud as it engaged.

Felt it. She didn't hear it. She couldn't hear anything except a shrill, continuous ringing that masked the sirens and aeroplanes. She put her fingers in her ears, jiggled them up and down, and pulled on her earlobes. Nothing helped; the ringing persisted. She was deaf and she was frightened. She wanted to get out of there but she couldn't. Only when she had secured the X-board in its locked box in the concrete safe, which she called the bunker, could she leave.

Lifting the box, keeping it level, Ena carried it across the room and placed it carefully on the counter. She prised the reinforced lid from the top of the bunker and-- 'What the--?' She jumped, dropped the lid, and watched it crash down next to the box containing her work. She whipped round. 'Dad? What the hell are you doing creeping up on me like that?'

'Creeping up on you? I called you half a dozen times. You ignored me.'

'What?' Ena pulled on the lobes of her ears again. 'I can't hear you.'

'Then we had better get you out of here,' her

father said, articulating each word.

Ena shook her head. 'Can't go yet.' Lifting the box, she carefully lowered it into the bunker and stood to the side while her father placed the concrete and steel cover on top. After snapping on the padlock, Ena put up her thumbs.

'Let's get out of here!' her father shouted.

Aware that she was holding her breath, Ena exhaled and followed him across the room.

As she reached the door, she felt the floor vibrating through the soles of her shoes. She held onto the doorframe and looked back into the room. As if she were a spectator in a silent film, she watched the windows blow in. The power of the blast ripped the blackout curtains to shreds, tearing them from their fittings, and shards of glass rained down on the desks and chairs.

Looking past the debris to the concrete bunker, Ena whooped with relief. It was still upright, still solid; the bomb blast hadn't touched it.

Turning and following her father, Ena ran across the factory floor, dodging lathes, boring machines, and other heavy apparatus. She was halfway between the annexe and the factory's main door when the lights flickered. Already feeling disorientated because she couldn't hear, Ena was plunged into darkness and quickly lost her bearings. She stopped and closed her eyes, hoping that when she opened them they would be accustomed to the dark in the windowless factory. They were not.

Unable to see or hear, Ena walked in what she thought was the direction of the door. She saw a flicker of light. A pinprick at first that grew into a faint beam – and she ran towards it. 'Damn!' she screamed, as her hip collided with the corner of a steel workbench. 'Dad? Is that you?'

'Ena? Stay where you are, love. I'm coming.'

'Dad, I can see a light. I'll make my way towards it.' Her words were lost in the roar of German planes thundering overhead. Arms outstretched, so she didn't walk into any other work stations, Ena made her way one tentative step at a time towards the faint beam of light emitted by her father's ARP lantern. Swinging like a pendulum, lighting up any obstacles in its path, the beam slowly moved towards her until her father was at her side.

Trembling, Ena threw her arms around her father. He patted her quickly before taking her hands in his and guiding them to the belt of his coat. Ena held on tightly as Thomas Dudley retraced his steps and led his daughter to safety. When the factory's entrance came into view, they ran for it.

Outside, Ena looked up in horror. Illuminated by a full moon, formation after formation of German bombers were silhouetted against a sapphire blue sky. Like flocks of migrating birds, the Luftwaffe soared over Lowarth before banking steeply to the west.

'Come on, Ena!' her father shouted. Mesmerised by the sight above her, Ena was unable to move. 'Come on!' he shouted again. He crossed his hands in front of her face. Ena shook her head. She could hear again. 'We need to put as much distance as we can between us and the factory!' he shouted.

The noise was excruciating. Ena put her hands over her ears. Nodding that she had heard, she followed him to the factory's air raid shelter. At the entrance, an explosion halted her. She looked back. A bomb had exploded next to the boundary wall, hurling bricks everywhere. Open-mouthed, she watched the factory's main door, which she and her father had just escaped through, bow and crumple. Then, as if it were cardboard, it disappeared into the building. Her father grabbed her arm and hauled her into the shelter.

'I thought they'd be going for Bruntingthorpe, or Bitteswell, but they're flying over the aerodromes. It's as if they don't know they're there.' Ena looked at her father. 'They must know, mustn't they, Dad?'

'They know all right, but it isn't the aerodromes they're interested in. Listen!'

Ena strained her ears for any changes in the notes of the planes' engines that might give her a clue as to where they were heading.

The realisation hit her and her father at the same time. They looked at each other. Ena shook her head, too shocked to speak. The distant rumbling of heavily-armed German bomber planes, interspersed with the high-pitched wail of air raid sirens, was followed almost immediately by the rumble of explosives.

A few minutes later, they heard the rat-a-tat-tat of anti-aircraft guns.

'Coventry!' her father said, with a catch in his voice. 'They're bombing Coventry.' The first crump of bombs was followed by a second, and a third, and so it went on.

Shivering in the cold November night air, Ena listened as wave after wave of German incendiaries tore through the city of Coventry.

Hours later, Lowarth's siren sounded the all-clear, and Ena's father, in his capacity as chief air raid warden, instructed the workforce to assemble at the factory gate.

When every employee of Silcott Engineering who had clocked in that morning was accounted for, Thomas Dudley handed over to the factory's owner, Herbert Silcott.

Raising his voice to be heard above the dull, continuous, sound of bombs exploding, and the chattering and cursing of the women, Herbert Silcott thanked them for the work they had done that day and told them to go home. 'Tomorrow!' he shouted, 'I shall get the builders in to assess the damage. If it is not too serious – and if they can begin work immediately – we should be back in production early next week, hopefully Monday.'

One of the women said she couldn't afford to lose a day's pay by not working on Friday. 'You'll be paid,' Silcott assured her. Several women, shouting at the same time, said they couldn't afford to go without their money either. Silcott put his hands up and called for hush. 'No one will be short in their wage packets. You will all be paid for Friday – and, if necessary, for any days you can't work next week. I give you my word.'

'That's all very well, Mr Silcott, but I'm

depending on my wages tomorrow as usual. The club-book man collects Friday night. I won't have his money if I don't get paid.'

'My rent has to be paid tomorrow,' another woman said.

'And my insurance,' said another. Half a dozen women called out in agreement.

'I understand!' Herbert Silcott shouted, above the assorted demands. 'If you come in tomorrow afternoon, after five o'clock, I will make sure your wages are here.' He looked at Ena, and she nodded. 'Is there anything else?' A couple of women shook their heads, and several muttered their thanks. The factory owner acknowledged them with a weary smile.

He looks all-in, Ena thought. She watched her boss take a handkerchief from the inside pocket of his jacket and sweep it across his face.

He raised his eyebrows, making the lines on his forehead appear deeper. 'Thank you ladies, goodnight,' he sighed.

Hugging her cardigan across her chest, Ena followed Freda and several other women to the factory's gaping entrance. Her father blocked their way.

'We need our coats,' Ena said. Marching on the spot, to keep the blood circulating in her feet, she blew warm breath into her cupped hands.

'It's too dangerous. The roof's damaged, it could come down. And there could be unexploded bombs about. Besides which, if the blighters need to offload any bombs before they go home to Germany, it may well be around here that they do it.'

'All the more reason for us to get our stuff and get out of here, Dad,' Ena said.

'All right! Does anyone need anything from the cloakroom that can't wait until tomorrow?'

'We need our coats and hats,' Ena said, shivering. 'It's too flippin' cold to bike home in just our overalls.'

A couple of women said they needed their handbags because their house keys were in them, but most had grabbed their belongings earlier as they ran to the shelter.

By the time Ena and Freda had collected their bicycles, Thomas Dudley was coming out of the factory with half a dozen gas masks and a selection of gloves, hats, scarves and coats. As soon as the women spotted him, they pounced. Grabbing their possessions, they called goodnight and went their separate ways.

'You all right, Dad? You look a bit shaken.' Ena relieved him of her gas mask and handbag, putting them in the basket on the front of her bicycle. The garments he had left in his arms – her hat, coat and gloves – she put on. 'Now you know what it's like going to the sales at C&A with our mam.' Her father raised his eyebrows. Standing on tiptoe, Ena planted a kiss on his cheek. 'See you at home.'

After assuring Mr Silcott that she had finished her work and secured it in the concrete safe, Ena said goodnight.

'Ena?' Herbert Silcott said, as she turned to leave. 'Would you come in tomorrow morning as usual?'

'Yes, Mr Silcott... of course.'

Arriving at Ena's side, Freda said, 'I'll be here in the morning to accompany you to--' She stopped short of saying where they were taking Ena's work and smiled at their boss conspiratorially.

'Yes, thank you, Freda,' he stuttered. Then turning to Ena, 'I'll check the work, make sure it is as you left it. As your father said, the Luftwaffe might offload their unspent bombs around here. If they do, and if there's any damage to your board, I'll need you to assess it and repair it if it's possible, before Freda, and I--'

This is my chance, Ena thought, remembering the number of times her boss had promised to take her with him to Station X. If she didn't speak up now, she might never get another chance. 'Perhaps I should come with you, Mr Silcott. With you and Freda,' she added, not wanting to put Freda's nose out of joint. 'I could bring my toolbox, and if any internal wires have been damaged...' Ena was sure there would be engineers wherever her work was going, but she didn't let that dampen her enthusiasm. 'I would be on hand if I were needed.'

Out of the corner of her eye, Ena saw Freda touch Herbert Silcott's forearm. He flinched, withdrew it immediately, and cleared his throat. 'After what has happened this evening – and what may happen in the night – it would have been an excellent idea. Unfortunately, I need you here to give the women their wages. Mrs Silcott will put the money in the wage packets, but I need you to check them against the overtime sheets. I'm sorry, Ena. It's important that it is done properly and confidentially.'

'Of course, Mr Silcott,' Ena said. 'Thank you.' Thank you, my eye. Anyone could check the wage packets against the overtime sheets and give them out. He just doesn't want anyone from the factory floor to know who earns what. Made sense, she supposed.

'See you both tomorrow. Thank you, ladies.'

Ena and Freda said goodnight to Mr Silcott, and set off together for their respective homes: Ena to a cottage on the Foxden Estate at Mysterton, just outside the village of Woodcote, and Freda to her lodgings on the Leicester Road in Lowarth.

Cycling in the blackout didn't usually bother Ena, she did it every night, but tonight she was glad Freda was with her. With the constant albeit distant rumble of exploding bombs in their ears, the two friends rode side by side along Coventry Road to George Street. Passing the Ritz Cinema, they said good night at the Ram Inn, where Freda turned left, and Ena right.

Ena stood on the pedals of her bike and pushed on down Market Street to High Street. The dark empty streets made Lowarth look like a ghost town. The shops with their blacked-out windows and brown adhesive tape, criss-crossing to stop them from shattering if a bomb fell nearby, looked sinister. A cross, Ena remembered from history lessons at the Central School, meant unclean. Samuel Pepys and the Great Plague of 1665 came into her mind.

Trying to remember how many people had died in the plague, Ena shook her head. To take her mind off biking home on her own, she often did mental arithmetic or thought about facts that she had learned in history at school. Tonight, having come close to death herself, she did not want to think about the outcome of the plague.

She free-wheeled down the hill, past the big white house at the bottom of Stony Hallow and the Fox Inn on Rugby Road, to the River Swift. Flying over the stone bridge, cold perspiration trickled down Ena's back and she shivered. The moon, full and bright in a cloudless sky, illuminated the grass verge, making a couple of potholes visible. As she negotiated her way round them, Ena's heart pounded. Out of the town, without the protection of the buildings, she would easily be seen from the air.

## CHAPTER TWO

Trying to ignore the burning sensation in her calves, Ena stood on the bicycle's pedals and pushed on up the hill. Her lungs felt as if they were going to burst, but she daren't stop. She turned off the main Rugby Road towards the village of Woodcote and flew under the railway bridge. Plunged into darkness, her legs tiring, she wobbled but she stayed on the bike.

Without thinking, she turned on the hooded lamp in the middle of the bike's handlebars, but turned it off when she was through the tunnel. The light, however faint, would pinpoint her location in open countryside. Besides, the moon was so bright she could see perfectly well without it.

Slowing down when she arrived on the crest of Shaft Hill, she veered to the left and coasted down Mysterton Lane.

Taking her feet off the pedals, Ena put the sole of one shoe, then the other, on the front tyre to slow the bicycle down. When she arrived at her parents' cottage, she lifted the handlebars and bumped the bike up the verge. Thick and uncut, the long grass further slowed the bike down until she was able to jump off.

The distant wail of Coventry's air raid sirens and the continuous crump of explosions had followed Ena all the way from Lowarth. She looked up at the sky. To the west, searchlights beamed into the cloudless night, in a desperate bid to illuminate enemy aircraft. She could hear the muffled crack and clatter of explosions, followed by the duller distant rat-a-tat-tat of anti-aircraft guns. The sky above Coventry was an orangey-red and looked as if the city was on fire.

Walking up the path, she saw the sitting room curtains twitch and a chink of light escape. By the time she had put her bicycle in the lean-to in the yard, her mother was at the back door.

'Thank God you're home and safe. Where's your father?' she asked, looking round Ena, straining to see in the darkness.

Ena stepped into the dark kitchen. 'Still in Lowarth.'

Lily Dudley tutted and giving Ena a gentle push, manoeuvred her ample body past her. Closing the door, Lily flicked on the light. 'Good God, girl,' she said, grabbing the clothes brush from a hook on the back of the door and thrusting it into Ena's hands. 'Get yourself back outside and brush down your coat. You'll never get the muck out of it if it dries.'

'I thought dirt was easier to brush off when it was dry.'

'Not when it's that caked in it isn't! And comb your hair while you're out there.' She pointed to a comb on the window ledge. 'You look as if you've gone grey.'

'Wouldn't surprise me if I had. The goings on at the factory tonight was enough to turn anyone grey.' Ena took the Kirby grips out of her hair, picked up the comb, and after switching off the light, opened the back door and went out into the yard.

\*

'Stew and dumplings for supper,' her mother said,

on Ena's return. 'Be a bit dried up by now.'

'It'll be fine, Mam.' While Ena set the table, her mother spooned dumplings, carrots, and a small portion of meat with gravy onto three plates. 'We'll keep your Dad's warm till he gets in.' Taking the plate with the largest helping, Ena placed it in the oven at the side of the stove.

'It's not right you being stuck in that factory on your own till all hours,' Ena's mother grumbled when Ena sat down to eat her supper.

'I wasn't on my own tonight, Mam.'

'Maybe not tonight, but there's been plenty of nights you have been.'

'Yes, but only when it's really necessary.' Aware that she mustn't say too much about her work but wanting to put her mother's mind at rest, Ena said, 'Silcott's do a lot of work for the military. There's no such thing as a nine-till-five working day anymore.'

'Why can't some of the other women stay late for a change?'

'They do. But the work Freda and I do is complicated. We're the only two who have been trained up to do it. Besides,' Ena said, 'I like my job and I'm good at it. Mr Silcott is ever so pleased with me. I might not be in the forces, but I'm working hard for the war effort, which,' she grinned at her mother, 'is why I sometimes have to work late.'

Lily shook her head and sighed, as if to say she had heard it all before, which she had. 'How much damage did the bombs do then?'

'What?' Her mother's question had taken Ena by surprise. She had hoped to distract her, stop her from worrying, by chattering on about work.

'I saw two explosions from your bedroom window. So you must have heard something while you were at work, or seen something on your way home.'

'Of course I heard the bombs. None fell on the town. At least I didn't see any bombed-out shops when I was biking home. Dad said, because Lowarth was directly under the Luftwaffe's flight path, the bombs were dropped by accident.'

Her mother leaned forward and tilted her head. She wants to know more, Ena thought, and carried on. 'Dad and I think it's Coventry that they're bombing. We could hear the bombs exploding and see the fires from Silcott's. Well, we couldn't actually see the fires, but the sky above Coventry was bright red. We wouldn't have seen or heard anything if it were Birmingham, it's too far away.'

Ena thought for a moment. 'You know, the air strike happened almost without warning. Air raid sirens are supposed to sound fifteen minutes before bombs are dropped, to give people time to get to a shelter, not when the planes are on top of them. Lowarth's air raid sirens were cranked into life before the Luftwaffe were anywhere near. We didn't hear Coventry's sirens until they were over the city.'

Ena wondered whether she should tell her mother that bombs had fallen near the factory. The grapevine between Lowarth and Woodcote, the nearest village to Foxden, was long and very active. Better any information about bombs came from her than from the village women in the post office the next morning.

'No one was hurt, most people were already in the shelter, but a couple of bombs did go off near the factory.'

Her mother put down her knife and fork and set her jaw.

'The planes were destined for Coventry not Lowarth. They didn't even bother with Bruntingthorpe or Bitteswell aerodromes. As I said, Dad thought the bombs dropped on Lowarth were accidents,' Ena said, trying to ignore the fact that she could have been killed by any one of them.

Her mother nodded, picked up her knife and fork, and began to eat. 'And your father? Did he say what time he'd be home?'

'No. The ARP wardens were still there when I left. I expect they'll help the Home Guard look for unexploded bombs. There aren't any of course,' Ena said quickly, not wanting to worry her mother, who shot her a concerned look and frowned. 'I'd have heard them fall, wouldn't I?' Ena concluded, with a reassuring smile.

Ena's explanation and her phoney relaxed attitude seemed to placate her mother, and she nodded.

When they had finished eating, they cleared the table, and washed and dried the pots together. 'Are you going to listen to the wireless, Mam?'

'I won't get a wink of sleep until your dad gets home, so I might as well.'

'I know. How about a glass of stout?' Her mother shrugged but Ena knew she would like one. 'You go through to the living room, tune the wireless, and I'll bring a glass in to you,' she said, putting the clean plates in the cupboard.

Her mother pulled herself out of her chair, took off her pinafore, and hung it on the back of the door. 'A drop of stout might help me to sleep,' she said, shuffling out of the kitchen in her old slippers. Ena smiled to herself. Her mother found a reason to have a drop of stout every time her dad was on ARP duty. And tonight, like all the other nights, it was to help her sleep.

After taking her mother a glass of beer, Ena returned to the kitchen, took a clean blouse from the washing basket and ironed it for work the following day. It was pale blue and looked smart with her new navy two-piece. If she was going to see the boss's wife she wanted to look her best.

'I'm going up, Mam,' Ena said. 'You coming?'

'No. I'm going to wait for your father. I expect he'll be hungry,' she replied, absentmindedly. 'I'll make him something to eat.'

'Don't forget the stew in the side oven.' Ena hung her blouse on the back of a dining chair. 'This feels a bit damp. I'll leave it down here to air.' Ena crossed to the fire and added a couple of logs to what was mostly ash and embers. 'Night night,' she said, bending down and kissing her mother on the cheek. 'Don't stay up too long.'

Her mother smiled, but Ena could tell she was worried by the deep lines on her forehead. 'Good night, love.'

Ena lay on her bed listening to the ferocious and unrelenting bombing of Coventry. So many bombs exploding at the same time made it impossible to distinguish one from another. Eventually, unable to sleep, she got up, threw her dressing gown round her shoulders, pulled back the blackout curtains, and looked out of the window.

The sky above Coventry was an even brighter red than when she had got home. Touching several objects on her dressing table, Ena came to her wristwatch. She picked it up, held it close to the window, and peered into its face. It was almost two o'clock. Conscious that she had to be at work at nine, she let go of the curtains. As they swung back into place, she felt her way across the room. Climbing back into bed, Ena pulled the blankets up to her chin, and closed her eyes.

Ena hadn't been asleep for long when she was woken by the roar of aeroplane engines. She sat up. 'What the...?' Diving out of bed, she opened the blackout curtains and looked up at the sky. Hundreds of German bomber planes were flying overhead.

She looked to her left. A steady stream of aircraft was coming from the west and heading east. Ena sighed with relief. The blitzing of Coventry was over. The Luftwaffe would soon be over the east coast and from there, Germany. She wondered how long it would be before the skies would be clear of enemy aircraft. She wondered too whether she should go down to her mother and insist they spend the rest of the night in the Anderson shelter at the bottom of the garden. The fact the planes would have to offload any bombs they hadn't dropped was the clincher.

Heading towards the door, Ena heard a change in the plane's engines. She ran back to the window. The entire German Air Force, or so it seemed, was banking to the right and turning south.

She heard the high-pitch wail of distant air raid sirens followed by the rumble of heavy aircraft. The nightmare of six hours before was being repeated elsewhere. She ran out of her bedroom, crossed the hall, and went into her brother Tom's bedroom. Watching from his window, Ena felt fingers of ice grip her spine as the Luftwaffe rose up from the south-west and began to bomb Coventry again.

With tears streaming down her face – and all thoughts of taking shelter gone from her mind, Ena stumbled back to her own room and fell into bed. Pulling the eiderdown up, she buried her head and tried desperately to ignore the terrifying, unrelenting, blitzing of Coventry for the second time that night.

In the morning, feeling as if she hadn't slept at all, Ena dragged herself out of bed. Yawning, she went downstairs and had a top-and-tail wash in the cold scullery. Before going back to her room to get dressed, she went to the living room and grabbed her blouse. She fully expected to see her mother asleep on the settee; instead, the room was empty, which meant her father had returned home safely at some point during the night.

After she had dressed, drunk a cup of tea and eaten a slice of toast with a scraping of margarine,

Ena crept out of the house. Closing the door quietly behind her so she didn't wake her father who had to be even more tired than she was, she put her gasmask over her head, placing the strap securely across her chest, and dropped her handbag in the bike's basket.

Wiping the winter dew from her bicycle's seat, Ena wheeled it down the path to the lane, mounted, and set off. She was about to turn onto the Lowarth Road when she saw her father cycling towards her. He looked exhausted. His face was pale and dirty, and his eyes heavy with dark circles under them. As they drew level, father and daughter dismounted.

'Mam said she was waiting up for you last night. When she wasn't downstairs this morning, I thought you'd come home and were in bed. Good Lord!' Ena said, leaning forward and examining her father's eyes. 'You need to get some sleep.'

'I will when I've been up to Foxden Hall and seen Bess.'

'Go home first, Dad. Mam's worried sick. She's in bed now, but I think she sat up most of the night waiting for you.'

'Alright. I need to change my clothes before I go up to the Hall anyway.'

Ena lifted her foot from the kerb to the nearside pedal of her bike and prepared to push off.

'You look smart,' her father said. 'Are you going out after you've been to the factory?'

'Kind of. I thought I had better look my best if I'm calling on the boss's wife at home.' Thomas Dudley's brow creased quizzically. 'I'm hoping to collect the wages from her, so I don't have to wait at the factory all day for her to bring them. Everyone else is having a day off with pay, except Freda and me. It's not fair. If all goes to plan, I shall go round to Madge Foot's at lunchtime, see if she fancies going to the pictures this afternoon. And there's a dance at Gilmorton Village Hall tonight that Madge and some of the other girls are going to.'

'It's time you had some fun, but be careful.'

'I intend to, don't worry.' Ena said goodbye. 'Oh, and have something to eat before you go up to Foxden.'

'When did you become so grown up?' Thomas Dudley asked, laughing. Ena watched her father cycle down the lane. 'See you later, love!' he shouted over his shoulder. As he neared the cottage, Ena set off for Lowarth.

Lifting her feet from the bicycle's pedals, Ena put one foot and then the other on the front wheel to slow the bike down. She had needed new brakes for a while and made a mental note to take the bike to Bradshaw's Bicycles later in the day.

Jumping off the bike, Ena wheeled it round to the bike-shed at the back of the building. She glanced at her watch. She was early, but she had planned to be. She wanted to check her work, make sure it hadn't been damaged in the bombing of the previous night, before Mr Silcott took it to… wherever he was taking it.

Every time he delivered Ena's work to this *secret location,* Ena hoped he would take her with him, but he always took Freda. It wasn't fair.

Freda was responsible for work that she delivered to a facility near Loughborough, so why did she have to go with him to this other place as well? Unless the rumours about Mr Silcott and Freda having an affair were true. If they were, he would want her with him. Ena tutted. She hated gossip and told everyone who talked about Freda behind her back that she would never sneak about with a married man. 'Besides which,' Ena would add, 'I work closely with Mr Silcott and Freda, I would know if there was any hanky-panky going on.'

Ena felt it her duty to defend anyone who wasn't there to defend themselves. She was sometimes wrong and this, she thought, after seeing the way Freda had touched Mr Silcott's arm the previous night, could be one of those times. She grimaced. Mr Silcott walking out with Freda occasionally was bad enough, but the thought of her being his mistress and *doing it* with him, that was too much for even Ena's imagination to contemplate. She shook her head to clear the image from her mind and giggled.

Peering into the factory through the gaping hole that until last night had been a steel frame and solid wooden door, Ena wrinkled her nose. The pungent smell of burnt oil and charred timber coming from inside the building was overpowering.

Taking her handkerchief from her handbag and holding it over her mouth and nose, Ena entered the main factory. She looked around and began to tremble. The events of the night before – bombs falling, losing her hearing, not being able to see when the electricity was knocked out –

overwhelmed her. The fact that she could easily have been killed, a reality that until now she had largely ignored, sent her running out of the building.

Outside, in the early morning mist, Ena sat on a pile of bricks and calmed herself while she waited for Mr Silcott. She didn't have to wait long. He arrived in his car on the dot of nine, Freda on her bicycle a minute later.

'Ena, I would like you to accompany Miss King... Freda... to Bletchley today.

'Bletchley?' Ena had never heard of Bletchley. Then the penny dropped and so did she, almost. 'Of course, Mr Silcott, but without you, I--'

'You'll be fine, Ena. I have to take my wife to Coventry. She is naturally worried about her parents. Williams Engineering, my father-in-law's factory, took a direct hit in the bombing last night. It has been reduced to rubble.' Ena gasped and put her hand to her mouth. 'Don't worry, my dear. Apart from the night watchman, who thankfully saw the planes approaching and was able to get to the shelter, everyone had left for the day. Hopefully they all made it home and were able to take cover in their Andersons before…' He shook his head. 'The night watchman telephoned my father-in-law after the first raid, and then my father-in-law telephoned us. He said it was too soon to know how many casualties there were, but the city centre was ablaze. He suspects the number will be in the thousands.'

'Do Mrs Silcott's parents live near the factory?'

'No, they live some miles away, thank

goodness. When we spoke to them the house only had a couple of broken windows and a few slates missing from the roof.' He sighed heavily. 'That, as I said, was after the first raid. Mrs Silcott telephoned her parents after the second assault, and again this morning, but couldn't get through. The BBC said the telephone lines are down.'

'She must be out of her mind with worry,' Ena said.

'She is. She's worried that her parents were caught up in the second bombing, which is why she wants to go to Coventry. And she's too upset to drive herself.'

'That's understandable.'

Mr Silcott smiled at Ena but didn't look at Freda. 'So I must take her. But first I shall fetch your work.' He disappeared through the gaping aperture and into the factory.

Although she had put on a smart suit and had ironed a clean blouse, Ena needed to be reassured. 'Do I look smart enough to go to this Bletchley place, Freda?'

'Of course you do.' Freda pulled at the buckle at the waist of her mackintosh. 'This is not what I would normally wear to go to Bletchley Park. To be honest, with everything that was going on last night, I didn't think you'd get the wiring on the rotors finished, so I didn't put on my best coat.'

'Ready, ladies?' Mr Silcott called, emerging from the factory carrying a large reinforced suitcase containing Ena's work. 'It's heavy,' he said, handing it to Ena, so she could get the measure of its weight.

'It's fine,' she smiled.

'Perhaps you can take it in turns. You won't have to carry it far. I'll take you to Rugby station in the car and as soon as I get home I'll telephone Bletchley, ask them to collect you from the station. So,' he said, looking from Ena to Freda, 'if you are both ready? We have half an hour to get to the station. If we leave now, you'll make the 9:45.'

Ena sat in the back of Herbert Silcott's big green Austin with the case containing her work on the seat next to her. Freda sat in the front passenger seat and chatted non-stop, telling Mr Silcott how sorry she was that the factory had been damaged in the bombing and that she hoped it would be back to full production very soon. 'And if there is anything I can do. Anything at all, Herbert,' she cooed.

Ena's cheeks flushed at Freda's blatant show of affection and she looked out of the window. As she turned, she caught Mr Silcott looking at her in the reverse mirror. He wants to see my reaction, she thought, and put on a smile of surprise, as if she hadn't heard what Freda said.

The train was ready to leave when they arrived on the platform at Rugby station. Ena carried the case to the train while Mr Silcott went to the ticket office. As soon as she saw him heading across the platform, she boarded. Out of breath, he handed Freda the tickets. 'I'll make sure someone's there to meet you when you arrive. Have a safe journey,' he said, glancing at the case at Ena's feet. Ena nodded, bent down, and took hold of the handle.

Freda jumped onto the train waving the tickets, the platform attendant blew his whistle, and Mr Silcott closed the door.

Waving goodbye to her boss, Ena suddenly remembered the wages. 'Mr Silcott?' she shouted at the top of her voice, 'Don't forget the wages at five o'clock!'

'Oh my God, I'd--!'

'The women are depending on you.'

Smoke and steam curled around Mr Silcott's legs. When it had devoured him entirely, Ena closed the window and followed Freda along the corridor.

## CHAPTER THREE

Holding the case with both hands, Ena struggled past several soldiers standing in the corridor smoking. 'How will we know them?' she whispered, catching Freda up. 'When we get to *you know where*?'

'We won't. They'll know us. At least they'll know me from going down before with Herbert.' The train juddered and Freda wobbled on her high-heels, falling against the window. 'Damn trains! I'd much rather go down by car.' She pushed herself off the window ledge and tutted at a smear of grease on her glove. Recovered, she walked on, leaving Ena trailing behind with the heavy case. 'This is it,' Freda called, opening the door to their compartment.

Ena looked through the window, fully expecting to see the compartment full of soldiers. First class carriages and compartments were ignored these days. It was often a free-for-all when troops were on the move, but today the overspill of servicemen only extended to the corridor. 'I hope Mr Silcott doesn't forget to telephone for someone to collect us,' Ena said, struggling through the door with the heavy case. Placing it under the window, she flopped into the nearest seat. Freda sat opposite. Ena was about to ask her friend what Bletchley Park was like when the door opened and two Wrens entered, followed by man wearing a dark overcoat and a black trilby hat.

The Wrens sat on the same side of the carriage

as Ena – one next to her, the other by the door. Both took documents from their shoulder bags and began to read. Leaning her legs protectively against her case of work, Ena watched the man drop his attaché case onto the seat next to Freda, and then haul his suitcase onto the overhead rack. As he took off his hat, a strand of blond hair fell onto his forehead. He ran his fingers through it, smoothing it with the flat of his hand into the rest of his brilliantined hair. He took off his coat and turned it inside out before folding it in half and putting it on the rack next to his suitcase.

Taking his seat, the man tugged at his trousers above each knee, lifting his feet to show highly polished black shoes. Her brother Tom did the same when he wore his best suit. He said it stopped his trousers from wearing shiny at the knee. When the man finally settled, he took *The Times* from his attaché case, shook it open, and began to read.

Good-looking but a bit fussy, Ena thought. With a sideways glance at Freda, Ena bit her bottom lip to stop herself from laughing. Freda rolled her eyes and looked out of the window. Trying not to giggle, Ena did the same.

The trees were bare of leaves and the hedges sparse. Cows and sheep grazed in the fields, and in the distance, women bundled up in thick winter coats were potato picking.

Ena shivered, grateful that she didn't have to work on the land. Her oldest sister Bess and a team of land girls had turned the Foxden Estate, where Ena's father had been head groom until the beginning of the war, into arable land. They worked every day from before dawn until after dark. Bess also had evacuees living at the Hall: her old landlady from London and her housemates – the youngest of them had a baby – as well as the children of her Jewish friends. They owned a theatre in London and had given Ena's second sister Margaret a job as an usherette.

Ena hadn't seen Margaret for some time. Shortly after marrying Bill she'd moved to London to be with him, and hadn't been home since. In a recent letter, Margaret said she and Bill would be home for Christmas. Bill's parents lived in Coventry, so they would probably come up sooner.

Ena's attention was brought back to the train's interior when the man sitting next to Freda laid his newspaper on his lap and took a pack of cigarettes from the pocket of his jacket. He opened the box and offered one to Freda. 'Thank you.' Taking a cigarette, she put it to her lips.

He offered the packet to Ena. 'No, thank you.' She enjoyed the occasional cigarette but not while she was travelling. She suffered from travel sickness and inhaling cigarette smoke would make her throw up. She swallowed hard. Just the thought of smoking made her feel queasy. She took a pear drop from her handbag and popped it into her mouth. She sucked pear drops on the train, the bus, or in a car. Like looking out of the window, it took her mind off feeling sick.

She watched the man flick the wheel on the side of his lighter. A small blue flame sprang up and Freda leant towards it. Sucking air through the cigarette, it soon ignited. Freda sat back in her seat, inhaled deeply, and returned her gaze to what was happening beyond the train's window.

'Ena? Got a pear drop?' her friend whispered five minutes later, after stubbing out the cigarette in the half-moon shaped brass ashtray under the window. Ena delved into her handbag, produced the cone-shaped paper packet, twisted it open, and gave it to Freda. 'Thanks.' Freda wrinkled her nose. 'Take the taste of the cigarette away.' She put a sweet in her mouth and returned the packet.

The man sitting next to Freda lowered his paper and looked at Ena. 'Would you like a sweet?' she asked.

'Thank you.' He took a pear drop, held it between his fingers, and looked at it curiously. After an encouraging nod from Ena, he put it in his mouth and crunched. 'Ah! You said sweet, but the taste is sharp.' His eyes sparkled with amusement, and after running his tongue along his front teeth, he said, 'It is good. Thank you.' He lifted his paper and resumed reading.

Ena was thinking how strange it was that the man didn't know what a pear drop tasted like when she heard the train's brakes hiss and engage. The train was pulling into Northampton station. She looked along the platform. People were standing two deep waiting to board. A group of soldiers were smoking cigarettes. After throwing the stubs to the ground, and stamping them out, they hauled their kit bags onto their shoulders and filed onto the train.

The door opened and Ena turned to see two men in black-belted mackintoshes and black trilbies enter. They looked so alike they could have been brothers. On closer inspection, the shorter of the men had a round face, the taller man's face was angular. They both had dark hair and blue eyes. She wondered if they might be Irish.

'Magazine, Ena?' Freda asked, forcing a *Woman's Own* into Ena's hands and frowning.

'What? Oh, thank you,' Ena said, realising that she had been staring at the two men. Opening the magazine, she glanced down at the case but then decided she shouldn't attract attention to herself. She lifted her head and turned a page of the magazine. Pretending to read, she sat back in her seat and mouthed, Sorry.

'Tickets please!'

Most people had their tickets ready. Ena didn't have one. Mr Silcott had given Freda both tickets, which she handed over. The ticket inspector ripped the tickets in half, put the Rugby to Bletchley section in a leather shoulder bag, and gave Freda the return stubs.

'I'm going to wash my hands, Freda,' Ena whispered, and carefully stepping round the feet of the other passengers, she left the compartment. Walking along the corridor, more to stretch her legs than anything, she saw the door to the toilet. The oblong panel by the handle said "vacant" and she entered. She didn't need to go to the toilet, but she went anyway. Better to go now than have to ask where the Ladies was when she got to--

She felt sick. She always did when she travelled, but this was different. Today, just thinking about where she was going made her tummy reel. She slid back the small window above the sink and inhaled. The acrid smell of soot and smoke filled her nostrils, stinging the back of her throat. She exhaled, then held her breath as the cold air rushed over her face.

Feeling somewhat better, Ena washed and dried her hands, refreshed her lipstick and combed the wave at the front of her hair back into place. She leant into the small mirror. She looked pale. 'Lack of sleep,' she said to herself then took a deep breath to settle her tummy. She didn't think she would be physically sick. Today she felt more nervous than anything. She had wanted to go to the *top-secret place* – where her work ended up – for months. Now she was almost there, she would give anything not to be going.

On the way back to the compartment, she felt the train judder and slow down. As she opened the compartment door, Freda was talking to the man next to her. She was telling him their cover story. 'We're going to visit a friend who we,' she motioned with her hand to Ena, 'used to work with. She married a chap from Bletchley and moved there. She's expecting, anytime now.' She looked at Ena, raised her eyebrows and nodded.

Oh heck! She wants me to carry on with the story. 'Yes, we're having twins.' The man laughed and Ena corrected, 'Not us. We're not having--' She looked at Freda.

'Now you're back, I'll go and wash my hands,' Freda said. Rolling her eyes as she passed Ena, she left the compartment.

Feeling she'd let Freda down, Ena absentmindedly took a pear drop from the packet.

She glanced at the man. He was staring at her. 'Would you like another?' He shook his head. 'I get travel sick, you see,' she said, putting a sweet in her mouth.

Freda returned as the train pulled into Bletchley station. It came to a juddering halt, catching her off balance. She lurched to the right as the man who had been sitting next to her was getting up. He put his arms out and Freda fell into them. 'Thank you,' Freda whispered, looking dreamily into the man's eyes. 'I'm not used to travelling by train.'

What a fib, Ena thought. Freda took the train to Northampton and back every time she visited her uncle for the weekend, which was at least once a month. Embarrassed by her friend's blatant flirting, Ena jumped up and busied herself by putting on her gloves. Hauling her gasmask onto her shoulder, she picked up her handbag. Perhaps Freda isn't having an affair with Mr Silcott after all, she thought, grabbing the handle of the suitcase. Perhaps she only flirts with him the way she's flirting with this man. Pondering her workmate's dalliances, Ena heard Freda call her. When she turned round the man had gone.

As they left the station, they were met by a powerfully built man in a dark blue coat and cap. 'Commander Dalton asked me to pick you up, Miss King,' he said to Freda. He looked at Ena. 'I'll take that, miss,' he said, standing almost to attention.

Freda nodded and Ena reluctantly handed over the case of work. 'Don't look so worried. Your work will be safe with Commander Dalton's driver.'

Ena smiled at the man. He didn't return the pleasantry.

The car was typical of the kind used by high ranking military officers. It was big and black, the kind she'd seen her brother Tom driving when he'd called at Foxden after taking army majors and generals to top-secret meetings in Northampton.

The man opened the back door of the car and laid the suitcase on the seat, pushing it gently into the middle. He motioned to Ena to get in. She sat down, lifted her feet up and swung them into the car. After closing her door, he went round to the other side, by which time Freda was sitting in the car with the door closed. He nodded and took his place behind the steering wheel.

During the short drive to Bletchley Park, Ena looked out of the window. On the left were allotments, on the right, a wire fence, and beyond that rows of single-storey buildings.

The car stopped and the driver wound down his window. Ena could see the security gate and the waist and legs of a man in uniform. She craned her neck and looked over the top of the driver's seat as the man's torso, and then his head, came into view. An RAF corporal, his face, framed by the driver's open window, looked first at Freda, and then at Ena.

'Got your identity papers, Ena?' Freda asked, hers already in her hand. Ena took the grey National Registration Identity card and Mr

Silcott's Bletchley Park pass from her handbag and gave them to Freda. When the man appeared at the back window, Freda wound it down and handed him their documents. He looked at Ena's papers and then at her face, keeping eye contact with her for what seemed like minutes but could only have been seconds. He glanced at Freda and nodded. Freda gave Ena her papers, and after a short exchange with the driver, who Ena heard explain why she was using Herbert Silcott's pass, the guard waved the car through.

As the car cruised along the drive, a huge red brick and sand-coloured stone building came into view. Ena looked at Freda and whispered, 'What a strange-looking building. I imagined it to be like Foxden Hall, a big country house. This looks like four country houses, from four different periods in history, all joined together. Look at the battlements, and the big green dome on the end.' Ena laughed. 'It looks like it belongs in the Hansel and Gretel fairy tale.' Freda nodded in the direction of the driver, put her finger to her lips, and mouthed shush. 'Sorry.'

The car pulled up outside the mansion's main entrance. The driver, first out of the car, opened Freda's door, before walking swiftly round the back of the car and opening Ena's. Clambering out, she looked up at the house and, overawed by the sheer size of it, stood on the drive in a daze.

She turned to Freda, but she wasn't there. She and the driver were standing in the doorway of the mansion waiting for her to join them. Ena ran and caught them up, side-stepping around one of two evil-looking stone griffins that stared at her from plinths on either side of the main entrance.

Before entering the mansion, Ena took her case from the driver and, breathless with excitement, followed Freda into the building. The inside was as dramatic as the outside. The stone arches and green and red stained glass windows reminded Ena of Lowarth Church. The floor was polished wood, and walls and ceiling wood panelling. Walking along the main corridor, their footsteps echoed, as if the building were announcing their arrival.

Ena offered Freda the case. She shook her head. 'I'll come with you, but you can sign the work in.' Ena felt the nerves in her stomach tighten as she followed Freda to the reception desk.

'This is work from Silcott's Engineering in Lowarth,' she said nervously to a man wearing an army officer's uniform with a security badge on the lapel.

The man smiled at her, stepped round the side of the desk, and took the work. Opening a large ledger, he turned it round so the pages were facing Ena and handed her a pen. 'If you'll sign here, miss?' He pointed to a blank line three-quarters of the way down the book.

Ena wrote her name in her best longhand and thanked the man. Pushing the large book back to him, she took out her identity card. The officer turned the ledger, and picked up the card. After studying both signatures, he said, 'If you'll take a seat.'

Ena and Freda crossed the reception area to a bench by the window and sat down. 'What happens now?' Ena asked.

'Commander Dalton, who commissions the work, may want to see us as it wasn't Herbert who signed in the work.'

'Oh.' Ena pulled a face and pretended to bite her nails.

Freda laughed. 'Don't look so worried. He'll only want to know where Herbert is.'

'Oh.'

'And stop saying, *oh*. You do an important job. If it weren't for us, and people like us, the boffins here wouldn't be able to do their jobs.' Freda nudged Ena. 'The reception chap's coming over.' As he drew near, both women stood up.

'Commander Dalton would like to speak to you, Miss King. Would you follow me? You too, miss,' he said to Ena, who was about to sit down again.

The two women followed the officer along a maze of corridors to an oblong hall. On the left was a window looking out onto a lake, in front of them a door, and on the right a young woman sat behind a desk furnished with a notebook and a telephone. Commander Dalton's secretary, Ena thought.

'If I can take your coats?' the young woman said.

Freda slipped out of her mackintosh and handed it over. Freda straightened the skirt of her suit with the flat of her hands, before pulling on the lapels of her jacket. Ena envied Freda her sophistication, her style. In a charcoal-coloured pencil skirt, with a kick-pleat at the back, matching jacket nipped in at the waist, and a dove grey blouse, she looked more like a model than an engineer in a factory.

Freda held herself in such a way that she appeared taller than Ena. She wasn't, but Ena was in the habit of slouching. She had spent so long hunched over machines, concentrating on drilling minute holes, soldering fine wires, and scripting tiny letters and numbers, that she was in danger of becoming round shouldered.

Ena took off her coat and gave it to the young woman who, after hanging it up, knocked on the commander's door. At the word 'Enter' she opened it and ushered Freda and Ena inside.

Pulling herself up to her full height, Ena followed Freda across the room to meet the man who commissioned the work she did, Commander Dalton.

The commander, a tall lean man with sandy-coloured hair, stood up as Freda reached his desk. She shook his hand and introduced Ena, explaining that it was Ena who did much of the intricate work for Bletchley Park.

The commander looked at her and smiled. Ena saw a flicker of surprise cross his face. He probably thought she was too young to have such responsibility. She had always looked young for her age, a disadvantage at times like this.

His focus returned to Freda. 'And Herbert? Not with you today?' He looked at the ledger that Ena recognised as the one she had signed.

'Mr Silcott sends his apologies. He was summoned to an emergency meeting at our parent company, Williams Engineering, in Coventry.' A slight variation on the truth, Ena thought, but it sounded better than *He's taken his wife to see her mum and dad*. But then Mrs Silcott's parents did own Williams Engineering.

Fully aware that the Luftwaffe had blitzed Coventry the night before, the commander sent his condolences, saying he hoped no one was hurt in the bombing. 'The work Williams Engineering has been doing will now be shared between the other Midlands factories. That will mean more work for Silcott's. Can you handle more work?'

'Yes sir,' Freda said, confidently. 'Mr Silcott will confirm as soon as he returns from Coventry.'

Before leaving, the commander gave Freda an envelope, which Ena could see was addressed to their boss.

After shaking Freda's hand, Commander Dalton turned to Ena. 'Goodbye, Miss Dudley.'

Ena took his outstretched hand and shook it nervously. 'Goodbye, sir.'

Leaving the mansion, Ena said, 'I didn't think we'd ever find our way out of the place.' She stopped and looked back. 'I wouldn't want to be stuck in there overnight.'

'It can be a bit scary after dark,' Freda agreed.

'Like the houses in horror films, all winding passageways and shadows in corners. I bet there's a ghost... Commander Dalton's a bit scary too, don't you think?'

'Not when you get to know him.'

Ena quickened her step and caught Freda up. 'Aren't we being driven back to the station?'

Freda laughed. 'We were only collected because we were carrying their precious work. Now they have it, we can whistle... Anyway, it isn't worth it.'

No sooner had they gone through the security gate than they were crossing the road to the station.

On the platform, Freda looked up at the clock. 'We've got twenty minutes to wait until the next train. Come on. Herbert gave me a ten-shilling note in case of an emergency. We'll have a sherry in the Station Hotel while we wait. The rest we'll spend on a taxi to Lowarth when we get to Rugby.'

Hooking her arm through Ena's, Freda steered her back through the portico columns at the station's entrance and along the pavement. The Station Hotel was dark red brick, with blue bricks arranged to make diamond shapes. The ledges of the sash windows were soot stained and a grimy film of coal dust coated the windows. It wasn't surprising. Bletchley station was a major railway junction and had been since Victorian times. Today, with hundreds of troop trains, goods trains carrying military equipment, as well as passenger trains, all pushing out clouds of smoke, it was no wonder the surrounding buildings were dirty and dull.

Freda pushed open the hotel door and strolled in as if she knew the place. Perhaps she did. Wondering if Freda had been to the Station Hotel with Mr Silcott, Ena stifled a giggle.

Freda sashayed into the lounge bar and dropped into an armchair to the left of the fireplace. Ena sat in the chair opposite. It was olive green with a high back and winged sides.

Leaning against a gold and green tapestry cushion, Ena ran her hands over the plush fabric on the chair's arms.

'Can I get you anything?'

Ena looked up to see a swarthy looking waiter in black trousers, white shirt and black tie standing next to her. He had directed the question at Freda.

'Two sweet sherries please,' Freda said, in a haughty clipped voice.

'Madam…' The waiter sounded bored, as if he knew Freda was putting on airs, which she was. With a tired nod to no one in particular, he turned and sauntered over to the bar.

Freda picked up one of several magazines from an oblong coffee table that stood between their chairs. 'This is better than waiting in that awful little buffet on the platform.' Clearly not expecting Ena to reply, she opened the magazine and began to read.

From the outside, Ena didn't think The Buffet looked awful at all. She would have been quite happy to have spent the time waiting for the train in there with a cup of tea. She had noticed a couple of cafés as they walked from the station to the hotel. One was called The Coffee Tavern which Ena presumed sold coffee and wondered how they managed to stay in business with coffee being in short supply.

She was miles away, pondering the difference between the coffee they would have sold before the war and the sweet sickly muck called Camp, when the waiter arrived with the drinks. He placed them on small cardboard coasters on the coffee table – one in front of Freda, the other in front of her. Ena thanked him, and the waiter left.

Taking her lead from Freda, Ena lifted her glass and took a sip of the sweet wine. It tasted strong at first but warmed her when she swallowed. 'This is the life.' Ena took another sip. 'I could get used to this,' she joked, relaxing in the comfortable armchair. Freda flung her head back and spat out a cynical laugh.

Startled, Ena put down her glass. Was Freda mocking her because she thought Ena was out of place in a hotel, which she certainly was not. Ena looked at her friend. It was more than that, much more. There was sadness in her eyes, anger too. And there was something else, but Ena couldn't put her finger on it. 'What on earth's the matter, Freda?'

She watched her friend knock her drink back in one. Freda banged the glass down on the table, attracting the interest of the people at the next table. 'On our wages?' Freda said with sarcasm in her voice. 'Not a chance!'

Ena didn't believe Freda's mood change had anything to do with money. She had been quieter than usual since arriving in Bletchley. She didn't like travelling by train, but surely that wasn't the reason for such an outburst. Ena looked at her watch. 'We had better go. The train will be here in a couple of minutes.' Getting to her feet, she picked up her gasmask and handbag. She no longer fancied the sherry and left it on the table.

At the door, Ena waited for Freda. She was gathering her belongings. Both sherry glasses were empty.

## CHAPTER FOUR

After three city types in dark overcoats and bowler hats left the train, Ena and Freda boarded. The train had come up from London Euston and there were as many businessmen as there were servicemen standing in the corridor.

Ena followed Freda, looking in each compartment for vacant seats. The train was full and they had to try two carriages before they found anywhere to sit, eventually finding a compartment with only one person in it. The passenger, an elderly woman wearing a tweed coat and a brown felt hat, was asleep.

As the train pulled into Northampton station, Ena glanced at the tag on the woman's carpet bag. 'Excuse me?' she said, tapping the woman on the arm. 'I think this is your station.'

Half asleep, the woman leapt to her feet and looked out of the window. 'So it is, my dear,' she said, in a voice thick with sleep. And in a flurry of browns and greens, she scooped up her belongings and fled the compartment.

Ena had begun to feel queasy and took the pear drops from her handbag. 'Want one?' She offered Freda the paper cone.

Freda shook her head. 'No thank you.'

Ena popped a sweet into her mouth, twisted the paper at the top to stop the rest of the sweets from falling out, and returned them to her handbag. With the sharp, tangy taste to enjoy, her stomach calmed down.

\*

By the time she had sucked the sweet to a smooth slither, she no longer felt sick.

Feeling better, Ena looked across the compartment at Freda and smiled. Freda cast her eyes down.

'Is something the matter, Freda? Are you angry with me?'

'No. I'm not angry with you. I'm angry with myself for spoiling your treat.'

'I don't care about a glass of sherry.' Ena waved her hand in the air, as if to brush the thought away. 'I care that you're unhappy. Is it the work we do? Is it Silcott's?'

'No. I like my job. It's nothing like that.'

'If you want to talk about whatever it is that's making you sad, I'm a good listener.'

'Thank you, but I'm being selfish. And I'm tired. I haven't been sleeping well.' Freda's eyes filled with tears. She looked away and cleared her throat. 'I'm sorry...' Ena took a handkerchief from her handbag, gave it to Freda, and sat in the seat next to her. Freda wiped her eyes. 'I'm upset because I'm worried about my brother.'

Brother? Ena had worked closely with Freda for six months and this was the first time she had mentioned a brother. 'I didn't know you had a brother.'

'Walter,' Freda said, with tears in her eyes. 'I'm scared that history will repeat itself and Walter will be killed, his body left to rot in a foreign country like Father.' Freda took a shuddering breath. 'Father was killed in France during the Great War. Mother never got over losing him. She shut out everything, everyone, and retreated to a place so deep in the recesses of her mind that we couldn't get through to her. She died a couple of years later, from a broken heart.' A faint smile played on Freda's lips. 'For a long time it had just been Walter and me. Walter is three years older than me and took on the role of father and mother. And for a time we muddled along happily.'

'You must have been very lonely.'

Freda turned and gazed out of the window, as if the answer lay in the darkening countryside. 'No, I was never lonely. I had Walter. We had each other.'

'Thank goodness you did.'

'Yes, thank goodness. Walter gave me the love my mother couldn't. It's strange, but as sad as those times were, Walter and I were very happy. But it wasn't deemed to be correct for two children to live on their own, even though Walter was fifteen. So after mother died, the authorities took us to live with my father's brother.'

'In Northampton?'

Freda gazed out of the window at the Northamptonshire countryside. 'Northampton? Yes,' she said, absentmindedly. A big tear spilled from the corner of her eye. 'My brother means more to me than anyone in the world. I miss him so much.'

Ena took Freda's hand in hers. 'Where is Walter?'

Freda's eyes lit up at the sound of her brother's name. But all too soon a dark shadow crept across her face and her eyes dulled.

'Somewhere in France. He's in the Army.'

'My brother Tom's in France too. He came home after Dunkirk, but he hasn't been home since.' Ena felt a lump in her throat. 'We haven't heard from him either. I suppose no news is good news?' She knew she hadn't sounded convincing and squeezed Freda's hand.

The two friends sat in silence, each nursing their own fears and worries. It was Ena who spoke first. 'You said you were tired earlier. So why don't you ask Mr Silcott if you can take a few days off? Go and see your uncle. You could make a long weekend of it. And you never know, he might have had news of your brother by then.'

'I don't know. With Silcott's having to take on some of Williams Engineering's work, I'll be too busy.' Ena could see from her friend's thoughtful expression that she was considering it. Freda wiped her tears. 'Whether I can get the time off or not, I shall telephone my uncle tomorrow.'

When the taxi dropped them off outside the factory, Ena offered to pay half the fare, but Freda wouldn't take her money. 'It's my way of saying thank you for listening to me tonight. I've never told anyone about that time in my life. I suppose it's because I have never felt close enough to anyone to confide in them, until now.' Ena bit her lip and swallowed her emotions. 'Besides, what's left of Mr Silcott's emergency fund will cover it.'

Arm in arm, the unpleasantness in the Station Hotel at Bletchley forgotten, Ena and Freda collected their bicycles. Pushing them across the car park towards the factory gates, Freda said,

'*Wuthering Heights* is on at the Granada. Fancy seeing it tomorrow?'

'Not half. I think Laurence Olivier is so handsome,' Ena crooned.

'When we've been to the Silcotts, we'll catch the bus into Rugby.'

Arranging to meet for a cup of tea, before taking the work order to Mr Silcott at his home, Ena and Freda pedalled off together, going their separate ways at the junction of Leicester Road and Market Street.

When Ena got home, her sister Bess was there. 'Any news about Coventry?' Ena asked, looking from Bess to her father.

'The BBC gave the names of the city's worst hit areas and thankfully the suburb where Bill's parents live wasn't one of them,' their father said.

'Thank goodness for that,' Ena said. 'Even so, Bill and Margaret must be worried to death. Have you heard from either of them?'

'Bill rang the Hall this morning,' Bess said, 'asked if we'd heard anything. His mam and dad don't have a telephone, so he couldn't get in touch with them.'

'And with him working for the Ministry of Defence, he can't get time off to come up, so Laura, one of the land girls, drove me over to see what was going on. She dropped me off and went up to the Hall to telephone Margaret at the theatre. Bill's on the road, but he's picking up Margaret after work. He'll be relieved to know they're all right,' their father said.

'And they are?' Ena asked.

'Yes, considering. Bill's father's faring better

than his mother. She's very tearful, but after her ordeal it's only to be expected. She put on a brave face and made us welcome. They were lucky,' Thomas lit a cigarette. 'They got to the Anderson shelter as soon as they heard the planes, and stayed there for the rest of the night. The worst they suffered was being cold.'

Ena shuddered, remembering the orange and red sky of the night before. 'What about the house?'

'Cracked windows, some slates off the roof. We boarded up the windows and Laura got on the roof. She repaired it in no time. Did a good job, too. They'll need to get a roofer eventually, but it's safe for now.'


'I wish I could have gone with Laura and Dad,' Ena said, walking Bess to the door.

'I think you have enough to do at the factory,' her sister said. Ena exhaled loudly. 'As bad as that is it?'

'Worse. There's a lot of damage. But,' Ena said, opening the door, 'it's only bricks and mortar. No one was hurt, thank goodness.'

Ena kissed her sister goodbye, watched her open the door of Lady Foxden's black Rover motorcar and drop onto the driving seat. She waved until Bess turned off the lane to drive up to the Hall. Before going inside, Ena looked up at the moon. A big round yellow orb, mottled like a marble, in a sky that was so clear, she could see every star. It'll be cold tomorrow, she thought. There may even be a frost.

## CHAPTER FIVE

Ena set out for Lowarth early. She was meeting Freda before going to Mr Silcott's house, and wanted to drop her bicycle off at Bradshaw's Cycles in Market Street first. Leaning the bike against the shop's window, she ran inside to ask if her brakes could be repaired.

Mr Bradshaw lumbered out of the shop. He pushed the bike along the pavement for a few yards before pulling on the brakes – and let out a raucous laugh. 'There's nothing to repair,' he said, shaking his head. 'Look here.' He lifted the front wheel. 'Worn down to the metal. Goodness knows how you haven't gone over the handlebars before now, Ena Dudley.'

Ena looked suitably aghast and scrunched up her shoulders. 'I didn't realise.'

'Come back at two.' Lifting the bike as if it were a toy, he returned to the shop.

'Not sure I'll be back by then,' Ena said, following him in. She handed Mr Bradshaw half a crown, he rang up 1/-3d on the till and gave her the change. 'Would you leave it in the alley for me?' She skipped out of the shop before Mr Bradshaw had time to refuse.

During the day, Mr Bradshaw chained and padlocked new and used bicycles in a metal bike stand bolted to the wall. After six he took the bicycles into the shop, leaving the stand empty for people to park their bikes if they were going to the pictures or to a dance at the Town Hall.

With the shortage of petrol, bicycles had

become the most popular mode of transport for the young people of Lowarth. Leaving your bike in the street after dark often meant it would end up at the gates of Bitteswell, or Bruntingthorpe aerodrome, but with Mr and Mrs Bradshaw living on the premises, the alley running along the side of the shop was one of the safest places in Lowarth to leave a bicycle at night.

Mrs Crabbe's Café was on the other side of Market Street. Ena could see Freda sitting at a table by the window. Ena waved as she ran across the road, but her friend was miles away and didn't see her. They had half an hour to kill before they needed to be at Mr Silcott's house, and ordered two cups of tea and two scones with margarine.

Refreshed, the two friends left the café arm in arm. Crossing Market Street, they followed the road round to George Street, and turned onto Coventry Road. The Silcott house was the fifth house on the right.

The pebble drive arced in a broad sweep to the front door. On either side of the door there were large bays with diamond-shaped leaded windows. On the left of the house was a garage with what looked like a flat above. Living quarters for a chauffeur, Ena thought. The Silcotts didn't have a chauffeur, but Mrs Silcott had aspirations.

The large detached house stood in an acre of neatly mowed lawns, those on the side and front of the house visible from the road. The back lawn, Ena remembered from having visited the house on previous occasions to collect the wages, was surrounded by colourful flowerbeds and evergreen shrubs.

Freda lifted the brass doorknocker and rapped twice.

A few seconds later, Mr Silcott opened the door. 'Good morning, ladies. Come in,' he said, leading them into a large sitting room. 'Please, sit down.' He showed Freda to an armchair, Ena to the settee, and sat in the remaining armchair himself.

'Goodness, where are my manners?' he said, leaping out of the chair. 'Mrs Silcott usually sees to the refreshments, but she stayed in Coventry last night with her parents. Would either of you like a cup of tea?'

'Not for me, thank you,' Ena said. 'I've just had tea at Mrs Crabbe's.'

'Nor for me,' Freda said, 'but I'll make you a cup if you'd like one, Herbert?'

Ena saw a band of scarlet creep up Mr Silcott's neck. 'Thank you, Freda, but I have to go to the factory to see how the builders are getting on before I return to Coventry, so I had better not.' He looked from Freda to Ena. 'I understand your visit to Bletchley was a success.'

Freda took the order form for the next job out of her handbag and, after giving Mr Silcott a short summary of the meeting with Commander Dalton, pressed the document into his hand.

'Thank you.' He scanned the worksheet and fabricated a frown. 'More work for you, Ena. I don't know what we'd do without you.' Ena sensed Freda stiffen, and ignored her. Crossing the room to a mahogany bureau, Mr Silcott took a key from his pocket, unlocked the pull-down top, and placed the papers inside.

As they were leaving, Mr Silcott thanked them again for taking the work to Bletchley and for returning with another order. He wished them both a good weekend and said, 'See you on Monday morning, Ena. Come in at nine, will you?'

'Nine o'clock,' Ena confirmed, and said goodbye. Freda walked on without her. Ena ran to catch her up. 'What's up with you?'

'Nothing,' Freda pouted.

'I don't believe you. You're mardy because Mr Silcott asked me to go into the factory on Monday and didn't ask you.'

'I'm his assistant! It should be me going into work on Monday, not you.' Freda sniffed. 'Herbert always asks you first these days.'

'No he doesn't. I'm only going in on Monday because we have a job order from Bletchley, and it's me who does their work.'

Freda shook her head and walked on. 'He doesn't think I'm capable of doing *your* work.' Ena didn't comment. 'But I am! I do all the stuff for Beaumanor, and it's just as difficult as the work you do for Bletchley.'

Ena needed to assure Freda that she was important to Mr Silcott. If she didn't, their evening together in Rugby wouldn't be much fun. 'Of course you could do my job. As his assistant, you could probably do his job. Oh, come on,' Ena cajoled, 'don't let's fall out about work. I expect I'll be up to my elbows in muck and dust, and opening boxes.' Ena tutted, linked her arm through Freda's, and jollied her along.

'Sorry, Ena. I'm not blaming you. I was just saying that's all…'

'I know. Freda, how fast can you run in those heels?'

'Why?'

'Because the bus is coming.'

Running and waving their arms to attract the driver's attention, Ena and Freda flagged down the bus and jumped on. Out of breath, they clip-clopped their way down the aisle to the back and joined their friends, Madge Foot and Beryl Clark.

Except for Freda, the friends left Rugby Granada Cinema in tears. 'Wasn't it sad when Cathy died?' Ena said.

Beryl sighed. 'If only Heathcliff had come back sooner.'

'His love would have saved her. She'd have got better,' Madge said, 'I know she would. Typical bloody man, getting there too late.'

'I like happy endings best,' Beryl said, 'when they kiss and you know they're going to live happily ever after.'

'I cry at them too,' Madge said. 'Happy or sad, I always cry. I know I've had my money's worth if I have a good bawl. Same with a comedy, but the opposite.' Ena looked at her friend and raised her eyebrows. 'You know what I mean.' Madge pushed Ena playfully. 'A comedy's meant to make you laugh, whereas a weepy is meant to make you cry.'

Freda stopped walking and stood with her mouth open. 'What is it?' Ena asked.

Freda laughed. 'Anyone would think, *Wuthering Heights* was real. It isn't Cathy and Heathcliff, it's Merle Oberon and Laurence Olivier, film stars who earn more money making one film than we earn in a year.'

'I know, but... Oh look,' Madge said, 'Next week it's *Gone With The Wind.* I love Clark Gable. We'll see it, shall we?' Everyone agreed.

'See her, Vivien Leigh?' Beryl said, pointing at the advertising poster of *Gone With The Wind.* 'She's walking out with Laurence Olivier.'

'Who is?'

'Vivien Leigh. It's been in all the film magazines. She's courting the film star who played Heathcliff in *Wuthering Heights.*'

'No!'

'Yes... Well, it said she was in my magazine.'

'I'll see what it says about them in *Starlet Magazine* when I get home.'

Ena yawned. 'I don't care who's walking out with who, I want my bed.'

'Don't be a killjoy,' Freda said. 'Who's coming for a drink?'

'No one. The bus is here.'

It had been a long day and the bus trundled along, making Ena feel even sleepier. When they arrived in Lowarth, the cold night air woke her up.

After saying goodnight, Ena and Beryl cycled off, leaving Madge and Freda, who lived in Lowarth, discussing which film they would see next, and when.

## CHAPTER SIX

Ena arrived at the factory just before nine o'clock on Monday morning. As she approached the main entrance, she was met by a young workman who clearly wanted to impress her. 'Good morning, Miss Dudley.' Not giving Ena time to return the greeting, the young man carried on, 'We started work on Friday, first thing, and we've worked all weekend.' He pointed to new slates on the roof, windows that now had glass in them, and the car park's rebuilt outer wall. 'All that's left to do,' he said, opening the door and standing back to let Ena go in first, 'is give the walls that have been plastered a lick of paint. We'll be doing that as soon as the plaster's dry.' He walked with Ena across the factory floor. 'You'll be back at work in no time, miss.'

'Not until the gas and the electricity have been checked, she won't, lad,' Herbert Silcott called from the doorway of the annexe. 'We need to make sure there aren't any cracked gas pipes or damaged wiring.'

'Yes, Mr Silcott.' The young man's cheeks flushed a deep red. 'Better get back to work.'

'When the factory is safe, and I am satisfied that the workforce isn't going to go up in smoke, we'll all be back.' Mr Silcott looked worried.

Ena rubbed her gloved hands together. 'Right, where shall I start?'

'I'm sorry. Ena, I'm afraid you are here under false pretences. I thought we would have lights and heating by now, but the utility companies can't get here until this afternoon.' He gave Ena a fatherly smile. 'My wife said I was overly optimistic.'

Ena returned Herbert Silcott's smile. She didn't mind being at work. She wanted to be of use. 'Surely there's something we can do?'

'Without heating, possibly, but not without lights.'

Ena followed her boss's gaze. The young workman was rubbing the flat of his hand back and forth across a newly plastered section of wall. 'Tomorrow morning, early, the telephone people are coming in. Hopefully they won't be too long, so if you come in at your usual time, Ena, I'll get you to check the work orders. If there is anything you don't think we'll be able to get out on time, I need to know, so I can inform the client. Hopefully, if I explain the situation, they'll extend the finishing dates.'

Ena was worried. If she wasn't able to start work on the current order for Bletchley Park tomorrow – and as things stood, it didn't look likely – it would be the beginning of a backlog. Ena blew out her cheeks. With extra work from Williams Engineering coming their way, delaying Bletchley's current job could have disastrous consequences. The commander's words ran through her head. "That will mean more work for Silcott's. Can you handle more work?" Freda had said, "Yes, sir," so confidently.

Ena did some mental arithmetic. The average Bletchley job took a minimum of four twelve-hour days – she had three. If she added four hours onto each day, worked sixteen hours, she would complete the job on time, and even if she had to do the last check on Friday morning, it would be at Bletchley by mid-afternoon. If it wasn't, and Silcott's lost the contract, there would be a lot of women out of work, including her.

Ena went to the safe. To her relief, the concrete bunker where she kept her work was undamaged. 'If you are sure you don't want me to check the work orders today, I'll go. But tomorrow, I am starting work on the order Freda and I brought back from Bletchley, and I shall finish it on time.'

'Thank you, Ena.' Herbert Silcott's eyes were moist, and he cleared his throat. As they left the annexe, he raised his hand to the workmen in a gesture of acknowledgement. 'I don't think there would be much work done today if you did stay,' Herbert joked. Ena looked over to where the workmen were having a cup of tea. They were all looking at her. Now it was her turn to blush.

When Ena arrived at the factory the following morning, the electricity was on and there was a team of maintenance engineers testing the machines on the factory floor.

'We're from Williams Engineering,' the foreman said. 'Mr Williams asked us to come over and check your machines, make sure they're safe for when you go back into production.'

'If you can get these three up and running first,' Ena said, pointing to Madge Foot and Barb Allyn's machines, and the one next to them, which she intended to use herself, 'You'll have saved us from losing our main contract.'

Something of an exaggeration, but it did the trick. The foreman called the other engineers over and they set about cleaning, oiling, and testing the three machines nearest the annexe. She then went over to the builder's apprentice, told him where Madge and Barb lived, and asked him if he would go to each of their houses and tell them that Ena needed them to come into work. She then went to the annexe where Freda was cleaning her tools. 'Any damage, Freda?'

'No. I've checked them all,' she said, scrutinising a small drill.

Ena went to the cupboard and took out her toolbox. Opening it, she lifted a hard leather pouch from the top, laid it on the workbench, and rolled out the length of chamois leather that protected her precision tools. Checking each one in turn, she heaved a sigh of relief. 'Mine are all right too.' She then took out the drills and bits, checked them and put them back. She wouldn't need her tools until later, so returned them to the toolbox and put it back in the cupboard.

As she was leaving the annexe, Ena saw Violet Wilson and her sister Rose talking to one of the maintenance men. When they saw Ena, they left the man and ran over to her. 'We were passing,' Violet said, 'and wondered if there was any news.'

'About us coming back to work,' Rose added.

Ena burst out laughing. 'Sorry,' she said, 'I'm not laughing at you. I'm laughing because you couldn't have asked at a better time. Come with me.' Taking the women back to the engineer who they had been talking to, Ena asked, 'How are you getting on?'

He wiped the sleeve of his overalls across his sweating face. 'Phew!' He blew out his cheeks. 'Hard going this is. Right! The three machines you wanted doing first are finished.' Ena put her hands together as if in prayer. 'The three on this bank are done, and the two next to them are almost finished.' He pointed to the far side of the room. 'And that lot'll be done next.'

'That's... that's incredible. Thank you.' Ena shook her head in amazement. Aware that Violet and Rose Wilson were waiting for an answer, she looked at her watch. 'How about after lunch today? One o'clock?'

'Why wait until one? I've got work started last week that I can carry on with,' Violet said.

'Me too,' said Rose.

'And,' Violet said, pointing at the machines the maintenance engineer had said were ready, 'I'll send my boys back to tell some of the other women to come up. They're outside. Won't be a mo. You get your machine going, Rose!' she shouted over her shoulder to her sister, and marched out of the factory.

Madge and Barb arrived within minutes of the Wilson boys running off to spread the word that Silcott's was back in production, and Ena took them to the annexe. By the time they had discussed what was needed to complete the work order for Station X, their machines were up and running.

When Mr Silcott returned that afternoon, the communal areas had been cleaned and were ready for use, thanks to a cleaning crew organised by Mrs Silcott. Freda had read and filed the invoices, petrol coupons, bills and statements, while a couple of girls waiting for their machines to be serviced had cleaned the annexe. The factory was working at seventy-five percent, which meant the work for Bletchley Park *would* be completed on time.

By the end of November, Silcott's Engineering was working to full capacity and by Christmas, the backlog of work had been cleared. Ena had Christmas Day off. She had to go into work for a few hours early on Boxing Day as the work for Bletchley was being taken down on Friday. As her sister Margaret had said in her last letter, the war didn't stop because it was Christmas.

Margaret and husband Bill had to work at Christmas, so were staying in London. The rest of the Dudley family, including Claire, who was home on twenty-four hours' leave from the WAAF, were spending Christmas Day with Bess and her ever-growing family of evacuees at Foxden Hall.

After church on Christmas morning, Ena, Claire, and their parents walked up to the Hall. The Dudley women went to the kitchen to help Mrs Hartley, Foxden's housekeeper and cook, to prepare Christmas lunch for the land girls and the evacuated children. Ena's father joined Bess and Mr Porter, Foxden's estate manager and his boss before the war, in the music room where the children were rehearsing for a concert that afternoon.

When lunch was ready, Mrs Hartley and Ena's mother brought two large chickens with homemade sage and onion stuffing into the main hall. 'We'll put a bird at each end of the table, Lily,' Mrs Hartley said. 'Thomas and Mr Porter are carving.' Ena and Claire brought dishes of vegetables, followed by two land girls carrying large jugs of gravy. Lunch was as chaotic as it was fun. And the tongue-in-cheek threat of not opening any presents until they had eaten every scrap of food on their plates worked so well that by the time they'd finished their main course, the children were full. Bess suggested they leave the Christmas pudding and the fruitcake until teatime and open their Christmas presents.

The girls were content to stay inside and play with the dolls that Father Christmas had brought them, but the boys wanted go outside. So, wrapped up warm in their winter coats, hats and gloves, the boys trundled off to build a snowman.

They hadn't been outside long when they came crashing back through the front door. An army lorry had ditched at the bottom of Shaft Hill on the Lowarth to Woodcote road.

Bess and one of the land girls dashed off on foot with instructions from Mrs Hartley to bring the boys back for tea, while Ena's father and Mr Porter followed on a tractor.

By the time the soldiers arrived, Mrs Hartley and Bess's mother were laying trestle tables with chicken and ham sandwiches, fruitcake and Christmas puddings. Ena and Claire brought in two pots of tea and a tray of cups and saucers – and giggled when the soldiers flirted and teased.

While the soldiers ate their meal, the children sang a selection of Christmas carols, recited poems and nursery rhymes, and danced jigs. The entertainment ended with everyone on their feet singing "Give A Little Whistle", followed by "Hands, Knees and Boomps-a-Daisy". The soldiers, clapping their hands when they should have been slapping their knees, made everyone laugh. Coincidentally, they conquered the moves at exactly the same time and everyone cheered. Then, after taking theatrical bows, all but one of the soldiers returned to their seats.

The sergeant stood at the top of the table and looked around the room until there was hush. 'On behalf of myself and the lads, I would like to thank you all. It's been a long time since any of us have sat down with friends to eat. And, because we're going overseas in the New Year, it may be a long time until we do it again. I think I speak for every soldier here when I say we will never forget what you did for us today. The next time we sit down with friends, wherever it is and whenever it is, we will remember today and every one of you.' He looked at his fellow soldiers. 'Look sharp, lads, it's time we were on our way.'

The soldiers pushed back their chairs and stood to attention. As they made their way to the door, they shook the hands of the children nearest to them and saluted those who were further away. At the door, they turned as one and saluted Bess and the women of the land army, who were gathered around the piano.

'Time we made a move too,' Ena's father said.

The Dudley family – except Bess, who lived-in at Foxden Hall – said goodbye and put on their outdoor clothes.

The walk home was pleasant. Ena and Claire, arm in arm, followed their parents along the lane, leaving their footprints in the newly laid snow.

The following morning, Bess arrived in Lady Foxden's Rover to take Claire to the station. Ena and her parents waited by the front door to say goodbye. 'Your coat,' her father said, taking it from the hook in the hall and helping Claire into it. 'Let me take your bag for you.'

He put the bag on the back seat of the car. 'Come home and see us soon, love,' her father said, opening the front passenger door.

'I will.' Claire kissed her father and mother goodbye, promising to write soon. Hugging Ena, Claire whispered, 'Keep up the *sensitive* work. I'm proud of you, our Ena.'

The relationship between Ena and Claire had always been competitive. They were close in age but opposites in temperament. No sooner had Claire arrived home on Christmas Eve than she and Ena were arguing. Both did work they couldn't discuss – Claire's secret, Ena's sensitive. Once that was established, they quickly became friends again.

Reading between the lines, Ena understood that Claire did a dangerous job. 'Be careful,' she said, doing her best not to cry.

Claire winked at her youngest sister. 'I always am,' she said, dropping onto the passenger seat. Bess put the car into gear and pulled into the lane. Ena waved until the Rover turned onto the main

Lowarth road and disappeared.

The winter was harsh. Snow fell almost every day, and for much of the time, the temperature was below zero. Because of black ice, which was causing havoc on the roads, Ena and her friends from the factory decided to stay in Lowarth and go to a dance for New Year's Eve.

Ena's friend, Beryl Clark, persuaded her father to take them into Lowarth before the dance and pick them up afterwards. He was one of only three taxis in the area, and as the Clarks lived in Woodcote and had to drive past Ena's parents' cottage on the Foxden estate, Mr Clark was often called upon to give lifts to the Dudley sisters.

Ena and Beryl met Freda and Madge in the smoke room of The Hind Hotel. Freda, already at the bar, shouted, 'Port and lemon, ladies?'

'Not for Beryl,' Ena mouthed.

'Yes please,' Beryl said, standing on Ena's toe. 'Sorry,' she giggled.

'It isn't funny, Beryl. You're underage. If Freda's caught buying alcohol for you, she'll be in trouble.'

'I'm not underage. I'm almost not.' Beryl leaned forward and looked into Ena's face. 'If I can drive Dad's taxi, I'm sure I can have *one* drink,' she said, her nose almost touching Ena's. The next round's on me,' she laughed, as she and Ena joined Madge and Freda at a table near the fire.

The four friends chatted animatedly, telling each other what they had done over Christmas.

Madge told them about a boy she'd met at her aunt's house on Boxing Day. 'He's the son of my aunt's neighbour, on leave from the navy, his name's Harry and he's asked me to write to him when he goes back to his ship,' she said, without taking a breath. Everyone was pleased for Madge who, although she was the prettiest of them, was so shy she found it difficult to talk to the opposite sex. 'It was just the best Boxing Day ever,' Madge sighed.

Ena told them about lunch at Foxden Hall, the army lorry breaking down, and the soldiers coming up to the Hall for tea.

'Christmas Day at our house was a washout,' Beryl said. 'What about you, Freda? What did you do over Christmas?'

'Sorry?'

'That good, was it?' Beryl joked.

'What?'

'Christmas. What did you do at Christmas?'

'I spent it with my uncle in Northampton. We had a traditional English Christmas. We went for walks, sat by a roaring fire, pulled crackers, and ate turkey.'

Madge, leaned forward. She's waiting for the exciting bit, Ena thought, but by the abrupt way Freda stopped speaking, she had nothing more to say. Ena looked across the table at Beryl. She could tell by the glazed look in her young friend's eyes that she was bored. 'It's seven o'clock. Time to make a move if we want to sit at a table. You know what the Town Hall's like; it gets busy really early.' Everyone agreed and gathering their belongings, followed Ena out of the Hind and across the road to the Town Hall.

The entrance hall was packed with girls queuing for the cloakroom and toilet. Ena, Freda, Madge and Beryl waited in line, shuffling forward every few seconds.

When Ena eventually got to the front of the queue, she took off her coat and handed it to the cloakroom girl who gave her a ticket with number 75 on it. Ena put the ticket in her handbag for safekeeping. She would need it at the end of the dance to reclaim her coat.

The four friends each paid the two shillings entrance fee and went upstairs to the dance room. Beryl, eager to find a table, pushed past half a dozen girls who were huddled together deciding which table would give them the best view of the band. By the time they had made up their minds – and chosen the table half way between the stage and the door, Beryl was sitting at it. With her handbag on one chair and her gasmask on another, she stood up and waved her friends over. The only other vacant table was on the far side of the room, which, looking daggers at Beryl, the indecisive group of friends sauntered over to.

Ena and Beryl went off to find something to drink. The bar, in an alcove on the opposite side of the room, offered a choice of dandelion and burdock or lemonade. They decided on lemonade.

They had no sooner arrived back to the table than Ray Walker's band began to play, "Why Did She Fall For The Leader Of The Band?" Cheering, everyone took to the dance floor.

The room was packed. There was an equal mix

of service men and women and civilians but as always, there were twice as many women as there were men. Ena and Freda, and Madge and Beryl were the first couples on the dance floor. Lots of women followed suit, leaving the men standing around the edge of the room like wallflowers.

Ena and Freda were soon parted by a couple of sailors. Ena's sailor, Arthur, was tall and good-looking, with sparkling dark brown eyes and a full head of black wavy hair. Freda's chap was as short as Ena's was tall, with mousy brown hair brought forward in a wave to cover a receding hairline.

Ena couldn't help but smile at the look of disgust on Freda's face as she and her handsome Able Seaman danced past. Freda, like Ena, was taller than average for a woman, stood on tiptoe, and looked over the head of her Very Ordinary Seaman. Ena giggled, and at the end of the third dance, excused herself, saying she needed to find her friend.

Madge and Beryl were sitting talking when Ena got back to the table, Freda joining them a minute later from the direction of the stairs. 'I swear that swathe of hair he wore across his head was to cover a bald patch,' Freda said, and shuddered.

Ena laughed. 'He might have been wearing a wig.'

Freda grimaced. 'Here,' she said, taking a quarter bottle of gin from her handbag, 'This will cheer us up.' Ena said she didn't need gin to cheer her up, getting back on the dance floor would do that, but it didn't stop Freda from pouring what must have been the equivalent of two measures of gin into her lemonade. 'Cheers!'

At the interval, Madge and Beryl knocked back their lemonades saying, as there was only beer at the dance, they were going over the road to the Hind. 'No need,' Freda said. And taking the gin from her bag, poured what was left of it between the four glasses.

'I can't drink neat gin,' Ena said. 'I'm going to the bar. Who wants lemonade?' Three hands went up.

'I'll help you carry them!' Beryl called after her, and leaping out of her seat, made her way through a crowd of people heading for the stairs, and the pub.

'Your sailor was a bit of all right,' Beryl said, catching Ena up.

Ena laughed. 'Don't say that in front of Freda. Her nose is out of joint, because she had to dance with the small, not so good-looking one.'

'She's a bit of an odd one, don't you think?' Beryl said, while they waited in the soft drinks queue.

'Odd? In what way?'

'She's friendly enough, but she never talks about her family, her mum and dad, or her friends. She must have friends outside the factory. Is it true she's sweet on old Silcott?'

'No it isn't!' Ena snapped.

'No need to bite my head off,' Beryl said. 'I only asked because Madge said she'd never seen her with a man, and Freda's never mentioned walking out with anyone.'

'As Mr Silcott's assistant, she has a position to keep up. She's all right when you get to know her.'

'And because she has a *position* to keep up, she thinks she's a cut above the rest of us.'

'If that were true, she wouldn't be sneaking a bottle of gin into the dance and sharing it with us, would she?'

'I suppose not.'

By the time they had shuffled to the front of the queue, asked for four glasses of lemonade, and waited for the woman serving to pour them, the hall was half empty. The band had gone to the pub for a break – they always did half way through the evening, along with most of their followers.

When Ena and Beryl got back to the table, Madge was peering into her powder compact's mirror applying lipstick, and Freda, staring into the middle-distance, looked as if she was a hundred miles away. 'Penny for them,' Ena said.

'The smell of juniper,' she said, waving the glass of gin back and forth beneath her nose. 'Reminds me of the Christmases I spent with my grandparents. My grandmother would crush juniper berries and add them to our food. She used to say it made bland food more flavoursome.'

'I don't think I've ever tasted food that smells like gin,' Ena said, lifting her glass and inhaling.

'The band's back,' Madge said. Taking Ena's glass from her hand, she pulled her out of her seat and dragged her onto the dance floor. Taking the man's part, Madge steered Ena to the far side of the room.

'Madge? What are you doing?'

'It's him. It's Harry Taylor.' Ena couldn't think who Harry Taylor was. 'It's the sailor I told you about. The one I met on Boxing Day.' Ena looked over Madge's shoulder as she twirled her round. 'Don't let him see you looking, or he'll think we're dancing over here on purpose,' Madge said, looking down.

Ena was just about to ask which one was Harry when Ray Walker announced the Gentlemen's Excuse-Me. Almost immediately, Ena felt a tap on her shoulder. 'Arthur?' The sailor who she had danced with earlier was at her side. Standing next to him, beaming at Madge, was a good-looking young man who Ena assumed was Harry.

1941 began with a lull in work. February was busier, but in March there was such an increase in orders that Silcott's had to set on more workers. With their husbands in the armed forces, most of them overseas, it was up to the women to pay the rent and put food on the table. Women who had never considered going out to work before the war were queuing up for it now.

By the summer, women who had started their training in the spring were given easy, straightforward, jobs, which freed-up the experienced members of the workforce so they were able to concentrate on the complicated jobs. After a few months, the workload levelled out, and for a while everyone, including Ena, went back to working a ten-hour day. There was even time for a social life. Ena and Freda often went for a drink together after work. They went to the Ritz cinema in Lowarth when a new film was showing, and at weekends they would get dressed up and cycle off to a dance in one of the villages.

Freda was in charge of the work produced for a top-secret facility called Beaumanor near Loughborough. Beaumanor was accessible by train from Lowarth station, but often delivery dates clashed. When that happened, Freda took her work to Beaumanor in Mr Silcott's car, dropping him and Ena – and Bletchley's work – at Rugby station first. It wasn't a long drive to Beaumanor, which meant Freda was always back at the factory in time to give out the wages.

As the war went into its second year, men in their thirties and unmarried women were called up. For every single woman who left Silcott's, there were two married women waiting to take her job. Life was hard. Work was hard. But for Ena and her friends it was not all doom and gloom. On the 7th of September, Ena's friend Madge Foot married her sailor, Harry Taylor.

Madge wore a cream two-piece. The skirt was straight and came to just below the knee, and the jacket was nipped in at the waist with a length of cream satin tied in a bow at the front. She wore matching gloves and shoes, and on her head, a cream saucer-shaped miniature hat with a fine veil. Her bouquet was blue delphiniums and trailing green fern, and her corsage was cream daisies and blue cornflowers.

Ena was Madge's maid of honour. Her dress was a blue floral print. She had cream shoes and gloves and instead of a hat, she wore a halo of cream daisies and blue cornflowers.

It was a beautiful warm, sunny, day. The only things in the sky, apart from a couple of Wellingtons returning to Bitteswell aerodrome, were fluffy clouds that were soon blown away by the Indian summer breeze.

As Ena walked down the aisle of St. Mary's Church behind Madge and her father, the sun burst through the East window and shone on Madge and her soon-to-be husband. A good omen, Ena thought.

# MARCH 7, 1942

## CHAPTER SEVEN

A squally March wind gusted along the platform of Rugby's railway station. Ena turned her back on it, dropped her head, and peered under the brim of her hat. What had begun as drizzle when she arrived at work that morning had turned into sheeting rain.

The railway tracks whined and Ena looked to the north. A black steam engine blundered into view, its brakes screeching as it slowed down before coming into the station. She looked across the concourse to the ticket office. Mr Silcott was next in the queue. She watched him bend down and speak into the round porthole in the glass window. Above him the clock said 9:40. They would make the 9:45 to Bletchley.

Ena stepped back from the platform's edge as the hissing train clunked to a halt. Before steam from its engine engulfed her, she looked at the ticket office again, expecting to see Mr Silcott. He wasn't there. She scanned the concourse, looked up and down the platform, but he was nowhere to be seen. Probably in the lavatory, she thought.

The reinforced suitcase containing her work was heavy. She swapped it from her right hand to her left, and rolled her right shoulder. Going to Bletchley Park with the boss made her feel important. And thinking about her work; the rotors and the complicated wiring, the casing on the X-board that only she was trusted to fit, made her feel even more important. Nervous too. Her stomach was doing cartwheels. She wished Mr

Silcott would hurry up.

Ena swapped the suitcase back to her right hand, looked through the steam and rain, and there he was. In his camel coloured overcoat and brown trilby, Mr Silcott was coming out of the Gentlemen's lavatory.

'Here we are, miss,' the station porter said, opening the carriage door. 'Can I take your case?'

'Thank you, but I can manage.' Ena hitched the string of her gasmask box further onto her shoulder and, holding her handbag in one hand, the suitcase in the other, struggled up the steps.

Standing in the doorway of the train, she let her handbag fall to the floor and put her hands up to shield her eyes from what was now heavy rain. Mr Silcott was running across the platform. She needed to attract his attention so, putting the case down gently, she waved out of the window with both hands. He was looking down, and didn't see her. Shielding his face with one hand and holding the brim of his hat with the other, he turned his back to the wind, as she had done a few moments earlier. Then he wrenched open the door at the other end of the carriage and disappeared inside.

'Well I never!' the elderly porter said. 'He's in a blinkin' hurry.'

'He is, isn't he?' Ena frowned. 'I shall have to cart this heavy case all the way to that end of the carriage now,' she said, turning and almost tripping over it.

'I'll pop it along for you, miss,' the old man offered, 'Won't take me a minute.'

'It's very kind of you, but I'll be fine.' The old man touched his cap in a friendly salute and slammed the door. The train clunked off its brakes and hissed, before beginning its journey south.

Winding the string of her gasmask through the handles of her handbag, and putting it over her head, Ena picked up the suitcase. Using both hands, she heaved the case along the narrow corridor, resting it every now and then on her knees to peer through the windows in the compartment doors.

In the last compartment, she spotted Mr Silcott sitting by the window reading his newspaper.

Breathing a sigh of relief, Ena pulled open the door. 'Thank goodness I've found you.' Hauling the suitcase into the compartment, she stood it down beneath the window, flung off her handbag and gasmask and, exhaling loudly, dropped onto the nearest seat. 'Oh!'

The man looked up from his newspaper, his fair eyebrows raised with surprise. 'Hello.'

'Hello?' Ena felt her cheeks blush with embarrassment. The man sitting opposite her was not her boss. Ena studied his face. His square jaw, blond hair and pale grey-blue eyes looked familiar. She had seen him before, she was sure she had, but where?

The man picked up his paper and shook it open. Ena leaned forward to read the front page. "AT LAST THE YANKS ARE HERE" and "IKE WILL SHOW HITLER".

'About time too!' the man said. Ena jumped. Embarrassed again, because looking at his paper felt as if she'd been looking over his shoulder. 'Mind you,' he continued, 'if the Japanese hadn't attacked the US Naval base at Pearl Harbor in

December they might still be dragging their feet.'

Ena nodded. She supposed he was right. 'Excuse me, but do I know you?'

'You don't know me exactly, but we have met,' the man said. 'You were with a friend. A fair haired young woman.' Ena had no recollection, and smiled through a frown. 'It would have been on this train,' he persisted. 'Of course, it wasn't actually this train,' he laughed. 'What I mean is, I go down to my company's head office in Bletchley every Friday, often on the 9:45, so if we have met, it would have been on a Friday and at around this time.'

The only female Ena travelled to Bletchley with was Freda. She traced back in her mind the times she and Freda had been to Bletchley. They had spoken to so many people... Then she recognised the man. He had spoken to them. At least he had spoken to Freda. Been quite pally, if memory served. Ena thought for some minutes, and then said, 'Yes, I do remember you. It was a long time ago.'

'I suppose it was. Time flies, doesn't it?'

Distracted, wondering where Mr Silcott was, Ena nodded.

'You look worried. Is there anything I can do to help?'

'No, it's all right. I saw my boss get on the train at this end of the carriage and, as this compartment is the nearest one to the door he boarded by, I thought he would be in here.'

The man dropped his newspaper onto his lap and opened his arms. 'No one here but me,' he said, looking around the compartment.

'I can see that!' Annoyed because the man was laughing at her, Ena got up to leave.

'I'm sorry,' he said, 'I didn't mean to be rude. What does your boss look like? I might have seen him.'

There was something about the man that Ena didn't like, but she needed to know if he had seen Mr Silcott. 'He's in his mid-fifties. He's an inch or two taller than me, so he's about five-ten. His hair is dark, almost black, with grey in it, and he's wearing a camel coloured overcoat and brown trilby.'

The man shook his head. 'Sorry.'

Ena blew out her cheeks. 'He's got my ticket, so I'd better go and find him.'

'I boarded in Birmingham, and I haven't seen anyone fitting your boss's description. If I had, I'd have said.'

'Of course you would. I'm sorry to have troubled you. I'll leave you in peace.'

'If you don't find him, come back. These seats are vacant now, but for how long?' He shrugged.

'Thank you, I will.'

'Tell you what!' the man said, stopping Ena, 'Why don't you leave your heavy case in here while you look for him. I'll keep my eye on it for you--'

'I can't do that. Thank you anyway, but I'll manage,' she said, picking up her belongings. She walked the short distance back to the next compartment. Mr Silcott wasn't in there, or the next. She described her boss to everyone, even people she passed in the corridor, but no one had seen him.

Her arms were dropping off by the time the train pulled into Northampton. Worried that the first compartment she went in to, the only compartment with vacant seats, would be full by the time the train left the station, Ena returned to it.

Putting her case under the window, Ena sat next to it and stared out. Not focussing on anything, she sighed heavily.

'You didn't find your boss then?'

'No. I suppose he could be in another carriage. I thought I saw him get into this one, but it was raining heavily... I could have been mistaken.'

Looking to the heavens in exasperation, a coat on the overhead rack caught Ena's eye. It had been turned inside out, and folded double, but she could see it was camel in colour. Her heart gave a couple of quick beats and she felt suddenly hot. Instinctively she leant forward and pulled the case nearer. As she did so, she saw the man's shoes. A cursory glance was enough for her to see they were wet, and the floor around them damp. If the man had been sitting in this compartment all the way from Birmingham, his shoes would be dry by now. If not dry, they wouldn't still be soaking wet, or would they? She wasn't sure how long the train took to get from Birmingham to Rugby.

'Do you have pear drops for the journey?' the man asked.

Startled, Ena repeated, 'Pear drops?'

'Yes. I have just remembered that you and your friend ate pear drops when we met. And, as you are looking a little pale, I wondered if you still suffer from travel sickness... Ignore me. I didn't mean to be personal.'

'It's fine, you're not being... Yes, we always suck pear drops when we travel.' Taking the cone-shaped packet from her handbag, Ena undid it and held it out to the man for him to help himself. 'Would you like one?'

'I would. Thank you.' The man took the packet out of Ena's hand and looked at its contents. 'Now, which flavour shall I choose?'

Ena laughed. 'Don't be fooled by the different colours, they all taste the same. If not the same, they are very similar.'

The man took a pear drop and put it in his mouth, before passing the packet back to Ena. Popping one into her mouth, she twisted the top of the packet, and returned it to her handbag. Leaning back in her seat, she looked out of the window.

The crick in her neck and the pain in her side made Ena think she had fallen sideways. She reached out to push herself up, but her hand, as numb as her feet, liquefied like an unset jelly. She screamed, but could make no sound. Her heart thumped and her pulse throbbed so loudly that she could hear the blood pumping in her ears. 'What the--?' was all she said before she gave into the pain in her head, which was followed quickly by silence, and then darkness.

Vaporous images floated in front of her eyes. She shook her head to rid herself of the ghostly apparitions. If she could lift her head, she would turn her back on them, but it was too heavy.

Ouch! Her forehead bumped against something hard and cold.

'Where am I?' a small voice deep in the recesses of her mind called out. 'Help me. Please,' she called again, but her voice refused to come forward and make itself heard. Her lips were dry. She tried to moisten them with her tongue, but it was stuck to the top of her mouth.

What was the matter with her? Why couldn't she speak, or move? Had she had some sort of stroke? Surely the man sitting opposite her would have noticed if she had. If only she could sit upright. She tried again to push herself into a sitting position but her arms melted in the same way that her hands had done, so she gave up trying.

Nausea washed over her in giant waves. She was always sick if she closed her eyes when she travelled. There was only one thing for it. Ena forced her eyes open, but instead of feeling better, a kaleidoscope of bright, piercing lights darted towards her and she closed them again.

In the darkness, Ena heard whispering. Relieved that her senses were returning, she strained to hear what the person was saying. She couldn't tell if it was a man, or a woman, but someone said, 'Damn!'

'Shush! She will hear you,' a man's voice warned. As the feeling in her hands and feet started to come back, Ena fought an overwhelming desire to sleep. Her head began to clear and her thoughts became more lucid. She heard a click, followed by second clink, as metal met metal. She lifted her head from the train's window, opened her eyes, and squinted under her eyelashes.

Lights still flashed across her vision, but they were not as bright and there were not as many. And there was something else. Dark at first and then lighter, but never light enough to see who or what they were, two forms loomed up in front of her. What the...? Are they ghosts? Am I dead? Perhaps I am. 'Hello?' Ena said, but they didn't answer. 'Please help me,' she called. This time they heard her, because the taller of the two shapes turned.

As if he was speaking from the bottom of a deep well, a man said, 'She is awake.'

'Give her another shot,' the shorter shape hissed.

Ena felt thirsty, dehydrated. Able to move her tongue, she licked her lips. It made no difference. She ran her tongue around the inside of her mouth to encourage saliva. It didn't work. She took a breath and opened her mouth to speak. Before she could form the word *help*, the tall shape was bending over her. A second later everything turned black.

## CHAPTER EIGHT

The platform on Euston station was a sea of people pushing to get to the exits. Ena spotted the buffet and weaved her way through the crowd to its entrance. She stumbled through the door and fell into the first empty seat. The buffet was noisy and as packed as the platform had been.

'Excuse me, miss, is this seat taken?'

'Yes,' Ena whispered. She took a shuddering breath. 'Please take it.' She looked up, her eyes red and swollen from crying, to see a tall dark-haired man in his early twenties. He made no attempt to take the chair. 'I'm sorry,' she said, and realising he wanted to sit down, took her coat from the seat and laid it across her knees. 'I thought--' was all she said before tears fell again. She looked away, reached into her handbag and rummaged around for a clean handkerchief. She always kept a spare in her bag, but there wasn't one in it today. The one bloody day she needed a spare hankie she didn't have one. She took the handkerchief that she'd used earlier from beneath her coat. It was sodden. She gave a shuddering breath. It was the last straw. Overwhelmed by a feeling of defeat, she put her head in her hands and sobbed.

'Excuse me?' the young man said, offering Ena a neatly folded white handkerchief. Ena lifted her face to him and pressing her lips together – she daren't speak for fear she would scream – took the handkerchief, nodded her thanks and wiped her tears.

She hardly noticed the young man get up from the table. When he returned it was with two hot drinks, tea for Ena and a black coffee for himself. He moved her empty cup and saucer to the other side of the table and replaced it with the full cup.

Dropping the handkerchief onto her lap, Ena put her hands around the hot drink to warm them. She had cried so much that she had exhausted herself and was shivering. Although the buffet was warm from so many bodies seated in such a small area, Ena felt cold. She ought to put her coat on, but just the thought of standing up and doing so exhausted her more. She took a sip of tea and felt better for it. 'Thank you,' she said, making a conscious effort to pull herself together.

'You're welcome, miss.'

Ena looked in her handbag again. This time for her purse. Taking it out, she opened it and offered the man a half-crown. 'For my tea.'

'There's no need,' he said, 'buying tea for a beautiful woman is a pleasure.'

'I insist,' she said. If it had been any other day, she would have been delighted to receive a compliment from such a good-looking man. She looked up at him and their eyes met. Fearing she had turned red, she said, 'First the handkerchief, and now the tea. What next?' she said, attempting a joke.

'You can tell me why you were crying. I'm a good listener.' He looked at his watch. 'I've got twenty minutes until my train leaves.'

If only I could, Ena thought. 'I'm afraid I can't. I mean, *don't* want to talk about it.'

'Okay, let's talk about something else. Not your English weather,' he said. 'There are so many things I love about England, my mom was English and I went to university here, but your weather,' he said, shaking his head. Ena laughed. 'What?'

'You're talking about the weather.'

'I am, aren't I? He laughed too. 'I'm Ben, by the way. Benjamin Franklin Johnson. Named after my country's most famous founding father, Benjamin Franklin.' He offered Ena his hand.

'You have a lot to live up to,' Ena said, taking Ben's hand and shaking it. 'Ena Dudley. Pleased to meet you.'

'Hi, Ena.'

'If you were named after Benjamin Franklin you were obviously born in America.'

'Yeah, Boston. But surely you could tell that from my accent.'

'You could have been Canadian.'

'I guess.' Ben laughed. 'Don't ever ask a Canadian if he's an American. The guys I work with don't like being mistaken for us Yanks. Though we're not that different from them.' Ben looked at Ena for a moment and smiled. 'Maybe one day when the war's over, you'll visit the US. It's a great country.'

'It's a large continent.'

Ben sat back in his seat, his eyes wide with surprise.

Ena laughed despite herself. 'Don't be too impressed. What I know about America is from geography lessons at school. The Rockies, Grand Canyon, and the Great Lakes... that's where my knowledge of North America begins and ends, I'm afraid.' Still feeling shaky, Ena picked up her cup. It was empty. She put it down.

'Would you like some more tea?' Ben asked, already on his feet.

'No. Thank you. If I have another cup, I shall be swimming to Bletchley.' Her hand flew to her mouth and she felt the colour rush to her cheeks. She inhaled sharply. She shouldn't tell a stranger she was going to Bletchley. She shouldn't tell anyone. Thank goodness she didn't say Bletchley Park. Her heart beat fast. She looked at Ben and told him her cover story. 'We have a friend who lives in Bletchley. That is, my boss and I. She used to work with us at-- anyway, we were going to visit her, but we got separated and I missed the stop. Stupid thing to do, miss the stop.' Ena tutted and rolled her eyes.

'Don't be so down on yourself. It's an easy thing to do if you're not sure of where you're going. Hey, I'm going to see some people in Bletchley today. We can travel together.' Ben looked at his watch. 'The next train is in fifteen minutes.'

Feeling the wings of panic beating in her chest, Ena opened her mouth to give the young American a reason why she wasn't able to travel with him, but couldn't think of one.

'That way I'll be able to get to know you, and you won't miss your stop. Okay?'

Was it really okay to travel to Bletchley with a man she didn't know? It couldn't hurt, Ena reasoned, as long as she didn't tell him anything about Silcott's Engineering or Bletchley Park.

And she would have to make sure that when they arrived, she walked away from the station in the opposite direction to him. 'Okay,' she whispered. It wasn't travelling with Ben to Bletchley that was worrying her. It was having to face Mr Silcott and Commander Dalton when she got there. The thought of telling them that her work had been stolen terrified her. She felt the tears welling up in her eyes, blurring her sight.

'Hey? What is it?'

Ena could see real concern in Ben's eyes. He would probably keep her secret if she told him, but she couldn't, she would be breaking the Official Secrets Act. But she had to tell him something. There had to be some reason for her tears. She wiped her face and thought of something that was close enough to the truth, without being the truth, that would make her cry.

'I was taking something important to my friend, the one I told you about, that I used to work with.' She looked around. No one was listening. The only people sitting near enough to hear what she was saying were engrossed in their own conversation. Keeping her voice low, just in case, Ena took a shaky breath. 'And it was stolen.' She knew she shouldn't go any further with the story, but the words kept tumbling out of her mouth. It was as if she couldn't stop. 'I shall be in terrible trouble. When my boss, who is also a friend of hers, finds out, he'll sack me. I won't be able to get another job, because no one will trust me again.'

Ben reached across the table and covered Ena's hands with his. 'Slow down and take a breath.' Ena nodded, and when she was calmer, he said, 'You were with your boss?' Ena looked down and nodded. 'So where is the guy? Did he get off the train at Bletchley?'

Ena shook her head. 'I don't know.' Ben's brow furrowed. He looked questioningly at her. 'I'm sorry, I shouldn't have said anything. There's probably a simple explanation, though what it is, I don't know. And it won't stop me from being in trouble for losing the case.'

'You said it was stolen.'

'It was.' *Oh Lord.* Ena bit her bottom lip. She hated lying. She never remembered what she'd said when she lied. 'It must have been, but...'

'But what?'

'I can't prove it. I had a terrible headache,' Ena said, rubbing her temples. 'It started behind my eyes.' She thought for a moment. 'The sun was shining through the window directly onto my face. It was so bright it hurt my eyes, so I closed them. I only meant to shut them for a second, to ease the pain. But I must have fallen asleep, because the next thing I remember was waking up in Euston. The carriage was empty and the bag had gone.'

Ben smiled at her sympathetically, then looked at his watch. 'Come on. It's 1.20, our train leaves in ten minutes. We'd better make our way to the platform.'

'I need to buy a ticket. My boss bought mine, when he got his own, at...'

'Do you have any money?'

'Oh yes. Mr-- my boss gave me enough money to get me home, if we got separated. And I've got an emergency ten-bob note. I didn't think I'd have to use it.'

They stood up at the same time. Ena put her handbag on the seat of her chair and Ben helped her into her coat. Grabbing her gasmask from the back of the chair, she picked up her handbag and allowed Ben to take her by the elbow and walk her out of the buffet. They went together to the ticket office and while Ena bought a single to Bletchley, Ben bought a newspaper from a vendor close by. Feeling more composed, Ena strolled down to the platform at the side of her new and incredibly good-looking friend.

As the train pulled out of Euston, Ena took the pear drops from her handbag. Looking at the cone-shaped packet, she felt the bitter taste of bile rise in her throat. She felt sick. It wasn't travel sickness, it was something else, she didn't know what. What she did know was, she didn't fancy a sweet and dropped them back into her bag.

Grateful to Ben for suggesting they travelled together, Ena watched him pick up his newspaper and settle back in his seat. As he opened it, he looked across the compartment at her. She noticed fine lines; the beginnings of a smile, playing at the corners of his eyes. But instead of smiling, he frowned. 'Are you okay? You're as white as a sheet.'

'I felt a bit queasy but I'm fine now. Really.' She looked out of the window.

A short while later, when the train was slowing down and Ena felt the grinding of the brakes, her stomach lurched again. 'Is this Bletchley?' she asked, praying it was.

Ben looked over the top of his paper. 'I thought you'd been to Bletchley before?'

'I have. From the north, not the south.'

'This is Willesden,' he said, 'We've got another half-dozen stations to go through before we get to Bletchley. Would you like part of my newspaper?' Without waiting for Ena to reply, Ben removed the centre pages. 'This will help you pass the hour.'

'Hour!'

'Almost,' he said.

Ena took the paper, opened it and began to read, but she couldn't concentrate. She was too worried about what she was going to say to Mr Silcott and Commander Dalton when they asked how the suitcase containing her work had been stolen. She'd tell them the truth of course – but what was the truth? She couldn't think. Her head felt as if it were stuffed with cotton wool. She felt woozy and confused, so angry that she couldn't remember what had happened to her. She wanted to scream. Tears of frustration threatened and she looked out of the window.

'Cigarette?' Ben asked.

'No thank you,' she said. Just the thought of smoking made her want to retch.

'Mind if I do?'

'Not at all.' She watched Ben take a cigarette from a pack of Chesterfields and put it in his mouth. He held it between his lips and flicked the small wheel on the side of his lighter. She caught the faint scent of petrol as the blue flame appeared. Lighting the cigarette, Ben pulled deeply before exhaling a long stream of smoke.

How am I going to lose him when we get to Bletchley? Ena thought. She felt a fluttering of excitement in her stomach. If it had been at any other time, in any other place, she would happily have gone with Ben to wherever it was he was going. Timbuktu, if he'd asked. But today she needed to go in any direction that was opposite to his.

'This is it,' Ben said, as the trained pulled into Bletchley station.

Ena handed him the section of his newspaper that she had failed to read. As the train pitched to a halt, Ben folded it and put it in his pocket. Ena stood up and put on her gloves and scarf. They had gathered other passengers along the way and, having sat next to the window, were last to leave the compartment. 'Will you be visiting your friend in Bletchley again?' Ben asked.

'I would like to,' Ena said, butterflies flying round in her stomach again. 'I don't know when, and it depends on a few things.' *Whether I'm sacked after today*, but she didn't say that. 'I will if I can.'

'Okay,' Ben beamed. 'I work shifts and don't get much time off, but if you could write and tell me when you're coming down?' Smiling happily, Ena nodded. He tore a piece of paper from a small notebook and scribbled down his address. 'If you give me some warning – say three days – I can get one of the guys to swap shifts with me, and I can take you to tea, or lunch, depending when you're here.'

'I should like that.'

'Okay then!' Ben's eyes sparkled. 'It's a date.'

'I suppose it is.' Holding Ena's arm, Ben helped her down from the train. On the platform, Ena looked up. They were standing so close to each other she could feel Ben's breath on her cheek. She thought he was going to kiss her. She wouldn't have minded if he had. She wanted to kiss him, and felt sure he wanted to kiss her. They did a little dance around each other, laughed, and shook hands. She watched him walk away. At the exit, he turned and waved. A second later he was gone.

She looked at the scrap of paper in her hand. *Benjamin F. Johnson, c/o The Ministry of Defence, Whitehall, London.* She read the address again. He works in London, but he must come to Bletchley often, Ena thought, because he'd said he would take her to lunch, or tea, the next time she was here.

She put Ben's address in her handbag and looked around the station. She needed to waste a few minutes. Although Ben had left the station, he might be waiting outside for a taxi or a bus and she daren't take the chance of him seeing which way she walked when she left. A little way along the platform was a waiting room, and next to that, the Ladies' lavatory. Ena wondered about sitting quietly in the waiting room for ten minutes. Instead she decided to go to the toilet.

Waiting in the queue, she caught sight of herself in the mirror above the sink. Having cried off her makeup, her face was pale with red blotches. And what was left of her mascara was streaked down her cheeks. She looked a fright and needed to wash her face and repair her makeup before she went to the Park.

Taking a step towards the basins, Ena took Ben's handkerchief from her handbag and gently rubbed at her face. When she had finished, she could still see faint lines of mascara and, on closer inspection, saw that rubbing her face had made it redder. Moving to the next basin, so she didn't lose her place in the queue, she turned on the tap, dipped a corner of the hankie under the cold water, and held it against her cheeks. It felt good, and when she looked in the mirror again, the dark streaks had gone and the red blotches had calmed down.

Satisfied that her face was at last clean, she patted it dry before putting on powder – she didn't need rouge. She took her mascara from her handbag, spat on it, and after rubbing the small brush across the black block, she applied it in sweeping movements to her top and lower eyelashes. Her eyes still looked puffy, but there was nothing she could do about that. She put on her lipstick and combed her hair.

Dropping her makeup into her handbag, Ena slipped into the queue and waited for a toilet to become vacant. When it did, she made for the door.

'There's a queue, you know!' A barrel of a woman in a fur coat and Cossack-style hat spat.

'Sorry, I thought as I have been waiting for some time--'

'But you haven't been waiting, have you?' The

old barrel said, 'You've been putting your slap on.' With that, the woman barged past Ena, almost knocking her over. The woman squeezed her huge frame into the narrow cubicle and slammed the door.

Ena felt tears of anger pricking at the back of her eyes. She gave the woman next in the queue a friendly smile, but she looked past Ena and shuffled forwards, filling the gap left by the furred barrel. Forcing the tears not to fall, so she didn't have to redo her makeup, Ena stormed out.

'Stupid woman,' she said aloud. She hadn't been so clever either, Ena thought. After two cups of tea, she was desperate for the toilet. Now she would have to wait until she got to the mansion.

Walking to Bletchley Park, Ena's mind wandered to when she was drinking tea with Ben, and she wondered if she would see him again. So, he worked at the MoD in London. Her steps faltered and she caught her breath. Her brother-in-law Bill also worked at the MoD. Ena wondered if he knew Ben. It was a big place; the chances of them knowing each other were slim. Even so, she might mention Ben the next time she wrote to her sister Margaret.

Forcing herself to smile, Ena approached Bletchley Park's security gate. She handed the guard her identity papers and pass. 'I'm here to see Commander Dalton. I believe my boss Mr Silcott is already here.' The guard checked the documents, and nodded her through. The walk along the footpath to the mansion was short, but Ena was so desperate to go to the toilet, it seemed like a mile. The nearer she got, the more nervous she was, making the need even greater.

At the door, Ena took several calming breaths. No good shilly-shallying; she would tell Mr Silcott exactly what had happened, or as much as she could remember, making sure he understood that the theft of her work was not her fault. She had no idea how it had happened, but she did not just fall asleep...

She walked briskly to the reception desk. 'I'd like to see Commander Dalton, please.'

'Certainly, miss,' the officer said. 'If you'd like to sign in, I'll take you to his office. I'm going that way.'

'Thank you.' Her legs felt like jelly and her hands were sweating. She wrote her name in the visitor's book and followed the man along the labyrinth of passageways to the commander's office.

The door stood ajar. When she entered, it closed behind her with a bang, making her jump. As much as she was dreading it, the sooner she told Mr Silcott and the commander what had happened on the train the better.

## CHAPTER NINE

'Come in, Miss Dudley. Take a seat.' Commander Dalton pushed himself out of his chair to a half-standing position, sitting down again when Ena did. Mr Silcott wasn't in the room. 'Now,' the commander said, 'what can I do for you?'

Ena's hands trembled. She put them on her lap. 'It's about my work,' she said, clenching her fists.

'On time as usual, Miss Dudley.' Ena's mouth fell open. 'Already taken through to the engineers.' He looked at his watch. 'They should be fitting it about now.'

Ena stared at the commander for some seconds. Eventually she found her voice. 'How did it get here?'

'Herbert Silcott, of course, a couple of hours ago.'

'Thank God! I need to speak to him,' Ena said, jumping up. 'Where is he?'

'He left after signing the work in, I think. Weren't you with him?'

'No. Did you see him?'

'What is all this?'

'Did you see Herbert Silcott sign the work in?' Ena persisted.

'No. I was in a meeting for most of the morning. By the time it finished, Herbert had left.' Ena put her hands up to her mouth to stop herself from crying out. 'Miss Dudley, it wasn't necessary for me to see Herbert. His credentials were in order, he delivered the work on time, and took an order for more work away with him. What difference does it make whether I actually saw him or not?'

Ena felt the colour drain from her face. 'Because Mr Silcott wasn't on the train.'

Commander Dalton picked up the telephone, 'Reception? I need to see the receipt book. Bring it in straight away, will you?' He dropped the receiver onto its cradle and drummed his fingers on the top of the large mahogany desk. Ena made an O of her lips and blew through them to try and calm herself. She didn't speak, nor did the commander.

A sharp rap on the door made her jump. 'Come!' the commander shouted.

'The receipt book, sir.' The officer from reception laid the open book down in front of the commander and stepped back.

Dalton ran his forefinger down the left side of the page. A faint smile played on his lips, which told Ena that he had found Mr Silcott's signature. He turned the book round, so Ena could see, and pointed to *H. Silcott*. 'There,' he said, 'you have nothing to worry about, Miss Dudley.'

Ena looked from the signature to the commander. 'That isn't Mr Silcott's signature.'

Dalton's eyes flashed with anger. He made a fist and brought it crashing down on the desk. 'Then who the hell delivered your work? More importantly, how in God's name did he get past security?'

Ena's heart was beating so fast she thought it would burst out of her chest. She lowered her eyes. The commander was angry now, but he'd be furious when she told him she was almost certain the work delivered today wasn't hers.

Ena had no idea what happened to her work once it arrived at Bletchley. Mr Silcott always said he couldn't tell her because that kind of information was need-to-know. But it didn't take a genius to work out that, with all the secrecy surrounding it, her work was important. She took a shuddering breath. What if it had been tampered with? Chances were it had. No one in their right mind would go to the trouble of stealing it only to deliver it. She looked up at the commander and pressed her lips together. If her work has been sabotaged any readings it gave would be distorted. She had to say something. If she didn't, by the time the people working with it realised, it would be too late.

She was terrified of telling the commander but she was more terrified of what the consequences would be if she didn't tell him. She cleared her throat. 'I don't think it is my work, sir.' Dalton shot her a look of outrage. She blanched and swallowed down the need to be sick. 'I'm sorry, sir, but your engineers won't be fitting my work, because my work has been stolen.'

The commander stared at her, his eyes penetrating and unblinking. 'Slow down, Miss Dudley, you are not making any sense.' Ena did as he asked, reminding herself that she needed to be clear and exact in what she was about to tell him. 'Are you telling me that an imposter delivered your work,' he looked down at the receipt book, 'more than three hours ago, and you are only telling me now?'

'Yes, sir. If I could explain...'

'You better had. And damn sharpish!'

Ena sat up, her back straight. 'First I'd like to say I had the case containing my work when I boarded the train at Rugby, and until... it *never* left my side.' The commander gave her an accepting nod. 'I thought I saw Mr Silcott get on the train and went to join him, but I couldn't find him. Thinking about it now, I don't believe it was Mr Silcott who boarded the train.' She cleared her throat. 'There was a man in a compartment who at first I thought was Mr Silcott. I am convinced that that man drugged me and stole my work, because after Northampton I remember nothing until I woke up in Euston and the case had gone.'

Commander Dalton snatched up the telephone. 'Put me through to the engineers.' There was silence for ten seconds, and then, 'This is Commander Dalton. Have you fitted the work that came in from Lowarth yet?' The answer must have been no, because he barked, 'Then don't. It may have been sabotaged.' He slammed the telephone down making Ena jump. She fought to regain her composure. 'Would you be able to tell at a glance if your work has been sabotaged?'

Not sure that she would just looking at it, Ena hesitated. 'I...'

'Would you, or would you not, Miss Dudley?'

'Yes, sir, I would.'

The commander picked up the telephone again. 'Get me the engineers again, will you? And then let Intelligence know that we may have a problem. This is Dalton. I'm bringing someone from the factory in Lowarth to look at the work.'

He put down the phone, pushed himself out of his chair and marched across the room to the door. Ena followed.

Running to keep up, Ena followed Commander Dalton out of the front door and along a narrow path to a large square building. Made of concrete, it was a complete contrast to the mansion, and looked out of place in Bletchley Park's grounds. As she went in, Ena heard the clack-clack-clacking of what sounded like typewriters in a typing pool and female voices calling out numbers at the same time. She glanced into the first room on the left. Dozens of women wearing earphones were sitting round an oblong table, scribbling ferociously on large sheets of paper.

The next room looked like a huge telephone exchange with women putting connecting plugs in and out of giant switchboards. Fascinated, Ena watched the women move around one another in swift, smooth movements.

She was miles away when she heard someone clear their throat. She looked along the corridor and saw Commander Dalton, grim-faced, disappear into the next room down.

Putting a spurt on, Ena soon arrived at the door. Although it was open, she knocked before entering. Commander Dalton and three other men stood around a wooden workbench. As she walked over to join them, all four men focussed on her.

'This is Miss Dudley,' Dalton said. 'She is responsible for...' Ena's heart almost stopped with embarrassment, 'for some of the work that comes from the Midlands. She is going to check this particular consignment, because she believes it may have been tampered with.'

Ena looked at the men in front of her. The two in overalls she assumed were engineers. Both nodded. She turned to the other man, and froze. Henry Green was from Lowarth. He had been the childhood sweetheart of her sister Bess as well as a friend of their family. Friend, or not, his face showed no sign of having known her. Ena smiled, as she had done to the other men, but didn't acknowledge him.

The X-board had been taken out of its box; the case it was delivered in stood open on the floor. 'If I could have some tools?' Ena said, pointing to a toolbox at the end of the bench. The engineer nearest the toolbox passed it along to her.

Trying to forget the four men watching, Ena looked at her work. She wondered which would be the easiest, quickest, part of the X-board to sabotage – wiring, or the dials? Wires would be easier, but the damage more difficult to locate. Dials not so easy, but any damage would be easier to see. She decided she would have to look at both.

'Does anyone have a magnifying glass?' The first engineer's hand shot up to the breast pocket in of his overalls and produced a finely-engineered magnifier.

She looked over her shoulder at Commander Dalton. 'I'll need to sit down.'

Henry Green fetched a chair from a desk by the window and placed it behind her. 'Thank you,' she said, pulling the chair up to the bench and sitting. It wasn't hot in the room but Ena was sweating and her hands felt sticky. She rubbed her palms down the front of her coat before unbuttoning it and letting it fall open.

Aware that every move she made was being noted, Ena took the diagram that she'd worked from at Silcott's out of the lid of the box and scrutinised it. She looked from the board to the diagram and back several times. There was a writing pad and a pen on the bench. Ena took it and made notes. The commander and the two engineers leant forward to watch what she was doing, making her feel even more nervous.

She looked over her shoulder at the commander. 'Could I have a little space, sir?' she asked, anxiously. Dalton mumbled a grudging agreement and ushered the three men to a small table by the window.

Analysing her work, cross-checking the diagram with the hard-wired wheels on the board, Ena made copious notes. Each of the wheel's twenty-six grooves – one for each letter of the alphabet – were equal distances apart and the letter 'D' had Ena's initials beneath it. She lifted the magnifying glass and looked closely. Her initials were not there.

She had no idea how long she had been examining the wheels, but her head ached from concentrating and her eyes felt as if they had sand in them. She looked away from the board and blinked rapidly. Commander Dalton and Co. had smoked so many cigarettes the air around them was a blue fug. Ena coughed. It was smoke, drifting across the room, that had made her eyes dry.

By the time she had finished checking her calculations it was overcast outside. She looked up to see a young Wren pulling the blackout blinds. Ena took advantage of the lack of light and sat back in her chair. When she had pulled down every blind, the Wren crossed to the door and switched on the lights. Ena closed her eyes as the harsh glare from a row of overhead bulbs flooded the room. Her neck was stiff and her back sore. She rolled her shoulders. She needed a break.

'Well?' Commander Dalton called, 'has the work been sabotaged?'

Ena opened her eyes, hardly daring to tell him what she had suspected all along. There was a shuffling of feet and a clearing of throats as the other men stubbed out their cigarettes and made their way to the workbench. When they were gathered, Ena said, 'Yes, sir. The work has been sabotaged. The wires of seven buttons on the top of the dials have been disconnected from their original positioning and reconnected to different letters. Pointing to each in turn, Ena said, 'They are, N. E. S. R. I. T. A. to E. T. A. I. N. O and S. The second group are the most commonly used letters in the English alphabet. The first group, I would guess, are the most used letters in the German alphabet.'

Ena offered the commander her notes. His face reddened and his eyes flashed with anger. He made no attempt to take them, but snapped, 'Proceed!'

'I don't know what the board is used for,' Ena

said, though she knew it had to be used in some way to receive translated communications, 'so I shall speak hypothetically.' She took a deep breath. 'If this were a telegraph or teletype machine, where information is input by a typewriter, what is received through this box now would be incorrect. And,' Ena scribbled on her notepad, 'if you were to multiply each corrupted letter by the rest of the letters in the alphabet…' She stopped scribbling, 'there would be millions, perhaps hundreds of millions of words that wouldn't make sense. They'd be gibberish.' Ena took a sharp breath and looked from the commander to Henry. 'Therefore it is my belief that the wires in these wheels have been deliberately muddled.'

An outburst of concerned exclamations followed. Dalton put his hand up. When there was quiet, he looked at the older of the two engineers. 'Can the wiring in the selector wheels be un-muddled?'

'Theoretically yes, sir. But by the time we've found out which wires have been scrambled and unscrambled them, the information would be useless, because it would be out of date.'

'How the hell could someone have done this much damage in such a short time?' Dalton hollered.

Ena gripped her chair's arms. She would have offered up a prayer but there wasn't time. 'They couldn't, sir,' she said, her voice shaky. She looked the commander in the eye. 'This is not my work. My work was not, as I first thought, sabotaged on the train, it was stolen and replaced.'

'Stolen?' he bellowed.

'And replaced. If I could explain, sir?' The commander gave a sharp nod. Ena swallowed, hoping it would lubricate her throat. It did, a little. 'I know it isn't usual. Well, it isn't the done thing at all, but--' *Damn it!* Ena said to herself. *Just say the bloody words and get it over with.* 'I engrave my initials on the metalwork.' The four men, having been eager to hear what she had to say, stood open mouthed. 'All the girls who work on the wheels and dials personalise them with their initials. Which no one is able to see. Apart from not being visible to the naked eye, they are concealed by wires running over the surface of the disks. It is not done for fun,' Ena said, which was only half true. The girls in the factory loved making their mark. Going down in history, they called it. Ena looked at each of the men in turn. Then, putting on her most serious face to make sure they believed her, she said, 'It is done at my instruction. If I find a fault when I'm checking the work, I can see at a glance whose work it is. It's a time-saving device. Instead of having to question everyone in turn, which is extremely time consuming, I speak quietly to the person whose initials are on the work. And,' she waited a couple of beats for the men to digest the importance of the signatures, 'the mistake is quickly and easily rectified.

'You see?' Ena handed one of the engineers the magnifying glass. 'There should be a small ED beneath the letter D, but there isn't.' She took the magnifying glass from the first engineer and gave it to the second.

At that moment, there was a knock at the door. Commander Dalton's secretary poked her head into the room and beckoned him out. Watching the commander leave, Ena breathed a sigh of relief. She had never been so in need of a distraction in her life.

A minute later, Dalton returned with two army officers. 'Miss Dudley, would you accompany these gentlemen?' Ena froze as she regarded the two giants standing before her. 'Tell them everything that happened to you on the way here today.'

## CHAPTER TEN

The two men, intelligence officers, Ena guessed, dwarfed her as they marched her out of the building and back to the mansion. On the left, along a short passageway leading off the main entrance foyer, one of the officers stopped and opened a door. He entered first, motioning for Ena to follow. The second officer entered after her, closed the door, and stood by it.

There was a young Wren in the sparsely furnished room. She saluted the two officers and acknowledged Ena with a nod. The officers retuned a hurried salute. Ena was so frightened, her face was numb, and could only stare.

The first officer waved the Wren to sit. She pulled a chair from under the large square table and sat down. There was a black Bakelite telephone on the table which the Wren moved to one side, pushing its braided cable out of the way to make space for what looked to Ena like a doctor's bag. She then took a notebook and pen from the bag and placed them on the table.

'Take a seat, Miss Dudley,' said the officer who had entered the room first, pulling out the chair to the Wren's right. Frightened and shaking, Ena did as she was ordered. 'Ring when you've finished,' he said to the Wren.

'Sir!' Pushing her chair away from the table, the Wren stood up and saluted again.

When the intelligence officers had gone, the Wren said, 'My name's Tilly Anderson. I'm a nurse.' She pointed to a medical badge on the lapel of her jacket.

'My name's Ena Dudley, but I expect you know that already. What's going to happen to me?' Ena asked, her eyes brimming with tears.

'Nothing you need worry about.' Still standing, the Wren opened the black bag. 'I'm just going to do a few tests.'

'Tests? What sort of tests?' Ena held her stomach. It hurt so much, because she desperately needed to go to the toilet, that she began to cry. And her head. She closed her eyes. Her head felt as if it had been hit by an axe. It had ached since she'd woken up at Euston.

'It's standard procedure when there has been a breach of security, especially when drugs are involved.'

'Drugs? Thank goodness.' Ena's suspicions were going to be proved. Now Mr Silcott would know that she had not been irresponsible, that it wasn't her fault the work went missing.

The Wren sat down and read her notebook. 'You fell asleep on the train and missed your stop?' Ena nodded. 'When you woke up, did you have a headache?'

'Yes, a blinder. I still have it. And I still feel fuzzy.'

Tilly gave a knowing nod. 'Were you thirsty when you woke?'

'Yes, and now I think about it, my mouth was really dry. I had two cups of tea on Euston station and I still felt thirsty. That reminds me, could I go to the lavatory before we start, please?'

'Of course, it's over there.' Tilly pointed to a door on the far side of the room. 'And, if you don't mind,' she said, stopping Ena when she leapt out of her seat, 'would you use this?' She produced a specimen jar from her medical bag and handed it to Ena.

'I thought there'd be a catch.' Ena wrinkled her nose and almost sprinted across the room to the toilet. 'There's no lock!' she called, from inside the sterile white room.

'Don't worry, no one will come in.'

There's no lock because they don't want people locking themselves in, Ena thought. She looked around. A tower of white paper towels sat neatly on a shelf at the side of the washbasin next to a pile of linen towels.

After using the toilet – and filling the small jar – Ena washed her hands, drying them on one of the freshly laundered towels. It felt soft to the touch. Before leaving, she wrapped a paper towel around the jar. Just looking at it embarrassed her.

When she handed it to Tilly, Ena felt her cheeks colour. Tilly took the bottle as if it were an everyday occurrence, which, Ena supposed, to a nurse it was. She sat down. 'What next?'

'I need to take your blood pressure and a sample of your blood. If you would roll up your left sleeve?'

Ena did as Tilly asked. She didn't mind having her blood pressure taken. At worst the feeling of tightening pressure made the procedure uncomfortable, but she hated the thought of a needle in her arm drawing blood. She looked away.

A second later, she felt a prick in the bend of her arm as the needle broke the skin.

'Not long now,' Tilly smiled. That was what the Red Cross nurse had said when Ena had given blood in Woodcote Village Hall, and she'd had to sit there for another ten minutes afterwards. 'All done.' Ena looked down at her arm to see Tilly placing a small square of lint over the spot where she had taken blood. 'Hold onto this and apply a little pressure, will you?'

A minute later she put a plaster over the tiny pin-prick and Ena pulled down her sleeve.

Tilly took the syringe and slowly expelled Ena's blood into a small bottle. After screwing the top on it, Tilly put it in her bag and wrote something in the notebook. 'I'll get you a cup of sweet tea,' she said, 'as soon as the intelligence officers get back.'

'Thank you.' Ena watched Tilly pick up the telephone. She asked for Intelligence, gave Ena a sympathetic smile while she waited to be put through, and then said, 'Miss Dudley and I have finished.'

Two minutes later, the intelligence officers entered the room.

'I'll take this to the medical hut. On my way back I'll call into the canteen and get Miss Dudley a cup of tea.' The man who had done most of the talking earlier nodded and walked round the table. He sat down opposite Ena. The other man sat on her right.

The man facing Ena put his elbows on the table and leaned forward. 'I want you to tell me everything that happened from the moment you left home this morning until you spoke to Commander Dalton here at the Park. Do you understand?' Ena opened her mouth to speak, couldn't find her voice, and nodded. 'Every detail – however small, or unimportant you might think it is, I want to know about it. Right?'

Ena nodded again and inhaled nervously. 'I cycled to Lowarth. I got to Silcott's Engineering, where I work, at half past eight. I parked my bicycle and went into the factory. No! I'm sorry. On the way I stopped at Newman's, the newsagents on Lowarth High Street, and bought a quarter of pear drops. Then I went to work.' Ena clasped her hands, gripping the fingers on her right hand with the fingers on her left, until her nails dug into the fleshy parts at the back. She winced.

The man opposite said, 'Take your time.'

Composing her thoughts, in order to recall every detail of the journey, Ena began again. 'After buying the pear drops, I cycled on to the factory and put my bike in the shed at the back. I went in through the main door and walked across the factory floor to the annexe where I work. Mr Silcott, my boss, was already there. I waited while he took my work from the concrete safe--'

'Was the safe locked?'

'Yes. I had locked it the night before. I'm sorry, Mr Silcott unlocked the safe and took out my work.'

The man made a note. 'Is the safe always kept locked?'

'Yes.'

'Who has keys?'

'Mr Silcott keeps the master key on his keyring with the annexe key, the key to the factory's main door, and his car keys. And there is one in his drawer, which only his assistant Miss King and I have access to.'

'Have you had reason to use the key in the past?'

'Yes. Every night. Before I leave, I unlock the safe, put in my work, and lock it again. I put the key back in the drawer.'

'And have you ever taken the key out of the office?'

'No.'

'Never? Not even when you've popped out to get a cup of tea? Perhaps there has been an occasion when you've dropped the key into your pocket and forgotten it was there.'

'No! Never! We make our own tea. Because we work long hours we have a kettle, milk, and tea in the annexe. But even if we didn't, the safe is next to Mr Silcott's desk, so there would be no reason for me, or anyone else, to take the key out of the room if we *popped* somewhere.' Ena felt a surge of anger. She knew she mustn't show it, and took a calming breath. 'I return the key to Mr Silcott's desk drawer every time I unlock, or lock, the safe.'

'And at night? Have you ever been there after Mr Silcott has left for the day?'

'Of course. But on those occasions, I put the key to the safe in Mr Silcott's desk, lock it, and put his desk key in his assistant's desk, which I have a key to, and I lock that. When I leave, I lock the only door to the annexe and I take both keys home with me. Only three people work in the annexe: Mr Silcott, Miss King and myself – and only we three have keys to the door. The last one out at night locks up. The first one in in the morning opens up.'

On the edge of peripheral vision, Ena saw the man on her left shift in his chair. 'Let's go back to this morning,' the man sitting opposite said. 'What happened next?'

Ena's mouth was dry. She licked her lips. 'Mr Silcott put the box containing my work in the suitcase and we left the factory. He then put the case in his car and Miss King drove us to the railway station in Rugby.'

'Did Mr Silcott put the case in the boot of the car?'

'No, on the back seat, next to me.' There was a knock at the door and Tilly entered. Ena was relieved to see the kind Wren and pleased when she placed a cup of tea in front of her. 'Thank you,' she whispered. She took a sip. It was just the right temperature and she gulped it down. 'I'm sorry,' she said, rubbing the back of her hand across her mouth. 'I didn't realise how thirsty I was.' She felt her cheeks redden and cleared her throat again.

'Why did you travel by train today? Doesn't the factory owner drive to Bletchley?'

'Yes, but we didn't have enough petrol. Mr Silcott tried all the garages in the area but he could only get a gallon, which wasn't enough petrol for a return journey to Bletchley. So, as Miss King had work to take to a facility in Leicestershire, he thought it best that she took the car and we travelled by train.'

The man consulted a second book that looked

like a ledger. 'It says here that the MoD supplies Silcott's Engineering with petrol coupons every week.'

'They do. But none arrived this week.' The man made a note, and nodded for Ena to carry on. 'It had been drizzling earlier, but it was raining hard by the time we arrived at the station – and it was windy. Mr Silcott stopped to get the tickets and I walked across to the platform with the case. When I got to the train, I looked back to see where he was. The first time he was in the queue, but the next time I looked I couldn't see him. Then I spotted him coming out of the Gentleman's lavatory. The train was about to leave, so the porter opened the door for me and I boarded with the case. Mr Silcott, coming from the direction of the Gents', ran to the nearest door, which was at the other end of the carriage.'

The man's eyes darted from Ena to the officer sitting next to her and back again. 'Go on.'

Ena's stomach lurched. She felt as if she was going to be sick and swallowed hard. 'As I said, the rain had turned into a storm and it was really windy. When Mr Silcott ran across the platform he had his head down and he was holding onto his hat.' Ena demonstrated with her own hand. 'I didn't see his face. He had his arm up, and I didn't see his face.' Ena's mouth fell open as the realisation hit her. 'His coat and hat were identical to Mr Silcott's, so I assumed it was him, but--' A wave of foreboding washed over her. She looked up at the intelligence officer who had been asking the questions. 'I don't think it was Mr Silcott who boarded the train. And if it wasn't him, who was it?'

The intelligence officer sitting next to Ena wrote frantically on his notepad. 'Oh my God!' Ena cried. 'If it wasn't Mr Silcott, what's happened to him? Where is he if he isn't here?' Ena jumped up. 'I've got to see Commander Dalton, tell him and ask him to telephone the factory. Find out if Mr Silcott's there, if he's all right.'

'Sit down, Miss Dudley,' the first intelligence officer said.

'But you don't understand.'

'I said, sit down!'

Ena fell into her chair, shocked at the way the officer had shouted at her. She looked at the telephone in the middle of the table and whispered, 'Could I telephone the factory in Lowarth?' The intelligence officer ignored her. 'I just need to know Mr Silcott's all right.'

'I'm afraid that won't be possible.' Ena looked at him, her eyes blazing. 'I understand how you must be feeling, Miss Dudley,' the intelligence officer said, 'And in due course you will be able to use the telephone. But it is very important that we know everything about the journey, who you met on the train, how you arrived at Bletchley. So please, just answer the questions.'

Ena looked down and nodded. 'I'm sorry,' she whispered, 'of course.'

'Tell me what happened on the train.'

'As I said, the man I thought was Mr Silcott boarded the train by a door at the opposite end of the carriage, so I went to join him – Mr Silcott that is, not the man.' Ena stopped speaking with shuddering breath and began to cry again. 'What if he's lying hurt somewhere? Please won't you ask someone to telephone to make sure he's all right?'

'The sooner you tell us everything that happened on the train the sooner you'll be able to telephone yourself, Miss Dudley.'

Ena shook her head in disbelief. 'I went into the compartment and there was a man in it. It wasn't Mr Silcott. I asked him if a man had entered the compartment at Rugby, and he said no. I asked him if he was sure and he said, or at least he implied, that he hadn't seen anyone fitting Mr Silcott's description before or after Rugby, which I took to mean he had boarded the train at one of the stations between Birmingham and Rugby. I think that is where the train came from.' Ena paused and frowned. 'But that didn't make sense.'

The man sitting opposite leant forward, as if to hear more clearly what Ena was about to say. 'The man was wearing a corduroy jacket, which at first I thought was odd in such bad weather. I noticed a heavy outdoor coat, camel in colour, on the rack above him, and his shoes were wet.' Pleased with herself for being observant, Ena said, 'If he had been sitting in that compartment all the way from Birmingham his shoes would have been dry, wouldn't they? If not dry, there wouldn't have been wet patches under them, and there were.' The man made no comment. 'Anyway, I went back along the corridor, looked in all the other compartments, asked everyone if they had seen a man fitting Mr Silcott's description, but no one had.'

'Where was the case containing your work while you were looking for your boss?'

'With me. I would never leave it anywhere,' Ena said, tersely. 'That's why I'm sure that the man sitting opposite me in the end compartment must have drugged me somehow and stolen it.'

Ena looked down and closed her eyes. Concentrating on events in the compartment of the train to Bletchley, she fought the throbbing pain in her head to get her thoughts in order. Tears threatened. She fought them too. The officer sitting across the table from her opened his mouth to speak, but Ena's eyes snapped open and she put her hand up. 'I'm sorry, but I needed to get the facts straight, and now I have.'

She looked at both men, and smiled for the first time since entering the room. 'That's it!' she shouted, 'That's it! I get travel sick. I suck pear drops in cars, buses, trains – especially on long journeys, to stop feeling sick.'

The officer opposite pushed his chair away from the table, leant back, balancing on the chair's back legs and blew out his cheeks. 'Is this relevant?'

'Yes it is relevant. It is very relevant!' Ena said. 'What I am about to tell you is the reason I went to sleep.'

'Go on, Miss Dudley,' the officer sitting next her said.

'I offered the man a pear drop.' Ena shook her head. 'No. That isn't right. Sorry!' The officer opposite was staring at her, a look of bewilderment in his eyes. If he was trying to make her feel uncomfortable, he was succeeding. Ena began again, this time directing her answer to the officer on her right. 'I didn't offer him a pear drop, as such, he hinted that he'd like one. He said he remembered that my friend and I sucked pear drops when we travelled.'

'So you knew him?'

'No. He said he had been on a train that we were on once, and that he remembered me because of the pear drops.' Ena felt her cheeks flush. The more she said, the more ridiculous the scenario on the train sounded.

'Go on,' the officer opposite said, finally showing some interest.

'I took the pear drops out of my handbag and asked him if he would like one. He said yes, but instead of taking a pear drop from the packet, he took the packet out of my hands. He said they looked good, and joked about which he should choose, before taking one. Don't you see? He held onto the sweets for… oh, I don't know, but it was a good few seconds before giving them back to me.'

'What did he do with the pear drop?'

'Put it in his mouth, of course.' Ena closed her eyes and took in a sharp breath. 'Oh, my God.' She looked earnestly from one man to the other. 'Putting a pear drop in my mouth was the last thing I remember until I woke up with a blinding headache at Euston Station.'

'Have you still got the pear drops?'

'Yes. They're in my handbag. I felt queasy on the way out of Euston and took them out, but I didn't have one. And thank goodness I didn't.'

The man sitting next to Ena who had taken her handbag from her earlier, left the table. He returned a minute later and handed it to her.

Ena thrust her hand into the handbag and produced the packet of pear drops. The officer sitting opposite reached over to take it. 'No, wait. These are not the sweets I bought in Lowarth.' Both men looked at her quizzically. 'Firstly, there are eight pear drops in a quarter. My packet would have four sweets missing.' She tipped the sweets into the table. 'I had one as soon as I bought them, I had one in Mr Silcott's car on the way to the station, I gave the man on the train one, and I had one myself on the train. 'Look – there's five left. If this were my packet, the one I bought in Lowarth, it would only have four pear drops in it.'

'Perhaps the shopkeeper made a mistake, put an extra sweet in.'

'Not possible, the bags aren't big enough. She looked at the packet and smiled. 'And it has been folded wrongly. The paper has been turned down at the top, you can see the ridge. It's the way the confectioner folds it. I twist the top after I've had one, to stop the rest from falling into my handbag. Look,' she said again, handing the packet to the man sitting opposite. 'The top has been carefully folded over, like they do in the sweet shop, but if you look closely you'll see the creases where I twisted the top after taking a sweet out in Mr Silcott's car.

'The man on the train couldn't have known that when he folded the packet,' Ena continued. 'He must have bought pear drops, poisoned them with some sort of knockout drug, and after taking one of my pear drops, swapped the packets, giving me the packet containing the poisoned pear drops.' A cold shivered ran through her as the realisation of what had happened on the 9:45 to Bletchley hit her. Ena looked from one intelligence officer to the other. 'Don't you see? I didn't have one of *my* pear drops, I had one of *his*, one that he had poisoned. That's why there's still five sweets in my packet. Then, when I was out for the count, he swapped them back again, closing the top of my packet by folding it over, the way the confectioner had folded his, which is not the way I close it. Look--' Ena demonstrated, 'I twist the top.'

Showing no sign of agreement, or even that he understood what Ena was saying, the man sniffed the packet. 'Pear drops have a distinctive taste. Didn't you notice anything different in the taste of the one you had on the train compared to the one you'd had in the car?'

'Not at the time. I don't remember anything after putting the pear drop into my mouth.' Ena trembled. Fear of what might have happened to her if she hadn't eaten the sweet, hadn't slept, engulfed her. Her stomach churned. She thought again that she was going to be sick. 'Could I have a drink of water, please?'

The officer next to her nodded to Tilly, who got up and went out of the room. She was back in a matter of minutes, with a jug and three glasses. She poured a glass of water and Ena drank it down.

'What do you remember about this man? How old was he? What did he look like?'

Ena looked up at the ceiling, trying to bring the man's face to mind. 'It's a bit of a blur, but he was around twenty-eight, thirty, with light hair… Blond. Yes, he had blond hair. I only saw him sitting down, but he looked fit – you know, muscular. And he was quite tall. At least he was taller than the other man, but not by much.'

The two officers looked at each other. 'What other man?' The officer opposite asked. 'This is the first we've heard about a second man.'

'That's because I've only just remembered him.' Ena squeezed her eyes shut and tried to remember. 'I'm only getting snatches, glimpses, of two shadowy figures. Sorry.'

'You're doing well, Miss Dudley,' the officer next to her said, pouring more water into her glass. 'Tell us what happened in London?'

Ena took a drink and wiped a droplet from her chin. 'When I woke up I was numb. I tried to move, to sit up, but my head felt as if it weighed a ton – and it ached. I had a terrible pain in my head and behind my eyes. Eventually I pulled myself up and looked out of the window in disbelief. I was in Euston. The first thing I did was look round for the case. I couldn't see properly, everything was blurred, looked wavy as if it were swaying. Anyway,' she said, 'my vision was good enough to see that the case had gone.'

Ena shook her head. 'It's hard to explain. It was a horrible feeling. I felt dizzy and disoriented, and I had this awful headache. It was as if my head was packed with cotton wool pressing on my temples. And my mouth was really dry. Anyway, I managed to get to the buffet on the station and I bought a cup of tea.'

'Did you speak to anyone?'

'Yes, but--'

'What did they say?'

'I only passed the time of day with a young American. The buffet was busy and there was only one spare seat. He asked if he could sit down and I said yes.'

'Did he ask you any questions?'

'No, not really. I had been crying and he gave me his handkerchief. And when he bought himself a cup of coffee, he bought me another cup of tea.' The officer sitting across the table from her raised his eyebrows. 'He was just being kind. Apart from his accent, he was just an ordinary young man.' Ena was dreading the questions that would follow. They were bound to include, What did you talk about, and did you tell him you were going to Bletchley? She was saved by the telephone ringing.

The man opposite reached into the middle of the table, pulled the phone towards him, and picked up the receiver. Still looking at Ena, he said, 'Yes?' A couple of seconds later, he replaced the receiver. Shuffling his papers into a pile, he put them into his attaché case and stood up. 'Time for a break. If you'd accompany Miss Dudley to the canteen, Miss Anderson?' Without waiting for Tilly to reply, he said, 'We'll resume in an hour.' He left the room. His associate followed.

## CHAPTER ELEVEN

The noise and clatter of hundreds of people met Ena and Tilly as they approached the canteen. Ena leant against the wall. She felt dizzy at the sight of so many people, and the smell of cabbage was making her feel sick. She closed her eyes, letting several women enter ahead of her.

'Would you rather have lunch in the interview room?' Tilly asked. Ena nodded. 'I'm not supposed to leave you, so you'll have to come with me to the counter. Will a sandwich and a cup of tea do?'

'Just tea for me, thanks,' Ena said. 'I don't think I could keep any food down.'

Waiting for her interrogators to return felt like an eternity. Tilly must have thought so too, because she looked at her watch several times.

'I'm sure you have better things to do than sit around here with me,' Ena said. Tilly smiled and shook her head. Blinking back her tears, Ena stood up and walked around the table. 'How long are they going to keep me here, Tilly?'

'I don't know, but they shouldn't be too long. If you want to talk, Ena, I'd be happy to listen.' Ena shook her head. 'I'm here if you want to get anything off your chest?'

Ena looked at Tilly, her eyes wide with disbelief. 'Get anything off my chest?' she said, with incredulity. 'I haven't done anything to *get off my chest*!' Ena's eyes filled with tears – and she didn't blink them back. 'I thought you believed me.' She fell into her seat and buried her head in her hands.

'I love my job,' Ena said, when she finally lifted her head. 'Not many people can do the job, because it's so complex, so.... intricate.' A hint of a smile crossed Ena's face as she thought about her work. 'It's a bit fiddly to tell you the truth. The fine wires-- I shouldn't be talking about it, I'm sorry. It's just that Mr Silcott... Oh God,' Ena cried, 'What will Mr Silcott say – and my friend, Freda. What will Freda think of me?'

Tilly Anderson put her hand on Ena's arm. A gesture that told Ena the young Wren was sympathetic to her predicament. 'I do believe you, Ena. I just thought, if you had mentioned your work to someone... Walls have ears, and all that.'

'But I haven't. And for the record, I wouldn't tell anyone. No one knows what I actually do in my job, not even my parents. They think I'm an apprentice engineer, which I am. I was only taken off the factory floor because I'm good at precision work, and I've got a knack with numbers and can work out stuff. And I couldn't tell them what happens here because, other than it having something to do with communications, I don't know.' Ena began to cry. 'I love my job, Tilly. I don't want to lose it. To tell you the truth, I am proud that I'm trusted to do sensitive work for a place like Bletchley Park.

'It's ironic,' Ena continued. 'I'm in trouble, suspected of all sorts by Commander Dalton, but if his people had sent the petrol coupons, as they should have, I wouldn't even have been on the train. Mr Silcott and I would have brought the work down by car.'

Lifting her head, Ena rubbed her eyes with the heel of her hands and turned to Tilly. 'What if the Ministry of Defence takes the contracts away from Silcott's? What I do is only a small part of the work the factory does for the different branches of the armed forces. If they don't give us any more contracts a lot of people will lose their jobs. Most of the workforce are women, mothers, whose husbands are away fighting. They depend on what they earn at Silcott's to pay the rent, the bills, and feed their children. What if--'

There was a sharp rap on the door. Tilly got up to answer it. Ena, worn out with emotion, leant back in her chair and closed her eyes. She could tell it was a man's voice, but she was not able to hear what he was saying because he spoke in a whisper. She wiped her hand across her face, too distraught to care.

'Commander Dalton would like to see you, Ena,' Tilly said, returning to the table. She picked up Ena's coat and handbag and offered her her hand. 'I'll take you to his office.'

Exhausted, Ena pushed back her chair, pulled herself to her feet, and let Tilly lead her out of the interrogation room.

Commander Dalton stood up when Ena entered. 'Sit down, Miss Dudley.'

Without looking at him, Ena sat heavily on the chair in front of his desk.

'One of our intelligence people has telephoned Silcott's Engineering.' Ena sat up, eager to hear news of her boss. 'On the pretext of requiring a quote for work in the future, he asked to speak to Herbert Silcott and was told by Miss King that Mr Silcott was away on business, not expected back in the office until later in the day.'

Ena's hand flew up to her mouth. 'Where is he?'

'Our man said he had spoken to a Miss Dudley on a previous occasion and asked if he could speak to her. Miss King told him that Miss Dudley had accompanied Mr Silcott and wouldn't be in the office until tomorrow. She asked if she could take a message. Our man thanked her and said he was getting quotes from other factories and would ring back. He then telephoned Mrs Silcott in case her husband had missed the train and returned home.' Ena crossed her fingers. 'He hadn't.'

Ena's eyes widened. 'The man with the wet shoes!' The commander tilted his head and looked at her curiously. 'Mr Silcott didn't return home because the man in the compartment must have kidnapped him or something. How else would he get Mr Silcott's hat and coat? I didn't see his face because he was holding onto his hat, Mr Silcott's hat, and his face was hidden. I thought the man who left the Gents' lavatory and ran for the train was Mr Silcott because he was wearing Mr Silcott's hat and coat. I didn't see the hat in the compartment but that only means he got rid of it. He could have thrown it out of the window for all I know. Or he could have put it under the coat. He'd tried to disguise it by turning it inside out, but I saw Mr Silcott's camel-coloured coat on the overhead rack.'

A worried frown crept across Commander

Dalton's face. 'I suspect you are right, Miss Dudley. I also suspect the man was a spy.' The commander gathered up the folders on his desk and stacked them into a neat pile. 'You were targeted, Miss Dudley. Targeted.' Ena felt fingers of ice grip her spine. She shivered. 'And, if what you say is true, you were lucky you were only drugged. These people can be dangerous.' Only half taking in what the commander was saying, Ena nodded mechanically. 'I'm sorry we had to interrogate you, but I'm sure you understand why it was necessary.'

Still thinking about Mr Silcott, Ena nodded again.

The commander pushed back his chair and stood up.

Ena took his cue. Then, realising what he had just said made her heckles rise. 'What do you mean, *if* what I say is true? Of course it's true.' The commander's eyes narrowed, but Ena was not going to be intimidated. 'What is it? What is it that I have told you that you don't believe?'

'*Pear drops*! The man in the compartment knew you had pear drops in your handbag. How could he possibly have known that?'

'I told the intelligence officers. He said he remembered me from the last time he travelled on the 9:45 train.'

'And that was--?'

'November 15th 1940.'

'You seem very sure of the date?' he said, a touch of sarcasm in the commander's voice.

'I am. Coventry, the nearest city to Lowarth, was blitzed to smithereens the night before. Mr

Silcott had to go to see his in-laws, so I came down to Bletchley with Freda King. It was my first time.'

'Of course.' The commander took a file from the middle of the pile and began reading. 'He went to see how badly the Williams Engineering factory had been damaged, is that right?'

'Yes. Williams Engineering is owned by Mr Silcott's in-laws. It is, was, our parent company. It's so long ago now,' Ena blustered, 'I can't remember the exact details.' The commander nodded slowly. 'Anyway, it was the day after the bombing that I accompanied Miss King to Bletchley. We travelled down by train and we sucked pear drops during the journey. I always do. I get travel sick and the pear drops...' Exhausted, Ena stopped speaking. 'You do believe me, don't you?'

The commander looked at her for a long minute. 'Someone must have told the man in your compartment – if it was him who stole the work – what you were carrying and where you were taking it. That same someone must have told him you had pear drops in your handbag.' Ena was beginning to see what the commander was getting at. 'And the man had to have been given this information well in advance of your journey, because you cannot buy drugs that put a person to sleep in the local newsagent's. Do you understand what I'm saying, Miss Dudley?' Ena nodded. 'So, if it was not you who told him, who was it?'

In shock, Ena slumped against the backrest of the chair. 'I don't know,' she said at last. 'But I don't believe it was anyone at Silcott

Engineering.' She looked sternly into the commander's eyes. She wasn't having him accuse her or her workmates of betraying the country. 'Have you considered that it might have been someone at Bletchley?' she asked. 'I suck pear drops when I'm here, and I offer them round. It could be any one of a dozen people.'

The commander's face turned scarlet and his eyebrows knitted together in a dark frown. For a second, Ena thought he was going to explode. Instead he leant his elbows on his desk, made a steeple of his fingers, and said, 'Go to reception, Miss Dudley, I shall arrange for a car to take you to the station.'

'I'd rather walk, thank you.' Ena got to her feet and looked around the room. Her belongings were on a chair by the door. Walking over to them, she could feel the commander's eyes boring into her back. She put her coat on as quickly as she could, swung her gasmask over her shoulder, and grabbed her handbag. She turned to face the commander. He was staring at her. He probably hadn't taken his eyes off her since he had told her to go.

'Goodbye,' she said, turned and opened the door. He didn't reply.

Closing the door behind her, Ena took a couple of faltering steps. She reached out for the window ledge, to stop herself from falling, and looked through tears of anger at the lake.

She wanted to scream with the injustice of it, the unfairness, especially from Commander Dalton who had blindly assumed it was her, or someone from Silcott Engineering, betraying the country. Ena clenched her teeth. She had known most of the women for years. They were ordinary wives and mothers working to keep a roof over their heads so there was somewhere for their husbands and sons to come home to. They wouldn't risk losing their jobs, they couldn't afford to. Then the reality of what would happen if Commander Dalton took the contract of work away from Silcott Engineering hit her.

Worried that the merest doubt about security at Silcott's would cost the women their jobs, Ena turned back to the commander's door, knocked, and went in. 'Forgive me for barging in like this, sir, but I need to explain something.' He reached for the telephone. 'Before you have me thrown out, would you please give me five minutes of your time?'

He looked at his watch. 'Five minutes!'

'Thank you. Firstly, I did not know the man on the train. I had nothing to do with the theft of my work, nor did anyone else at Silcott's.' Trying to ignore the look of fury on Dalton's face, she said quickly, 'Secondly, I am asking you not to take work away from Silcott Engineering. The workforce, mainly women whose husbands are overseas fighting for our country, depend on the money they earn at the factory to pay the rent, bills, and to feed and clothe their children.' Dalton made a show of looking at his watch. 'But it isn't only for them that I'm asking, it's also for me. I know you think I was somehow involved in the sabotage of my work, but I was not. I can't go into what my sister and brother are doing in the war, except to say that my brother is on the front line and my sister's work, also overseas, is highly classified. I should not have told you that, but I think I can trust you.' Ena thought she saw a twinkle of a smile in the commander's eyes. She didn't react. 'I just want you to know that I am proud of them both, and I hope that one day they will be proud of me.'

The commander looked at his watch, again.

'I'll get to the point. Please don't stop the work Silcott Engineering does for the MoD and for Bletchley Park. If you don't trust me, I won't do any more sensitive work. I'll go back to the factory floor.' Ena felt tears stinging the back of her eyes. 'And if that isn't good enough for you, I'll hand in my notice, I'll leave. I'm sure, in time, Mr Silcott will find someone else to do my job. Please,' Ena begged, 'don't make everyone at Silcott's suffer because of me.'

Commander Dalton pushed back his chair and stood up. His lips twitched. Ena thought he was going to speak. When he didn't, something inside her snapped. 'All those women, mothers, will be out of work.' Her eyes widened with anger. 'If that happens, I hope you'll be able to live with yourself, Commander Dalton. I know I shan't!'

Turning away, Ena marched to the door, opened it, and left without looking back.

## CHAPTER TWELVE

'Ena?'

A man was calling her name. Pretending she couldn't hear him, Ena picked up her step and walked on.

'Ena?'

She shot a look over her shoulder. The man was waving. Recognising him, she stopped. Henry Green was running towards her. Having ignored her in the hut, Ena wondered what he wanted with her now.

'Hello?' Henry beamed her a smile. 'I could hardly believe my eyes when I saw you with Horace Dalton.'

'Oh? I didn't think you recognised me.'

Henry laughed. 'Of course I did. But I thought if you were in some sort of trouble, I'd be better placed to help you if no one knew we were friends. I had no idea you worked at Bletchley.'

'I don't really.'

'But the X-board?'

'Well yes, but...' Ena wondered if Commander Dalton had asked Henry to come after her and trap her in some way. Thinking about it, there hadn't been much time for such a conversation. Even so, not knowing who she could trust and not wanting to get into more trouble, she decided to tell him what he already knew. 'I did some work for Bletchley that was sabotaged. Now my credibility is in question, which I'm sure you are aware of.' She stopped and checked herself. 'I work at Silcott

Engineering in Lowarth, and what I do there ends up here.' Her vision blurred as her eyes filled with tears. 'Oh, Henry,' she cried, 'I've got myself into terrible trouble.'

Before she could tell Henry more, a mountain of a security guard came lumbering towards her from the mansion's main door. 'Oh no!' Ena wiped her tears with the back of her hand.

The guard arrived red faced with beads of perspiration on his forehead. 'Excuse me, sir,' he wheezed, 'I have been looking for this... Miss Dudley...'

'Why?' Henry asked.

'I have orders to escort her off the premises. If you'd like to come with me, miss, I'll take you to the railway station.' The security man clamped a hand the size of a plate, with sausage-like fingers, around the top of Ena's arm. 'There's a car waiting to take you.'

'Hold on a minute, old chap,' Henry said, seizing the man's hand and removing it from Ena's arm. 'Who ordered you to take Miss Dudley to the station?'

'Commander Dalton, sir.'

'Then go and tell the commander that Miss Dudley is an old friend of mine, Henry Green,' The security guard nodded as if to say he knew who Henry was, 'and that I shall take her to the station.'

The security guard looked from Ena to Henry. 'But my orders are to put Miss Dudley on the next train to Rugby.'

'Damn your orders, my friend. I shall put Miss Dudley on a train to Rugby. So be a good chap and go and tell Horace.'

'If you're sure, sir?'

'I am.'

As the security guard walked back to the mansion, Henry winked at Ena.

'You won't get into trouble, will you?'

'No. Horace is a bit of a stickler for protocol, but he's a good sort. I poked my head round his door and said goodbye. So he knows my shift has just finished. And he knows the station is on the way to my digs, so he'll be fine about me escorting you. I'm afraid I don't have a car, so we'll have to walk.'

Ena laughed. 'I'd rather walk five miles with you, than sit in a security car for five minutes with that gorilla.'

Arriving at the station, Henry checked the times of the trains. 'There's a train to Rugby in two minutes, or,' he raised an eyebrow, 'we could have a cup of tea in the buffet. But if we do that, you'll have to get the 4:25 and you'll be late getting back. What do you think?'

'Tea please. I'm parched.'

There was a vacant table by the window and one against the back wall. Ena didn't want to risk being seen by the security man, if he had followed her, and made her way to the table at the back of the room. The thought of a hot drink, in the company of someone who wasn't there to accuse her of anything, made Ena feel better.

Henry joined her after ordering them both tea. When the waitress brought the cups over, she also had a thin slice of Victoria sponge on the tray.

'I wanted to buy you something nice by way of a peace offering, but that's all they had left.' He turned his attention from Ena to the waitress and grimaced. 'It looks a bit dry.'

The waitress looked down her nose, and with more than a little sarcasm in her voice, said, 'If it isn't good enough for you, sir, I'll take it back.'

'No! Please don't do that,' Ena said. 'It looks wonderful.' She frowned playfully at Henry before taking a bite of the cake. 'It's delicious. Thank you,' she said to the waitress, who swooped down directly in front of Henry to pick up a used cup and saucer. Ena put her hand up to her mouth and smothered a giggle as she watched the waitress flounce back to the counter. 'You deserved that,' she laughed.

'Her performance has cheered you up, I'm pleased to see.'

'It has. So has this cake.'

'Am I forgiven then, for not letting on earlier that I knew you?'

Making a show of deciding whether or not to forgive Henry, Ena looked at him steely-eyed and bit into her cake. 'All right then. I didn't have any lunch; I'm too weak to argue!'

Henry laughed. 'You didn't miss much. The food in the canteen...' He shook his head. 'So, how are your mother and father? And how's Bess and your other sisters?'

'Dad's working at the Foundry in Lowarth. When the lads and grooms were called up, Lord Foxden had the horses taken to his estate in Sussex, so Dad lost his job as head groom. Mother's well. She worries because Dad joined the ARP and is always in the thick of it. Bess worked in London, as a teacher, until the children were evacuated at the end of 1939. But she's home now. She turned the Foxden Estate into arable land. Not on her own,' Ena laughed. 'She's got what they call an army of land girls working with her.'

'And Tom?'

Ena's expression became serious. 'Tom's in the army, in France. We haven't heard from him for a while. Margaret's in London,' she said, brightening. 'She married Bill Burrell. I'm not sure you'd know Bill.' Henry shook his head. 'Anyway, Margaret's a dancer now in a West End show. She started as an usherette, then got a job in the chorus. She's having a whale of a time. And Claire's in the WAAF.' She thought it best not to mention Claire's work. She didn't know anything about it anyway, so left Claire stationed at RAF Morecambe in Lancashire.

Ena ate the last of her cake, washing it down with a drink of tea. She picked at the crumbs on the plate. 'Thank you, Henry,' she said, then burst into tears. 'I'm sorry.' She fished in her handbag for her handkerchief.

'What is it?' Ena shook her head. 'Come on, it can't be that bad.' Finding and discarding the ball of sopping handkerchief from her tears earlier in the day, Ena picked up the paper serviette that the cake had been on, dabbed at her eyes, and pushed it into her pocket. She sat for some time staring at the condiments in the middle of the table. Absentmindedly she lifted her cup. It was empty.

'Would you like more tea?' Without waiting

for a reply, Henry got up and made his way to the counter. Ena wondered whether it would be safe to tell Henry what had happened. He was a friend of Commander Dalton's, which might help. On the other hand it might not.

'Was it that oaf of a security guard who upset you?' Henry asked, returning with two cups.

'No! Well, a bit.' Ena took a sip of her tea. 'Can I talk to you in confidence, Henry?'

'Of course you can, Ena.'

'Commander Dalton had two intelligence officers interrogate me and it's left me... I was going to say tearful, but truthfully it's left me terrified. It wasn't the intelligence officers' fault; they were only doing their job. No,' she sighed, 'the fault was mine. Well, it wasn't my fault, not really, it was Mr Silcott's. But he couldn't help it because he wasn't there. And,' Ena let out a loud sob, 'I don't know where he is.'

Henry put his hands up. 'Slow down, Ena, you're not making sense.' He took a handkerchief from his coat pocket. 'Dry your tears, and when you're ready, tell me what happened.'

Ena wiped her face, looked at her sister's old boyfriend for several minutes, and decided against it. She desperately wanted to tell Henry, but she had told Commander Dalton that she hadn't spoken to anyone about the work she did for Bletchley, and she'd promised him she never would. 'I can't tell you, Henry, I've signed the Official Secrets Act.' Tears began to well up in her eyes again. 'I can't tell anyone.'

'I've signed the Act too,' Henry said, sympathetically. 'I work with the machines you make parts for at Silcott's. That's why I was there when you discovered your work had been sabotaged.'

Unable to keep it to herself a second longer, the words poured out of Ena's mouth in a torrent. 'I am suspected of espionage; of leaking information to the person who stole my work.' Henry's eyes widened. 'Which I didn't do! I would never do anything like that, Henry. And,' she took a shuddering breath, 'now I'm petrified that because of me, the commander won't give Silcott's any new contracts. If he doesn't, the women who work there will be unemployed and their families will go hungry – and it will be my fault.'

Henry took hold of Ena's hand. 'If you tell me what happened, I might be able to help.'

Ena looked into his kind face. The skin at the corners of his brown eyes creased when he smiled, as he was doing now. She ached to tell him, share the burden, but shook her head. 'I've said too much already. Please don't press me.'

They heard the train come in to the station. 'I'd better go,' Ena said. Henry helped her into her coat. She picked up her handbag and gasmask, and the two old friends left the buffet.

'Thank you for the tea and cake, Henry,' Ena said, when they were on the platform. 'I'm sorry I couldn't tell you more--'

'Don't be sorry.' Henry opened the door of the train and gave Ena a warm smile. 'Will you come to the Park again?'

'After today? I doubt it,' she shrugged, 'but you never know.' The brakes released and the train jolted, catching Ena off balance. She stumbled. Henry caught her and she looked into his eyes. 'I'd better board,' she whispered, 'or I'll miss this train too. Goodbye, Henry.'

'Goodbye, Ena. I'm sorry I can't send my best wishes to the family, but no one knows I'm here.'

'Don't worry, I won't say anything.' She laughed. 'They don't know I'm here, either.' The whistle sounded along the platform. 'I'd better get on the train.'

Henry bent down and kissed Ena on the cheek. His lips were soft and warm. She smiled up at him. A tingling sensation in the pit of her stomach almost took her breath away. It was a strange, exciting feeling. 'Take care,' he said, as she mounted the steps.

'I will,' Ena called, from the train's open window. She waved until she could no longer see Henry, then found a seat.

By the time the train arrived in Rugby, it was dark. The air smelled of engine oil and damp coal, and fine drizzle made patterns like spiders' webs on her woollen coat. She turned her collar up against the wind and looked along the platform. Fog as dense as a blanket hovered above the northbound tracks.

She walked quickly down the station tunnel and up Railway Terrace to the bus stop. She didn't have to wait long. Sitting on the first seat inside the door, she gave the conductor a shilling. 'Lowarth please.' The bus conductor turned the handle on his ticket machine: out came a ticket. He tore it off and handed it to Ena, with sixpence change.

With the ticket in her hand, Ena relaxed and looked out of the window. It was too dark and too foggy to see anything. She was tired but daren't close her eyes in case she fell asleep. Worse still, she might be sick.

The bus wound its way along the Rugby to Lowarth Road, lurching to stop and pick up or put down in every village. Instinctively, Ena went into her handbag for pear drops. They weren't there. They were being analysed somewhere by one of the commander's medical people. Ena took a shaky breath and swallowed down the feeling of nausea. The journey to Lowarth seemed to take forever and by the time Ena left the bus on Coventry Road she felt very sick and very tired.

She was certainly too tired to concentrate on cycling home through blacked-out Lowarth and low-lying fog. She had enough money left to pay for a taxi home to Foxden and decided to telephone Clark's Taxi from the factory.

Ena walked up to Silcott's. She had her own set of keys but she didn't want a repeat performance of the last time she had let herself in after dark. Charlie Dawkins, the night watchman, had been dozing in his chair. He woke up, thought the Germans had invaded, rang the alarm, and in no time the air-raid sirens were wailing and Lowarth's entire ARP brigade, including her father, were swarming all over the factory.

Ena knocked on the door and peered through the glass to see if Charlie was about. She rested her forehead on the door, sighed through a yawn, and closed her eyes. When Charlie opened the door, Ena fell into his arms. 'You all right, Miss Dudley?' he laughed.

Ena took a couple of stumbling steps before regaining her balance. 'I am now you're here, Mr Dawkins. Would you be a love and take me through to the annexe? I'm too tired to bike home. I'm going to see if I can get a taxi.'

'Anything for you, Miss Dudley.' The night watchman gave Ena a fatherly smile, and shining his torch on the floor, escorted her through the factory to the annexe. Ena took her keys from her bag, unlocked the door, and flicked on the light. 'I'll leave you to it, miss,' he said. 'Give me a shout when you're ready to leave and I'll see you out.'

Already at Mr Silcott's desk, Ena picked up the telephone. She watched Charlie Dawkins amble back into the factory. When he had disappeared into the darkness, she put the telephone back on its cradle and closed the door.

Standing in the middle of the room, Ena looked around. She didn't believe Mr Silcott or Freda were traitors. She knew them both too well. They were not spies, nor would they help a spy to steal her work. If it weren't such a serious business, it would be laughable. She picked up the telephone again and waited for the operator. 'But someone did,' she said aloud.

'Would you repeat that, caller?'

'Oh, sorry. Clark's Taxi, please. Woodcote 835.'

'One moment.' Ena heard the phone go dead and then, 'Putting you through, caller.'

'Thank you,' Ena said, but the operator had

already pulled the plug.

'Clark's Taxi,' Ena heard her friend say.

'Hello Beryl, it's Ena. Would your dad be able to fetch me from Silcott's?'

'Dad's finished for the night but I'll come. We're just having supper. Be with you in twenty minutes, all right?'

'That'll be fine.' Twenty minutes would give her time to have a look around. 'Thanks, Beryl,' she said, putting the telephone down. Snooping on her friends felt wrong, but she knew that she hadn't told anyone that she was taking work to Bletchley today or that she sucked pear drops when she travelled. She hated the thought that Commander Dalton could be right and someone she worked with had helped a German spy to sabotage her work, so she set about to prove him wrong.

With one eye on the door in case the night watchman returned, Ena opened the top drawer of Freda's desk. Her cheeks burned with embarrassment as she fingered through documents and worksheets regarding work assigned to herself and her friend. There wasn't anything there that she hadn't seen before.

Closing that drawer, she opened the next one down. Dockets and notes attached to petrol coupons from the MoD. Several a month, dated and signed, going back to April of last year. Nothing unusual there.

She pulled on the bottom drawer. It was stuck. She tugged again and it sprang open a couple of inches. Forcing it open further, until she could get her hand in, Ena ran her fingers along the wooden runners. She touched something. It felt like paper. On her knees, she peered into the cavity behind the drawer. An envelope was trapped between the back of the drawer and the back of the desk.

On her side, her arm stretched as far as the gap between drawer and desk would allow, Ena tugged the envelope free. With the drawer fully open, she sat back on her heels and read the envelope's contents.

No wonder Commander Dalton had looked shocked when Ena told him they had to travel down to Bletchley by train because they hadn't received any petrol coupons this month. Here they were. Ena put the coupons back in the envelope, and placed that on top of Freda's desk.

Except for several letters which had already been opened, the drawer was empty. Ena picked them up and glanced through them. Two were from Freda's brother, Walter. She read the first page. Walter had referred to Freda as *Dear sister*. In the body of the letter he said that he was working hard, might have to go overseas soon, and ended with *Hope to see you at Uncle's in Northampton before I leave.* He signed off with *Keep up the good work, Walter*. The second letter from Walter was much the same as the first.

The last letter was from someone who signed off as *H*. A close friend if the salutation *Dearest* was anything to go by. It was clear from reading the letter that H and Freda were a little more than friends. But again, there was nothing out of the ordinary in the body of the letter. She returned all three letters to their respective envelopes and put them back in the drawer, making sure she put them in the order they were in when she had taken them out.

Ena blew out her cheeks. Strange that Freda hadn't told her that she was walking out with someone, if of course she *was* walking out with the man who signs himself only as *H.* Mysterious, Ena thought, but not a capital offence.

Pulling herself up, Ena remembered the crumpled envelope containing the petrol coupons on the top of Freda's desk. She couldn't leave it there or Freda would know she'd been looking through her desk. The only thing she could do was put the envelope back where she found it and hope it would eventually fall into the bottom drawer where Freda would see it. Satisfied that there was nothing sinister in Freda's desk drawers, Ena pushed the drawer closed.

She went to Mr Silcott's desk. The top drawer where the safe key was kept was always locked.

Returning to Freda's desk, Ena took the key that opened her boss's desk from the top drawer. Again, there were only worksheets and documents stamped *Top Secret* in red, which she didn't read. The second drawer was deeper than the first and held staff information. Ena fingered through the files until she found Freda's details. Previous address Number 7 Manning Street, Oxford, Current address, since 1939, 24 Newbold Street, Lowarth. No Northampton address. But then it was her uncle's home, not Freda's. Ena put the file back and nudged the drawer to with her knee. In the bottom drawer were maps, train timetables, insurance documents and other business papers, but nothing that even hinted of espionage or spies.

Locking the top drawer, Ena returned the key to Freda's desk then looked at the clock. Beryl would be here in the taxi any minute. Ena needed to leave. As she turned the key in the door of the annexe she called Mr Dawkins. 'I'm off home,' she said, 'would you lock me out, please?'

'Is that you, Ena?'

'Yes, Mam. Just taking my coat off.' Ena looked in the hall mirror and tutted. Her hair was a mess. The usual deep wave at the front was so damp it stuck to her forehead in rats' tails. She ran a comb through it and held it in place with a Kirby grip. It didn't look any better, but it would have to do.

'Thank goodness you're here,' Ena's mother said. 'I was beginning to worry.' Putting her knitting down, she held onto the edge of the table and pulled herself up. 'There's a bit of stew left. I'll get a bowl.' But first she turned to the kitchen dresser. 'This came for you a bit ago.' She handed Ena a plain brown envelope. Ena felt her pulse quicken. What now? Her mother, looking over Ena's shoulder, said, 'I thought it was Bill come to give us bad news.'

'Who? Margaret's Bill?'

'Yes, on that big motorbike of his. I mean with him and Margaret living in London, in all the bombing.' She clicked her tongue. 'I was relieved when it wasn't Bill, I can tell you. Go on then, open it.' Ena ran her finger along the flap at the top of the envelope. 'And then I thought it might be about our Tom.'

'Don't worry so, Mam. If anything had

happened to Tom, you'd have been sent a telegram. And it wouldn't be addressed to me, it would be addressed to you and Dad.' The adhesive on the top of the envelope eventually gave way to the pressure Ena was applying. She took out a single sheet of white paper. It had neither the name of the sender nor a signature. It didn't need one, Ena knew exactly who had sent it and where it had come from. 'It's an order for work,' she said, returning the letter to its envelope.

'Why did they bring it here to you?'

'I was at their offices today.' She waved the envelope as if in some way it backed up her story. 'I took some work over.' To Ena's relief, her mother didn't ask where the offices were, so she carried on. 'They should have given me the order when I was there, but the boss was in a meeting. Anyway, we've got the work, that's all that matters.' Ena folded the envelope in four and put it in her pocket.

If she hadn't been so hungry, Ena would have gone straight up to her bedroom to read the document. but having only eaten a round of toast at breakfast and a slither of sponge cake at teatime, she was ravenous.

Lily Dudley ladled stew into a bowl and placed it in front of Ena. It was mostly carrots and parsnips, which her father had grown in his allotment. Because of rationing there was no meat in it, but it was hot and it smelt good. While her mother cut and buttered a slice of bread, Ena tucked in. The document was burning a hole in her pocket but whatever Commander Dalton had to say would have to wait until she had eaten.

At eleven o'clock, her father came in from a night on ARP watch. Too tired to do more than wash her face, Ena kissed her mum and dad goodnight and went up to bed.

In her bedroom, she closed the door and undressed. She took the envelope from her jacket pocket, and hung the jacket up next to her skirt in her small wardrobe. Pulling on her nightgown, she jumped into bed.

The letter was clearly not an order for work or it would have been stamped *Top Secret* and sent from the Ministry of Defence in London. Ena had never been privy to any personal correspondence from Commander Dalton at Bletchley Park but she was certain if she had it would have been signed. This document wasn't. Pulling the blankets up to her neck, leaving only her hands exposed to the cold air in her bedroom, Ena began to read. *Green vouched.* Ena leant back against the headboard of her bed and looked to the heavens. 'Thank you, Henry,' she said aloud, before reading on. *Do not speak to anyone about the events of today.* The word 'anyone' was underlined in red. *Imperative that no one learns of the loss on the train.* 'No one' was also underlined in red. *Work order to follow. Proceed as usual. Will be in touch.* Ena stared at the letter in disbelief – and read it again.

## CHAPTER THIRTEEN

Freda was already at her desk when Ena arrived at the factory on Saturday morning. 'Herbert didn't come back here yesterday,' she said, lifting her head and swivelling round in her chair to face Ena. 'I was so worried, I telephoned the house, but there was no reply. Any idea why he didn't come in?'

Ena's mind was blank. She needed to say something – to stop her friend from worrying, if nothing else. 'I don't know. I--' The telephone on Mr Silcott's desk burst into life. Ena put her hand up and mouthed, Hang on.

'Silcott Engineering. Can I help you?'

'This is Commander Dalton.'

Ena's mouth went very dry at the sound of the commander's voice. He had never telephoned at the weekend before. She swallowed. 'Ena Dudley speaking,' she said, in as normal a voice as possible.

'Are you alone?'

She wondered how she could let him know that she was not, and said, 'Mr Silcott hasn't arrived yet.' Her heart beat so loudly she felt sure Freda would hear it. 'Can Miss King or I help you?'

'He telephoned from the hospital.'

Hospital? Gripped by panic, Ena felt the colour drain from her face and turned sideways, so Freda didn't see. 'I'll get Mr Silcott to telephone you as soon as he comes in,' she said, hoping her voice didn't betray her fear.

'He won't be coming in today.'

'I see...'

'Mrs Silcott will ring to say he has the flu and is staying at home. I'm biking a work order to you. When you've completed the work, I want *you* to deliver it. Understood?'

'Understood, sir. Thank you.'

'Don't thank me until you know what it is I want you to do, Miss Dudley.'

Ena laughed nervously. 'I'm confident that we will do whatever is necessary to get the job done and delivered on time.'

'Goodbye, Miss Dudley.'

'Good bye, Commander.'

'Is he giving us more work?' Freda asked.

'Yes. He's biking up a work order.' Ena pulled a mock-worried face. 'We should have waited until he was out of his meeting yesterday and brought the order with us. Still, no harm done.' The telephone sprang into life again, making Ena jump. 'We're popular today,' she laughed, more from tension than humour. She picked up the receiver quickly in case Freda offered to answer it. 'Silcott Engineering, Can I help you?'

'It's Dorothy Silcott here.'

The boss's wife sounded tearful. 'Good morning, Mrs Silcott. I'm afraid Mr Silcott hasn't arrived yet.'

'He won't be coming in today. He has the flu. The doctor says he must stay in bed until his temperature is back to normal.'

'Oh, I am sorry, Mrs Silcott.' Ena glanced across the room at Freda, who was about to fill the kettle but had stopped to listen to the call, and mouthed, Mr Silcott is ill. 'Wish him a speedy recovery from Miss King and I, won't you? And tell him not to worry about the factory. We all have plenty of work to be getting on with. Oh, and would you tell him that Commander Dalton has just telephoned. He's biking a work order up, which I shall be dealing with.'

'I will.'

'Thank you, Mrs Silcott. Good bye.' Ena put the receiver on its cradle and turned to Freda. 'Mr Silcott isn't coming in. He's got the flu. Still, we can manage without him, can't we?'

Freda nodded, 'Of course. Poor Herbert,' she said. 'Was he showing any signs of illness yesterday when the two of you were at Bletchley?'

Pulling a thoughtful face by turning her mouth down at the edges and tilting her head, Ena said, 'Now you mention it, he did look a bit peaky, but he didn't say anything. The flu can come on without any warning, can't it?' Ena went over to Freda and took the kettle out of her hand. 'The kettle won't boil itself,' she laughed, giving it a shake. There was enough water in it for two cups. While her friend was worrying about Herbert Silcott, Ena set the kettle down on the stove, lit the gas ring under it, and wondered what it was the commander wanted her to do.

'Feeling ill explains why Herbert didn't come into the factory yesterday afternoon,' Freda said, suddenly. 'But why didn't you?'

Deep in thought, Freda's question had taken Ena by surprise. It took her a second to gather her wits. 'I bumped into an old friend. You might have met him when you were at Bletchley. Henry Green?' Freda pushed out her bottom lip and shook her head. 'He and our Bess used to walk out together.' Ena smiled as the memory of Bess and Henry came into her mind. 'It was a long time ago now. He's very nice.'

Freda turned sideways, looked over her right shoulder, and batted her eyelashes. Ena felt herself blush. Freda had clearly taken her meeting Henry to mean she was sweet on him. 'Not my type, so you needn't start fishing for information,' Ena laughed. 'Anyway, Henry went off to university and met someone else.' Ena felt it best not to mention that the someone else was thought to be a man.

'Bess didn't see much of Henry after that, but they stayed friends. They wrote to each other quite often, I think. So when he invited me to tea I said yes, which is why I forgot about the new work order.'

'And your sick boss, by the sound of it.'

'I didn't forget Mr Silcott,' Ena said, laughing. 'When I saw him at the station he looked fine.' Which, in a way, was true. The last time Ena had seen Herbert Silcott was at the station – Rugby station, not Bletchley – and it wasn't after they had finished work, it was before they'd even started. 'Do you want to know what happened or not?'

'Of course I do. I want to know all the juicy details. Don't leave anything out,' Freda said, tapping the side of her nose with her finger.

'We went to the buffet on Bletchley station. Henry bought me tea and a slice of Victoria sponge, which was very nice of him. He was always a nice fellow,' Ena said, as much to herself as to Freda.

'And?'

'And the train that I had intended to catch was delayed.' Freda looked disappointed and Ena let out a loud sigh. 'I don't know, the trains get worse. And when it did eventually arrive, it was packed to the gunnels with soldiers. I had to stand all the way to Northampton. My own fault, I should have caught the earlier one.' She realised she was waffling and was grateful when the kettle whistled.

'So, what time did you get back?' Freda asked as she ladled two spoons of tea into the pot. Ena poured boiling water onto the tealeaves and, to give herself time to think, took the spoon from Freda and swished the leaves around a couple of times.

'Seven or thereabouts.' Ena squinted into the middle distance as if she was trying to remember the exact time. She was actually racking her brains for something credible to say – and couldn't think of anything. 'It might have been a bit later. It took an age to get from Rugby to Lowarth. The bus from the station stopped at every bus stop whether there was anyone to pick up or not. The driver probably didn't want to get back to the depot too early in case he was sent out on another run.' Freda nodded, put milk into two cups and Ena poured the tea. 'I was too tired to bike home, so I telephoned Clark's Taxi to fetch me.'

They carried their drinks to their respective desks and sat down. 'How did you get into work this morning?' Freda asked, taking a sip of her tea.

'Beryl was driving the taxi last night, and as luck would have it, she had an early morning pick up in Bitteswell, so she called for me on the way and dropped me off. What is this,' Ena said, laughing, 'some sort of interrogation?'

On Wednesday morning, Ena found a letter addressed to her among the post. It was from Ben Johnson asking when she would next be visiting her friend in Bletchley. She slipped into her handbag and at lunchtime, read it again. She was taking work down to Bletchley on Friday and wondered if she should write and tell him.

'Penny for them?'

'What? Oh, my thoughts. Nothing in particular,' she lied.

Freda eyed her with playful suspicion. 'Are you sure?'

'All right. Yes. I was thinking about someone I met recently.'

'I thought as much. You've been quiet all morning. Come on then,' her friend said, nudging Ena's arm, 'spill the beans.'

Omitting anything to do with Bletchley and having her case stolen – and pretending it was on the train from Bletchley to Rugby that she met her American friend and not in the buffet on Euston station – Ena told Freda everything she knew about Ben, which wasn't much.

'So when are you seeing him again?'

'I don't know. He works in London. But he said he had an aunt in Bletchley who he visits now and again, and that if ever I was in that part of the world to get in touch.' Ena took a bite of her sandwich. 'I don't suppose he meant it.'

'You're in that part of the world at the end of this week. How will you let him know?'

'By letter. He gave me his address.' Ena looked at her friend who was nodding in an exaggerated fashion. Ena laughed. 'All right, I'll write to him. But I'd better do it now, so it goes in the lunchtime post, or he won't have time to arrange cover where he works.'

The two friends returned to the annexe, giggling like schoolgirls. Before she settled down to work, Ena wrote a short note to Ben. She looked at her wristwatch. If she was lucky, she would make the lunchtime collection. She did, just.

'I'm going to Beaumanor again on Friday,' Freda said, turning up her nose. 'It takes hours on the train. And they collect me from Loughborough station in a bloody troop carrier. It isn't so bad when I drive up in Mr Silcott's car. Even so,' she sighed, 'I wish I could come down to Bletchley with you.'

Ena wished Freda was going to Bletchley too. She wasn't looking forward to travelling on the train on her own. But there was nothing she could do about it. 'Perhaps we can go together next time.'

'Yes! Then I can meet your American.'

'He isn't my American,' Ena said, blushing.

'But you wish he was, don't you?'

The next morning, Ena and Freda met at the factory gates. After parking their bicycles, they walked to the factory, entered by the main door and walked across the shop floor to the annexe. Mr Silcott was at his desk.

Knowing the real reason why her boss had been off work, Ena held back a little to let Freda greet him first.

'Herbert!' Freda gushed, 'Thank goodness you're better.'

'Good to have you back, Mr Silcott,' Ena said.

'Thank you.' Herbert Silcott nodded as Ena drew level. 'It is good to be back. And thank you,' he said, looking from Ena to Freda, 'for holding the fort while I've been off sick.'

'You *are* better?' Ena asked, concerned that her boss looked extremely pale, had dark shadows under his eyes, and appeared to have lost weight.

'I'm fine, thank you. I've been fit enough to come back for days, but Mrs Silcott wouldn't have it.' Ena smiled that she understood.

Freda fussed about, offering to make cups of tea and asking if *Herbert* would like anything from the canteen. He said he didn't want any food but would like a cup of coffee. There was a tin of tea, dried milk and sugar in the cupboard, but no coffee. So, promising not to be long, Freda dashed off to the canteen.

'I've spoken to Commander Dalton,' Mr Silcott said as soon as Freda was out of earshot. 'He tells me he wants you to take the work to Bletchley tomorrow.' Ena nodded. 'I'll be with you of course. I wouldn't let either of you travel to the Park alone. Not after what happened last time. I feel responsible--'

'You shouldn't, sir. It wasn't your fault. You

couldn't have known what was going to happen.'

'That's as maybe, but it won't happen again. I shall be on my guard in future.'

Ena looked at her boss's gaunt face. 'Are you sure you're fully recovered, sir?'

'I'm fine. What about you? They drugged you, the commander said.'

'Yes. There's no other explanation for what happened.'

'Horace Dalton had you put through your paces by his intelligence people, I understand.' Herbert Silcott didn't pause for Ena to reply. 'Bloody man!' He looked briefly at the door. 'The petrol coupons,' he whispered, 'came through this morning, before you arrived, but I shall take them home. Commander Dalton wants us to travel to Bletchley on the same train as before. Don't worry, we shall go to the ticket office together and board the train at the same time. I will not leave you on your own for a single second.'

Ena's heart sank. If Mr Silcott stuck to his word, there would be no chance of her seeing Ben. 'You're sure you're well enough, Mr Silcott?'

He put his hands on either sides of his ribcage, pressed slightly and breathed in. 'The damage to my ribs wasn't as bad as the hospital first thought. My body is still black and blue, and my ribs are still bound up, but they are only badly bruised, not broken. I had concussion from the blow to my head. Because of it I was seeing double, which worried the doctors. ... I just couldn't shake it off,' he said, loudly, 'I thought I'd never feel well again.' Ena hadn't a clue what her boss was talking about until she spotted Freda, carrying a cup of steaming coffee.

Ena left her colleagues to it and went to her own work desk. Damn! Why had she written to Ben telling him she'd meet him on Friday? Unable to concentrate, she slumped back in her chair. What if she got a letter off this afternoon, explaining that her boss would be with her at Bletchley and she wouldn't be able to get away to meet him. These days there was no telling when post arrived at its destination. And even if the second letter was delivered tomorrow, he might already have left London for Bletchley, in which case he wouldn't see it. But it was a risk she would have to take.

Ena took a writing pad and pen from her desk and wrote a short note. Reading it back to herself, satisfied that the message had conveyed her disappointment in not being able to meet Ben, she put it in an envelope and stuck a stamp on it. 'Be back in a minute,' she called, picking up several letters from the post tray and taking them to the post box.

On the train to Bletchley, Ena told Mr Silcott everything that had happened on the day her work was stolen.

'Some parts of the X-board would have been almost impossible to copy for anyone who didn't know what they were doing. I can only think whoever stole it had worked on the same, or similar, boards before – perhaps in another factory. But what really bothers me, what I still don't understand,' she confided, 'is how the thieves were able to make an identical case to the ones we use. Perhaps it wasn't identical, but it was good enough to pass as one of ours when it was signed in at Bletchley Park.'

'They must have been watching you, Ena, sizing up the case.'

'What, travelling on the same train as I did? On the occasions we didn't take the work down by car? A bit of a coincidence, don't you think?' Mr Silcott nodded thoughtfully. 'No,' Ena said, 'I'm convinced someone at Bletchley Park was in on it.'

'The commander mentioned something about that,' Herbert Silcott said.

Ena bit her lip. 'He wasn't very happy at the suggestion. Did he tell you I had met an American in the buffet on Euston station?' Mr Silcott nodded and smiled. 'He was very kind to me. Of course, the commander could only see a German spy who befriended me to turn me. That's the phrase they use in popular spy thrillers, isn't it?'

Ena sighed. 'He invited me to tea today,' she said, 'when I finish at the Park. And no, before you ask, he doesn't know I have anything to do with Bletchley Park. I stuck to the cover story. Anyway it doesn't matter now. I wrote yesterday and said I couldn't make it.'

'That's a shame, Ena,' Mr Silcott said, 'You spend so much time at work, and often on your own, being taken out for tea by a young man would be a nice treat. Still, if he's a decent sort, he'll invite you out again.'

Ena hoped he would. She also told Mr Silcott about Henry Green being in the room with Commander Dalton and the engineers, and how he had vouched for her to the commander. Mr Silcott knew Henry, as Ena's family did. Henry's father was the only butcher in Lowarth, and he and Herbert Silcott regularly played golf together.

## CHAPTER FOURTEEN

Herbert Silcott and Ena took the case containing the work to reception, showed the security officer their passes and work permits, and Mr Silcott signed his name – adding the time and date as proof of when the work was delivered.

'Commander Dalton is expecting you, sir... Miss Dudley,' the officer said. 'If you'd like to go on through…'

Leaving the case of work with the officer to take to Bletchley's engineers, Ena and Herbert Silcott made their way along the familiar corridors to Commander Dalton's office. Ena knocked on the door.

'Enter.'

'Welcome,' the commander said, striding over to meet Mr Silcott at the door. 'And Miss Dudley. Thank you for coming down today. Come in, come in. Take a seat, both of you.'

When they were seated at Commander Dalton's desk, he opened a folder, looked at it for a moment, and then slowly closed it. Spreading his fingers wide, he laid his hands palms down on top of the folder as if to protect it. He looked from Herbert Silcott to Ena. 'More work has been sabotaged,' he said at last.

'When? Where did it come from?' Ena asked.

'We have several X-boards in reserve, as back-ups. They're routinely checked, but not often enough it seems. Our engineers were checking them against their blueprints, as you had done, Ena, when they came across anomalies in two of the boxes. The rotors were signed, and remained correct.' The commander raised his eyebrows and Ena held her breath. 'However, the wiring in the selector wheels had been deliberately muddled.'

'Do you want me to check them?'

'Thank you, but no. We've decided to leave them as they are. Two clever young women in Hut 3 are going to try to unscramble the results. It will take hours – rendering any recovered text useless, because by then it will be out of date. But we must try, and we must carry on as normal. We don't want whoever is doing this to know we've cottoned onto them.'

Ena frowned. 'If you don't mind me asking, sir, why did you bring me down here, if you don't want me to check the work?'

'To ask for your help in another matter.'

'Anything, Commander,' Ena said, sitting forward, ready to hear her instructions.

'I want you to find out who is sabotaging your work. It has to be someone from Silcott Engineering.' Ena opened her mouth to defend her workmates. 'Or,' the commander said, raising his voice, which stopped her interrupting, 'someone from Bletchley Park.'

'But… How? What can I do?'

'I am sure that you did not sabotage your own work, or anyone else's. As that is the case, you and Herbert are the only people outside Bletchley that I can trust.'

'I'm glad you believe us innocent, sir.' Ena felt the heat of a blush rise to her cheeks.

'I haven't actually found Herbert innocent,' the commander said with a wry smile, 'but as he was in a hospital bed, I think we can eliminate him from our enquires.' Ena looked from the commander to Mr Silcott. The commander's lips were twitching, and her boss was doing his utmost to look serious.

'Seriously, my dear, there is only one person who I am sure did not sabotage your work – and that is you,' Commander Dalton said. 'Your blood and urine tests showed traces of a rare sleeping draught that's used by veterinary surgeons to put animals to sleep. I was told it is difficult to administer, so it is added to treats. An incorrect dosage could have been fatal.'

Ena felt a wave of heat surge through her. 'Fatal?' She thought for a moment, hardly able to take in what the commander had said. 'You mean I could have died?'

'But you didn't, my dear. Thank goodness, you didn't,' Herbert Silcott said, patting Ena's arm.

'If you don't mind me saying, Mr Silcott, that isn't the point. I could have…' Ena shuddered. Herbert Silcott opened his mouth to speak but she didn't give him the chance. 'I'm sorry, Mr Silcott, but some damn *spy* almost beat you to death, and nearly killed me! The only reason I'm here today is because of my good luck and his bad judgement. One or two grains more of whatever it was he gave me and I'd be dead.' Tears pricked at the back of Ena's eyes, but she was damned if she was going to weaken and cry. She turned to Commander Dalton and looked him squarely in the eyes. 'What do you want me to do, sir?'

'Nothing for now. Just be yourself. Go about

your business as normal. Stick to your routine. Don't make any changes to the plans you've already made, especially not to plans that involve other people. Whatever you were going to do here today, or somewhere else later, do it.' The commander leaned forward and resting his elbows on his desk, made a steeple of his fingers. 'And while you are being yourself, be vigilant. Keep your eyes and ears open. Watch and listen to everyone. You're a pretty young woman, if a man smiles at you, smile back.' Ena was about to react to his suggestion, but thought better of it.

Dalton sat up, put his hand in his jacket pocket and pulled out a ten-shilling note. 'Take this,' he said, pushing it across the table to Ena. 'Ask him, or her, but preferably him. Women carry handbags, so are more likely to have the change in them. Men on the other hand only have pockets, so are less likely to carry a lot of change around.'

Ena was baffled. Thinking she had missed something, she said, 'What is the money for?'

'The telephone. Ask for change for the telephone! Ten shillings in change would be too much to carry about, so chances are a man will be chivalrous and give you a few coppers.' Ena felt a dull ache behind her eyes from frowning. She blinked a couple of times and shook out her hair. 'Then, the next time you see that person, you give them what they lent you back.' The commander looked pleased with himself. 'It's a good way to meet people.'

'Get to know the people here, join in their conversations. Listen for anything you think irregular, out of the ordinary. I can't tell you who to listen to or what to look for, but if you see anything you think is unusual, questionable, out of character, however small or insignificant you think it is, I want to know about it. All right?' Ena nodded. 'Make mental notes of anything that doesn't ring true. Especially if it is something done by someone you have recently met. Someone who has befriended you. Practice on your young American. I believe he is taking you to tea today?' The commander looked at his watch, 'In an hour.'

'Excuse me?' Ena was furious that Ben had been dragged into this. 'I can assure you that my American, as you call him, has nothing to do with any of this. It's immaterial anyway,' she said tersely, 'I wrote and cancelled our appointment.'

'He didn't get the letter, I'm afraid.'

'How do you know?'

'How I know is not important. What is important is that Mr Johnson will be waiting for you in the station buffet as arranged. He probably came to England at the beginning of '42, so you could use Pearl Harbor as an opening.' Ena felt anger boiling up inside her. 'I really don't care how you do it, just find out as much as you can about him. I'd like to know exactly what he does at the Ministry of Defence, if indeed he works there at all.'

'You intercepted my letter to him, so you know he works there.' The commander raised his eyebrows but didn't speak.

Exasperated, Ena said, 'Why would he tell me to write to him at the MoD in Whitehall if he didn't work there? What would be the point? He wouldn't get my letters. He wouldn't have got the letter telling him I was coming to Bletchley today if he didn't work at the ministry, but you said he did. So how can you doubt that he works there?'

The commander looked at Ena, his eyes hard and unflinching. 'Because no one by the name of Benjamin F. Johnson works for the Ministry of Defence in London.' Ena's mouth fell open with shock. 'What I am about to tell you stays in this room, Miss Dudley, is that clear?'

'Yes,' Ena said, looking from the commander to Mr Silcott and back again.

'Your friend could be with American Intelligence. The Office of Strategic Services are working with our Military Intelligence, which could explain why he isn't listed as working for the MoD. However, until we know that for sure, we must assume he is a threat to British security and find out as much as we can about him. That is your job. Do you understand?'

Ena dropped her head, giving a faint nod.

'If you would rather not be involved in this investigation, you must say so now, Miss Dudley, because once you leave this office I shall expect you to see the job through to its conclusion, whatever that is.'

'I want to carry on. I need to clear my name and the names of the people I work with.'

The commander looked at Ena for a long minute. 'I need to be a hundred percent certain you are not going to change your mind, Ena. I need to know you are not going to turn around somewhere along the line and say you won't investigate Mr Silcott, say, if something suspicious happens, or your colleague, Miss King.' Ena looked at Mr Silcott, nodded that she understood, and he gave her an encouraging smile. 'You have to be fully committed or you are no good to me, or the job.'

'I am fully committed, sir,' Ena said, sitting upright and looking him in the eye.

'Good. So, to reiterate... Assume everyone you know, especially anyone who has befriended you since your work was sabotaged, is a potential threat to the country and the work we do here at Bletchley. And today, find out all you can about the young American.' Ena nodded. 'Listen for contradictions, or inconsistencies in what he tells you.'

'Yes, sir.'

The commander stood up. 'Time you left. You don't want to be late for your appointment. Do you want a car to drive you to the station?'

Ena looked at her wristwatch. 'No thank you, sir. I have time to walk down. The fresh air will do me good. Goodbye.' She picked up her coat and turned to her boss. 'I'll see you at the station, Mr Silcott.'

'Five o'clock, or thereabouts.'

Ena could see in his eyes that Mr Silcott was worried.

'And Ena,' Commander Dalton said, as she opened the door to leave, 'Be careful.'

'I will, sir. Thank you.'

When she was through the main gates, Ena stopped to breathe some fresh air. She was annoyed with the commander for assuming she would allow herself to be picked up by a spy. How would she know someone was a spy? They didn't exactly go around wearing a badge with *spy* pinned to their lapel.

She didn't know anything about spies. She didn't really know anything about Ben Johnson either. Walking on, Ena went over Commander Dalton's instructions, reminding herself that, as much as she liked Ben Johnson, she mustn't lose sight of what someone did to her on the train. Cold perspiration ran down her back. Could Ben have been the second person in the carriage? She strained to recall his voice, his demeanour, anything at all that would give her a clue as to who the other man was. But it was no good. All she could remember was a shadowy figure.

She spotted Ben gazing out of the window as she approached the buffet. Opening the door drew his attention and before she had time to close it, he was on his feet.

'Hi,' he waved. 'I thought you'd changed your mind.'

'Am I late? It must have taken me longer than I thought to get here from my friend's house. I'm sorry.'

'No need to apologise, you're here now.' The waitress came to take their order. 'Would you like tea?'

'Yes please.'

'Anything to eat?'

Too nervous to eat anything, Ena said, 'Thank you, but I've already eaten.' The waitress made a note on her pad and returned to the counter with their order.

'Wow! You're even more beautiful without tears running down your cheeks.'

'I should hope so,' Ena said. 'What a fright I must have looked that day in Euston.'

Ben batted the suggestion away. 'I don't remember.' Lowering his hand, he rested it on Ena's hand and looked into her eyes. Ena felt her cheeks flush. 'But I'm sure glad I was there.'

'Two teas!' Ben sat back and the waitress plonked the tray down with a clatter.'

'I was glad you were there too. I don't mind telling you, I was scared. Ending up in Euston on my own. I'd never been to London before.' Ena bit her bottom lip and laughed. 'You must think I'm a real baby. I was only a hundred miles from home and you are thousands of miles away from yours. Do you miss your home, your family?'

'I guess, but my mom died when I was real young and my dad married again.' Ena didn't comment, hoping Ben would carry on talking about himself. He did. 'I resented Grace, my stepmom, at first.' He raised his eyebrows. 'I gave her a real hard time.'

Ena tried to imagine how she would feel if her mother had died when she was little. She couldn't. 'It's understandable. You must have missed your mother terribly.'

'I did, and Grace understood that. She treated me like her own kid.' Ben poured milk into their cups and lifted the teapot. 'I'm real fond of my stepsister. She writes me every week,' he said, laughing. 'She was so cute when she was small. Smart too. She's grown now, of course. I was six when she was born, so I'm her big brother.'

Commander Dalton's words, *"No one called Benjamin F. Johnson works for the MoD in London"* came into her mind. 'What brings you to England? Are you with the military? Were you sent here after Pearl Harbor?'

'No, I've been here a while.' Ben took a drink of his tea. 'When I was at high school there were a couple of rival gangs in our town and I got mixed up with one of them, so before I got into real trouble, Dad sent me over to England to visit with my grandma in Oxford. She's my mom's mom.' A bright smile spread across his face. 'She spoilt me rotten. She still does,' he laughed. 'I came over here after fifth grade, finished my schooling, and got into Oxford University.' Ben reached out and took Ena's hand again. 'I have a confession to make.'

Ena held her breath. 'What is it?'

'I don't live in London. I live here in Bletchley.'

'Is that all?' she said, exhaling with relief.

'All? Ben laughed. 'What did you expect me to say, that I was the Brighton Trunk Murderer?'

'Not exactly. But I'm pleased you're not.' A draught cut across Ena's ankles as the buffet door opened and Mr Silcott entered. 'Sorry to interrupt,' he said to Ena, and taking in Ben.

Jumping to his feet, Ben put out his hand. 'Benjamin Johnson, sir.'

'Pleased to meet you, Mr Johnson. Herbert Silcott.' The two men shook hands. 'I was wondering if you were ready to leave, Ena, or if you had decided to catch a later train?'

'I have to go to work, sir,' Ben said. Then, taking Ena's hand, he said, 'I would rather you didn't travel on the train alone. Perhaps I could see you again, when you next visit your friend?'

'The train leaves in two minutes. I'll wait for you outside, Ena,' her boss said, clearing his throat. 'Nice to meet you, Mr Johnson.'

'You too, sir,' Ben said.

'I'd better go then,' Ena said, disappointed that she couldn't stay longer with Ben. 'Thank you for the tea.'

'Will you write to me?'

'I will,' she said, looking up into Ben's big brown eyes. He stepped closer, put his arms around her and lowered his head until his face was level with hers. Ena's heart leapt with excitement. She stood on tiptoe, her mouth ready to meet his, when a sharp blast from a whistle sounded. 'You'd better go.'

'Yes.' Ena giggled.

'What is it?'

'I can't go until you take your arms from around me.'

They both laughed. Ben held his hands up as if he was surrendering. 'Bye, Ena.'

'Goodbye,' Ena said, and ran out of the buffet. Mr Silcott was waving to her with one hand and holding the door open with the other. Ena jumped onto the train as the station master blew his whistle again.

Closing the door behind her, Ena pulled down the window and looked out. Steam hissed and smoke billowed from the train's engine, enveloping everyone on the platform. She knew

Ben wouldn't be able to see her. She didn't care and waved until the train was out of the station.

## CHAPTER FIFTEEN

Taking work to Bletchley Park had become a regular event for Ena. She accompanied Mr Silcott who, when the MoD's petrol coupons came on time and the garages in the area had petrol, drove them down in his motorcar. She still went down with Freda by train. But when the delivery date for work going to Beaumanor clashed with Bletchley's delivery date, Freda took the car, and Ena and Mr Silcott caught the 9:45 train from Rugby.

When Ena knew in advance that she was travelling by train, she wrote to Ben saying she would be in the buffet on Bletchley station at 4 o'clock. Once or twice he didn't make it. He either had to work or her letter didn't get to him on time. When they did meet, they held hands across the table and talked about their families and friends. Ben read Ena letters that he'd received from his stepsister. In one letter, she'd written, "I can't wait until the war is over, so I can meet the beautiful girl who has stolen your heart, Benny."

Ena blushed. Stolen his heart? She had no idea Ben felt so strongly about her. 'I love you, Ena.' She looked at him and a self-conscious laugh escaped her lips. He went back to reading his sister's letter, but Ena was no longer listening. She was embarrassed by his declaration of love. It was much too early in their relationship to know how she felt about him. She liked him, cared for him, but love? And meeting his sister? Did that mean his sister was coming to England, or did Ben expect Ena to go to America? If he did, it was a huge step, and one that Ena had never considered. Ben finished reading the letter, looked at Ena, and said, 'Well?'

'Well?' she repeated, taken aback. 'Your stepsister seems to think I shall be going to America when the war's over.'

'Maybe sooner than that,' Ben said, his eyes bright with excitement. 'I shouldn't be telling you this, but my boss and I have been working with the British on a special project. I can't tell you what it is, but the US top brass are sending us home. Not home exactly, we're going to Washington to build the same kinda facility there as you have here at Bletchley.

'Your guys do a great job, but the operation's too small. We have the money and the manpower to set up a much bigger operation. We'd be able to do ten times what they do here. So,' Ben's eyes brightened, again, 'if the British agree to what we want, I shall be going back to the States. And when I go,' he said, leaning forward and looking into Ena's eyes, 'I want you to come with me, as my wife.'

'Oh!' Ena gasped, shocked this time by Ben's out-of-the-blue proposal. 'I don't know what to say.'

'Don't say anything now,' he said, putting his forefinger to her lips. 'It takes time to get these things okayed by Washington. We may have months.' He told her again that he loved her, and told her again that she didn't need to give him an answer today. 'Take your time, Honey, there's no rush.'

Holding her at arm's length, Ben leaned back, as if Ena was a painting that he wanted to admire from a distance. 'You're gonna love it in the States. You won't have to work in a factory anymore, you won't have to work at all. You'll be able to stay home all day, visit friends, go shopping.' Ben pulled Ena to him and kissed her. 'My kid sister's gonna love you,' he whispered, burying his face in her hair and rocking her gently, 'and I know you'll love her.'

Marriage, America, his sister? Ben had presumed too much. How could he think she would want to leave her job, her family, her friends, and go off with him to the other side of the world when her country was at war? He may not know how important the work she did for Bletchley was, or even care, but he must think her very shallow to want to up and leave while her friends and family were risking their lives fighting.

Ena heard the train rattle into the station. 'I must go.' Grabbing her handbag and gasmask, she flew out of the buffet with Ben at her heels.

'I'm sorry,' he said, opening the train door, 'I didn't mean to pressure you.'

'You didn't,' she lied.

'That's great. So you'll think about it?' Ena mounted the steps. 'Ena?' Ben called.

'What? Yes,' she called back, and shut the door.

'I'll write you as soon as I get back to my billet!' Ben shouted as the train clunked off its brakes and began to chug north.

On the journey home, Ena thought about her

relationship with Ben. She liked him very much, but marriage? Going to live in America? Ben's feelings for her were greater than hers were for him – and his plans were moving at a far greater speed. He said he wasn't rushing her, but he was. He was suffocating her.

Thinking now about what Ben had said, what he had presumed, it struck Ena that the man she had been seeing for the last several months didn't know her at all. And by the time the train pulled into Rugby station, Ena's feelings for Ben had begun to change.

Ena wasn't able to see Ben when she went to Bletchley with Freda, which wasn't a bad thing. She needed to put some time and space between them. She still wrote to him several times a week, which she had done since they had first met, but the letters were less intimate. She now signed off with *Yours, Ena*, instead of *Love, Ena*.

Going to Bletchley with Freda was always fun. They had recently got into the habit of having a sherry in the Station Hotel before catching the train back to Rugby. Or they would walk up to the Market Tavern on Station Road and have a port and lemon, until it was time to catch the bus to Lowarth.

Ena liked Freda, and had told the commander at the beginning of the investigation that she wouldn't spy on her colleague and friend. He'd said she had no choice, that it was an order. He reminded her that not only had she agreed to find out if there was a mole at Silcott's Engineering, or at Bletchley Park, but she had wanted to – and more importantly, it had been sanctioned by Mr Silcott. Ena was watching Freda closely, not because she thought she was a spy, but to find evidence that she wasn't, so Ena could prove Commander Dalton wrong.

She hated spying on her friend, going through her desk, reading her private letters, eavesdropping on her telephone calls, which Ena thought was the worst thing she had to do. She didn't mind watching people at Bletchley, listening in on their conversations. It was what she had to do if she was ever going to find out who had sabotaged her work. Commander Dalton didn't believe it was anyone from Bletchley Park. But Ena needed to find out – and crossing people off the extensive list of suspects was as important as adding them to it.

Ena leaned back in her seat and gazed out of the window at the Buckinghamshire countryside. Of the detective books she'd read, she mused, which of the amateur sleuths would she most like to be. She wouldn't want to be Agatha Christie's Marple. Clever, always worked out who had done it, but Miss Marple was too old. She could be Tuppence Beresford. She was more Tuppence's age. And Tuppence had a handsome husband called Tommy. Tuppence and Tommy Beresford. She racked her brain, trying to remember what the name Tuppence was short for. Prudence, she remembered. No, she didn't want to be a Tuppence or a Prudence. They were both silly names for a detective.

Ena, like her sisters, had been encouraged to read books from an early age by their father. Her favourites were Dorothy L Sayers' mystery stories. But Sayers' detective was a man, Lord Peter Wimsey. Wimsey was as whimsical a name as Tuppence. But there was a female in some of the books called Harriet Vane. Sayers described her as a detective novelist with a husky voice and dark eyes. That's who I shall be like, Ena decided, dismissing Tuppence Beresford from her mind. Besides, she thought, Harriet Vane ends up with a lord. Tuppence's husband was a crook, a blackmailer, before becoming an amateur detective.

Ena sighed at her own silliness, brought her attention back to the carriage and looked across the aisle at Freda. Her friend enjoyed reading out snippets of interest from her *Woman's Own* magazine: today they had been how to make rayon nylons last longer, a knitting pattern for the gayest girl in town, and how a jacket can turn an ordinary day-dress into a dressy outfit. Ena would have liked the chance to put all three ideas to the test. She hadn't been out for ages. All work and no play, her dad had warned.

She was about to suggest to Freda that they went to the flicks at the weekend when her friend said, 'Next stop Bletchley. Want the magazine?'

Ena shook her head. 'I'll read the short story on the way home, there's no time now.'

'All right.' Freda stood up and dropped the magazine on the seat. 'I'm going to the lavatory. Won't be a minute.'

Ena looked at her wristwatch. Fifteen minutes and they'd be in the station, another two and they'd be at the Park. Although she had been there lots of times, Ena still had the collywobbles until her work had been verified and passed as perfect by Commander Dalton's engineers.

Ena relaxed back in her seat and thought about Henry telling her that he loved her and smiled. It was sweet of him, but... Good Lord! She shook her head. She meant Ben – she thought about Ben telling her he loved her, not Henry. It wasn't the first time Ena had thought about Henry Green recently. She'd been thinking about him while getting ready for bed during the week. She put it down to having spent time with her sister Bess, who had walked out with Henry before he went to work at Bletchley Park. An association, not of words, but of people, Ena told herself. She blew out her cheeks and put both Henry Green and Ben Johnson out of her mind.

She looked at her watch again. Freda was taking her time. Getting up, Ena stretched and crossed to the door. She reached out to slide the door open and froze. The man who had drugged her, who had stolen her work, was walking past the compartment. She turned her back on the door and gasped for breath. She only saw him for a second, from the side, but she remembered his profile clearly. She remembered everything about him.

He hadn't seen her. He hadn't looked into the compartment. Ena turned round and faced the door, half expecting him to be there, but he had gone. Not daring to leave the work, but needing to warn Freda, Ena grabbed the suitcase's handle. Her heart was thudding. She left her handbag and gas mask and returned to the door. Without making a sound, she slid the door open and poked out her head. The man was standing in the corridor with his back to her, smoking a cigarette. She ducked back into the compartment and waited a couple of minutes. When she looked again, he was opening a door at the end of the corridor.

As the man disappeared into his compartment, Ena saw Freda walking towards her from the direction of the lavatory. She beckoned Freda to hurry. Freda smiled and lifted her hand as if to wave, but before she had time, the man who Ena recognised as her attacker came out of his compartment and bumped into Freda. Ena took a step back and, peering round the door, saw Freda move to her left. The man moved to his right at the same time, blocking Freda's way. They both laughed. Then the man said something, which Ena couldn't hear, and Freda shook her head, as if to say it was all right. The man bowed, returned to his compartment, and Freda walked on.

Ena exhaled with relief. She was about to go to Freda, tell her who the man was, when she saw him again. He was directly behind Freda, his face a scowl. Freda didn't realise and kept walking. Ena opened her mouth to shout a warning, but she was too late. The man grabbed Freda from behind, putting his hand over her mouth. Ena watched her friend struggling, trying to fight the man off, but he was pulling her backwards, dragging her into his compartment.

Carrying the suitcase, Ena made her way along the corridor to the compartment where the spy, for that was what Commander Dalton had called him, had taken Freda. Craning her neck, her back as flat as she could make it against the nearside wall of the corridor, Ena looked through the window. The blinds were drawn, but not fully. Crouching, she could see the man's back. He had pushed Freda up against the window. He had his arm around her neck and was talking into her face.

'Freda?' Ena shouted, sliding the door open with such force it crashed home, rattling the glass in the windows.

The man spun round, loosening his grip on Freda. She wriggled free. He lunged at Ena. 'Be careful!' Freda shouted, and put out her foot. The man tripped and Ena swung the case as high as she was able. It connected with his chin and he staggered backwards. As he fell, he caught his head on the brass ashtray attached to the window ledge and his head jerked.

Near hysterics, Ena watched his eyelashes flutter and his eyes roll back in their sockets. He let out a horrible rasping breath, closed his eyes, and slumped sideways, hitting his head again, this time on the floor. 'Oh my God!' Ena screamed, 'What have I done?'

'You've saved my life, Ena, that's what you have done.'

'Why isn't he moving, Freda?' Ena's friend bent down and felt the man's wrist for a pulse. She shook her head. 'No!' Ena screamed, again. 'Please don't say I've killed him. Please God, no!'

'We've got to get out of here,' Freda said, stepping over the man's body. Staring at him, still gripping the case of work, Ena shook uncontrollably. 'Ena, we've got to go. Now!' Freda shouted, taking Ena by the shoulders.

'Come on. Don't look at him,' she said, steering Ena out of the compartment.

In shock, but still clutching the case, Ena allowed Freda to push her along the corridor to their compartment. Inside, Freda took the case from her, put it by the window, and forced Ena to sit down. 'Stay here and don't move. Ena, are you listening?' Ena looked up in shock and nodded. 'I'll be back in a minute.'

'No! You can't go. Please don't leave me, Freda.'

'I won't be long. I'm going to check he's all right, and have a quick look through his pockets, see if he has any ID on him.' Freda knelt down and looked into Ena's face. 'Promise me you'll stay here? Ena? Promise me.' Ena nodded.

As Freda left, Ena heard the brakes grumble and felt the train slow down. Shaking, she gathered her handbag and gasmask, and hugged them to her. As the train pulled into Bletchley station, Freda returned. 'Are you ready?' she asked, collecting her own handbag and gasmask.

Ena nodded, picked up the case of work, and followed her friend into the corridor. As they passed the end compartment, Ena saw the blinds were fully drawn. Freda had pulled them down to stop people from looking in. Ena thought she was going to be sick and gagged.

Freda armed Ena into the buffet, sat her down at the back of the room, and ordered two teas. 'Drink this,' she said, when the waitress brought their cups. 'You'll feel better.'

'Was he all right?' Ena whispered, 'When you went back, I mean. Was he all right?'

'Don't worry about him. He won't be hurting anyone again,' Freda said, keeping her voice low so she wouldn't be heard.

Tears rolled down Ena's cheeks. 'Are you saying that I-- Is he?'

'I don't know. I couldn't find a pulse but I'm not a doctor. He might just be unconscious. I pulled him round and sat him up. He looked as if he was asleep. With a bit of luck, he won't be found until Euston.'

'With a bit of luck?' Ena shook her head. 'I've killed a man. I need to report it, tell the police. They'll understand if we tell them he was attacking you, and he--' Ena almost said, *was the man who drugged me and stole my work last year*, but she stopped in time. She hadn't told Freda about the incident, Commander Dalton's orders. But after what Freda had done for her today, Freda was the one person Ena knew she could trust.

'Listen to me, Ena.' Freda held Ena's hands and waited until she had her attention. 'It was as much my fault as yours. You lifted the case but it was me who tripped him up. I killed him as much as you did.' Ena shook her head and bit down on her bottom lip. 'Think about it, if you hadn't come into the compartment – hadn't stopped him when you did – he might have killed me. Chin up,' Freda said, with a sad smile, 'We're in this together.'

Commander Dalton sat behind his desk and listened without interrupting Ena and Freda's account of what had happened on the train that day. When they had finished, he asked to speak to each of them separately. Ena asked why, when their account was the same. The commander said that sometimes going over something as important as this, on your own, you remembered things that you perhaps didn't think of, or thought unimportant, when you were with someone else, listening to their account.

After asking Ena if she was happy to carry on without taking a break, Commander Dalton suggested Freda might like to go to the cafeteria and get something to eat. His suggestion did not require her to answer. 'Give us half an hour,' he said. Freda looked at Ena, smiled supportively, and left.

Ena leant forward and braced herself for an interrogation but the commander picked up the telephone. 'Get me Sir James Hillingborough at MI5 will you? His private line.' Ena's mouth was suddenly very dry. She licked her lips – it didn't help. 'Good afternoon, Sir James, it's Horace Dalton here. Very well thank you. And you? Jolly good. Sir James, I have favour to ask.' There was a short pause and the commander laughed. 'Now I shall owe you two.' Another pause, this time Ena suspected it was Sir James who was laughing. 'Thank you. It's a rather delicate matter. There's a body on a train that is due into Euston station in the next--' He looked at his watch, 'half an hour. It's the 9:45 from Rugby. Could you get someone at Euston, someone who will keep this under his hat, to locate the body and stay with it until your chaps get there?' Horace Dalton nodded and said, 'A spy. German we think. Fell over and hit his head. Probably caused a heart attack.' The commander laughed again. 'Thank you, Sir James. Goodbye.' Dalton put the receiver on its cradle and looked across the table at Ena. 'MI5's problem now. They'll deal with it discreetly. The death certificate will say heart attack. So there's nothing to worry about.'

'What will happen to him?'

'When MI5's medical examiner has finished with him, he'll be sent to the morgue. There'll be no way of tracing his next of kin, even if he has one. These people are professionals. His identity card, ration book, petrol permit and driving license will be forgeries. Did Miss King find any papers on him?'

'I don't know. I didn't ask her.'

The commander shook his head. 'They'll be false anyway,' he said. 'If there's an address it won't exist. If on the off chance the address is real, I can promise you that whoever lives there won't have heard of him.' Dalton leaned back in his chair, put his hands on the desk palm down, and spread his fingers. 'Even if he was carrying something that was traceable, no one will admit to knowing him.'

'What? No one will come forward to claim the body?'

'No. Spies know what's in store if they are killed. If they're caught they kill themselves anyway, by cyanide capsule.' Ena sat wide-eyed, hardly able to take in what the commander was saying. 'Better to be dead than risk giving up their handler and fellow spies under interrogation. It sounds harsh but spies are well aware of the rules before they sign up for the job.' Dalton shook his head, 'Don't feel too sorry for him, Ena. He would have killed you without a second thought if you hadn't…'

'Killed him,' Ena whispered. She felt tears well up. 'I can't get it out of my mind that I have killed a man. I keep seeing him on the floor, his eyes staring up at me but not able to see… I know he was a spy, and I know he would have killed Freda if I hadn't stopped him, but he's still someone's son.' Ena burst into tears.

Commander Dalton picked up the telephone again. He pressed down several times on the receiver's cradle. 'Get someone to bring in a cup of strong sweet tea, will you? Then find some bloody sugar!' he barked. He banged down the receiver. 'Ena?' No sooner had she looked up at him than the phone rang. 'Dalton! What is it? Yes of course, put him through.'

## CHAPTER SIXTEEN

There was a tap at the door. Ena rose instinctively. The commander nodded and, wiping her eyes, she crossed the room. She opened the door to see a waitress from the canteen holding a cup of tea. 'Thank you,' she whispered, taking the cup shakily. When waitress left, Ena closed the door and returned to her seat. She sipped the tea. It was just as the commander had ordered; strong and sweet. When he put down the phone, she said, 'What is it? You look worried. Is it the man on the train?'

'There wasn't a man on the train, dead or alive, that fitted the description you gave, Ena.'

'There must have been. I saw his lifeless body on the floor of the compartment. He was dead. I wish he hadn't been, but he was. It was exactly as I told you. His eyes were open, but they were dull and staring. He was dead, I tell you.'

The commander got up slowly and walked over to the window. He looked out for some minutes before speaking. 'And you're certain that the man on the train today was the same man who stole your work last year?'

'Yes. Absolutely certain.' Ena put down her tea, pushed herself out of her chair, and joined the commander at the window. 'I'd have known him anywhere. I don't think I'll ever forget him. His face, grinning when he gave me back the pear drops. Every time I closed my eyes, I saw his face. I had nightmares for months.' Ena stared out of the window. A flock of wild geese flew overhead and landed on the lake. She watched the water wave and settle to a ripple. 'I recently began to sleep better.' She shuddered. 'I expect the nightmares will start again now.' She lowered her gaze as tears fell onto her cheeks.

The commander laid his hand on her arm. 'Ena?' She lifted her head and looked at him through her tears. 'You mustn't tell anyone that MI5 met the train and didn't find a body. Do you understand?'

Ena nodded. 'I wonder what happened to it... to him?'

Commander Dalton shrugged. 'He might have had an accomplice on the train who got the body off before it arrived in London. There are plenty of stations between here and Euston. Or he could have planned to meet someone at one of the smaller, less busy stations. If that was the case, when he didn't get off the train, the person expecting him would probably have boarded – and when he found the body, got rid of it.'

'What, threw it off the train?'

'He'd have had no choice,' the commander said. 'And if his accomplice threw him out where there was dense foliage or woodland, we may never find it.'

Ena jumped at the sound of someone knocking on the door. 'Remember,' Dalton hissed, 'Not a word about MI5 to Miss King! Come in!' he called, as soon as they were seated.

A Wren opened the door and ushered Freda into the room. Ena got up to leave. 'I don't think I need to speak to Freda on her own,' Commander Dalton said, smiling. He looked down at the notes he'd made earlier. 'There's just one thing. Did you find any ID on the man?'

'No Commander. Not even a train ticket. But I only had a quick look in his jacket pocket.'

'Thank you, Miss King. You were lucky Ena was with you.'

'I was, sir. I dread to think what might have happened if she hadn't come to my rescue.'

The commander nodded and looked at Ena. 'A clear case of self-defence.'

'That's what I told her, sir.' Holding her hand out to Ena, Freda said, 'You saved my life, my friend.'

Ena opened her handbag and plunged her hand inside. 'Where's my damn hankie?'

'You should have a medal,' Freda said, taking her own handkerchief from her handbag and giving it to Ena.

'Here, here. Now dry your eyes, Ena. The man is not worthy of your tears,' the commander said, lifting the telephone again. 'Would you get someone to bring in tea for three and something sweet if they can find it,' he said, politely this time.

While they waited, Freda brought Commander Dalton up to date with what was going on at the factory. She wasn't aware that Ena gave him regular updates. Nor did she know that Ena was watching everything the staff at Silcott's did, even what she did. Ena felt disloyal. Freda had just helped her cover up… She couldn't bring herself to even think the word.

The door opened and the Wren brought in a tray with three cups of tea and a plate of digestives. Ena took a cup of tea but refused a biscuit.

When they had finished their refreshments and were leaving, the commander shook Freda's hand. 'Look after her, won't you?'

'Of course.'

While Freda collected their coats, Commander Dalton shook Ena's hand. He held it for a little longer than usual. 'The friendly chat changes nothing, Ena. You do understand that, don't you?'

'Yes, sir,' she said, 'I understand.'

On the way home, Ena cried again.

Freda put her arms around her. 'When we get to Rugby I'll treat you to a drop of brandy.'

'A drop? I could do with a large one. Do you think Mr Silcott would notice if we had a drink or two from the bottle he keeps in the annexe for medicinal purposes?'

'Not when he knows why we drank it.'

Ena burst into tears again. 'Oh Freda, I killed a man.'

'No Ena, he killed himself when he fell.'

'But it was because I hit him with the case that he fell.'

'Ena,' Freda said, exasperation in her voice, 'you have to stop blaming yourself. You hit that madman because he had me round the throat.'

'But I didn't mean to kill him.'

'Of course you didn't. As the commander said, it was self-defence.'

Ena felt a little better knowing that the commander and Freda agreed about the man's demise. But that was all they agreed on. Freda thought the man was a madman, the commander and Ena knew he was a German spy who would think nothing of killing them both.

Freda knew nothing about Mr Silcott being attacked the year before, the man stealing his clothes, drugging Ena on the train and stealing her work, replacing it with sabotaged work, posing as Mr Silcott, and delivering it to Bletchley Park. Ena wanted to tell her. She thought she owed it to her friend to warn her, so she knew how dangerous people like the man on the train were, but the commander had strictly forbidden her to tell anyone.

Over the next six months, Freda helped Ena to come to terms with what had happened on that terrible day, reminding her every time she talked about it that she didn't have a choice, that the man who attacked her would have killed her if Ena hadn't intervened.

'It was him or me,' Freda would say – and Ena would agree. She didn't know what she'd have done without Freda during those months. Sometimes, although those times were getting fewer, Ena would find herself remembering vividly what happened. Out of the blue, she would see the man's face, his eyes, and it would make her tremble. Freda was a Godsend when Ena got the shakes. And when Ena had to talk it out, Freda would listen patiently, never interrupting, until Ena had got it out of her system. Freda would tell her over and over that what had happened was not her fault. She helped her to be strong, to come to terms with what had happened, and to live with it.

A couple of times when they were talking, Ena had come close to confiding in Freda that the man's body hadn't arrived in Euston. She wondered what she'd say if she knew he had most likely been thrown from the train and lay rotting somewhere along the railway embankment? After six months he still hadn't been found or Commander Dalton would have told her.

For all this time, the man had been exposed to the elements and to wild animals. He had probably been eaten by foxes. Ena felt the bitter-sweet taste of bile rise from her stomach to her throat. Breathing deeply and slowly, she stopped herself from being sick.

She banished all morbid thoughts of animals and corpses from her mind. There was a time when she saw his face every time she closed her eyes. When she slept, she would see him on the floor of the train, his eyes open, dull and staring. He would sit up and his chalky face would come towards hers. It would get nearer and nearer – until she woke up clenching her teeth, drenched in sweat.

The nightmares happened less as time went on. In later months, Ena had even started to accept that the man's death was unavoidable. A terrible accident that, unless she could turn back the clock, she couldn't change. The man was going to kill Freda. Ena had to do something to save her.

Ena knew she would never be able to forget what had happened, that it was something she would have to live with for the rest of her life, but she was at last trying to forgive herself.

*

It was early summer when Ena received a telephone call from Commander Dalton telling her that work sent to Beaumanor had been compromised. Her heart sank with frustration. She was no nearer to finding out who had stolen and sabotaged her work eighteen months before, and now she had the added problem of Beaumanor.

Since she was the last person at Silcott's to check the work before putting it into the concrete safe, Ena had at first thought it was someone at Bletchley changing a few wires around when the opportunity arose. But at Beaumanor as well? Ena didn't believe in coincidences. Nor did she think there were two independent saboteurs at work.

The two engineers at the Park, who were in on the problem from the start, checked every delivery of work against Ena's diagram before fitting it. On the odd occasion when there were muddled wires, the engineers informed Commander Dalton before quietly getting on with the job of correcting them. Except for Ena, the commander, and the two engineers, no one, not even Herbert Silcott or Freda, was told when there were problems. It was imperative that no one knew when the problems were found and corrected.

Ena met Commander Dalton every Friday when she delivered new dials for the X-boards. One of the engineers had let slip that the work she did was for a decoding machine. Ena had worked that out for herself while explaining the number and letter confusion the muddled wiring would cause on the day her work was stolen. But because she had never been told officially, she referred to the parts she delivered as being for X-machines, especially when speaking about her sabotaged work to Commander Dalton.

She had been working on jobs where parts ended up in machines at Bletchley Park for three years, but she still wasn't privy to the work they did there, still hadn't been given higher security clearance. It didn't matter, as she answered to Commander Dalton. There was no one higher.

Having come to the conclusion that she needed to spend more time at Bletchley Park, Ena rang in sick one Monday morning and caught the 9:45 down there. A couple of Mondays after that, she was off with a head cold, the next time a dental appointment. She also took a couple of days of her annual holiday.

The extra time spent at the Park was working. She began to recognise people, and they began to recognise her. She got to know several people well enough to say hello and pass the time of day. Some would only smile. On the whole, the people who worked at Bletchley were polite enough, but they didn't talk about their work. And when Ena asked what they did, they all said the same thing, communications. One too many questions and they clammed up, so she would change the subject.

Asking too many questions opened the door for whoever was sabotaging the work to befriend her, use her as what Commander Dalton called a mark, or try to turn her into a spy. Good God, what had she got herself into?

Most of the time, Ena felt as if she was running round in circles. In the crime and thriller books she read, detectives would have had a 'breakthrough' by now. She needed to talk to someone, discuss with them what she'd found out so far, but apart from Commander Dalton there was no one. She couldn't talk to Ben, even though she didn't think he was involved. She couldn't tell Henry either, or could she? Ena decided she needed to move things on, and the only way to do that was to get to know more people at Bletchley. And for that, she needed to spend more time there.

In the first week of July, she asked Mr Silcott if she could take a week of her annual holiday, explaining that with working on Saturdays, and often Sundays, she was exhausted. Her boss agreed that she needed a break, but with several of the single women waiting for their call-up papers to join the WAAF and Auxiliary Ambulance Service, the workforce was thin on the ground. He also said that if Ena was away when work came in from Bletchley, there would be no one at the factory capable of doing it.

'I'll tell you what,' Ena said, 'I'll telephone Bletchley and if there is any work on its way, and it needs to be completed by next Thursday night, I'll stay and do it, deliver it on Friday, and take my holiday the week after.' Herbert Silcott rubbed his chin. He didn't look convinced. 'I won't be going to the seaside or anything. I'll only go on days out. I'll ring in every day and I'll come in if we get a work order for Bletchley,' she assured him.

Herbert Silcott said he would telephone Commander Dalton and ask if he was sending any work. Ena crossed the room and put on the kettle.

She made tea while she waited for the two men to finish speaking.

'What did he say?' Ena asked, sure that she knew the answer.

'A courier is on his way. Apparently a faulty X-board from a factory in Shropshire is arriving tomorrow and the commander wants you to look at it, put it right if possible.' Ena nodded that she understood. She didn't. 'Not a lot of work involved, Dalton said, but it's needed on Friday. You'll have to put your holiday off, Ena. I'm sorry my dear.'

The courier arrived from Bletchley with a letter from Commander Dalton. It was short and to the point. *X-board to follow. Work as usual. Do nothing to cause suspicion. Deliver on Friday and prepare to return to the Park on Saturday. There is a dance you might like to attend. I have booked a room for you at the Station Hotel on Saturday night.*

Ena whistled. 'Blimey!'

Mr Silcott still didn't allow Ena or Freda to travel to Bletchley Park on their own. 'Freda will accompany you on Friday,' he said, 'I'm not having you carrying top-secret machinery on the train alone, it's too dangerous.'

## CHAPTER SEVENTEEN

Ena had telephoned the commander during the week to tell him that she and Freda would be at the Park on Friday, and that she needed half an hour on her own. It was important that she got to know a few people, men or women, who were going to the dance on Saturday night. With a bit of luck, someone would invite her to go with them, or at least agree to see her there. So, she explained, since the canteen was the place where almost everyone went for lunch, she thought she'd have her lunch there too.

She told him that she felt awful going behind Freda's back. He reminded her that it was necessary – and reluctantly Ena agreed. She felt even worse about going to a dance and not telling her friend. Freda would have told Ena the minute she found out about it. They'd be discussing what they were going to wear by now. Ena sighed. Freda was bound to find out about the dance, but Ena would just have to cross that bridge when she came to it.

Commander Dalton had said leave it to me, so on that Friday when a Wren brought Freda a message from the commander asking her if she would spare him half an hour, Ena wasn't surprised.

Freda dove into her handbag and took out a small satin makeup wallet. After checking her hair in the mirror of a compact, she dabbed powder on her nose and put on some lipstick. Dropping everything back into her handbag, she got to her feet. 'How do I look?' Ena gave her the thumbs up. 'I wonder why he wants to speak to me on my own?'

'He's spoken to you on your own before, hasn't he?'

Freda thought for a moment. 'Yes, but... Oh!' She took a sharp breath. 'You don't think he wants to talk to me about you, do you?'

'Me?' Freda's question had taken Ena by surprise.

'Yes. After you-know-what.' Freda looked round to make sure the Wren wasn't listening and whispered, 'The man on the train.'

Ena knew that wasn't the reason, but said, 'I didn't think of that... but you never know.'

'See you in half an hour.' Freda pulled a face, pretending to be scared. Her cheeks were flushed. Worried because she had been singled out, Ena thought. It was usually her that the commander asked to see about Freda, not the other way round. 'I'll get myself a cup of tea.'

'Aren't you going to wait here for me?'

'I feel a bit peckish. I thought I might go to the canteen, get a sandwich,' Ena said casually. 'I'll be back by the time you've finished with the commander. And don't look so worried.'

'I'll tell you *everything* when I get back.'

In the canteen, Ena picked up a tray, took a cup and saucer from a recently washed stack, and poured tea from a big urn. Balancing the full cup, she queued for a sandwich. There was a choice of cheese and pickle or cheese and tomato. She plumped for the cheese and pickle. While she waited in the queue to pay, she overheard an interesting conversation between several women sitting at a nearby table.

'Excuse me?' Ena said, putting her tray down on the table closest to the women. Three of them looked up at her with mild curiosity, one with annoyance. 'I'm sorry to interrupt,' Ena said, taking them all in, 'but did I hear you say your regular hairdresser was off ill?' The four smartly dressed women in casual but expensive-looking clothes looked at each other. No one spoke. This was not going to be as easy as Ena had first thought. 'It's just that I do hair.' The annoyed-looking woman exhaled and raised her eyebrows. Ena cleared her throat. 'And, as I shall be here again tomorrow, I was wondering if I could be of assistance?'

'You're a hairdresser, are you?' a beautiful woman with hair as black as raven's feathers and bright green eyes said, smiling.

'Not exactly.' The annoyed woman shook her head and, looking at Ena with indifference, pushed back her chair and started to get out of her seat. 'I was before the war!' Ena spat out the lie for fear it would choke her.

'That's different,' the tall one said. The other women looked at Ena now with interest. The miserable one sighed loudly and sat down again. 'If Marcel has the flu today, there's not much chance of him being here tomorrow. We could at least give…'

'Ena.'

'Ena a try. I'm off for the rest of the day. Why don't you come to Hut 23 in say, ten minutes, and have a go on me? Call it a trial run.' Standing up, the beautiful woman offered Ena her hand, 'Honor Brinklow. Everyone calls me Binkie.'

'How do you do,' Ena said, shaking Binkie's hand.

Binkie, who looked twenty-five or six, was clearly the leader of the group. She pointed to the others around the table, who had remained seated. 'Eleanor Woodrow, Woody.' An attractive young woman with chestnut hair, hazel eyes, and freckles on her nose that were so pale they were hardly noticeable, put up her hand and saluted. 'Camilla Robertson, Bertie.' With her peaches and cream complexion, blue eyes and naturally blonde hair, Bertie looked the same age as Woody. Ena thought about twenty-two. Bertie jumped up and shook Ena's hand vigorously, giving her a warm smile. 'Last, but by no means least, our very own, Honourable. Lady Arabella Crofton-Dimbleby. Dibbs to all who know and love her. She is always first in the queue when there's food in the offing, aren't you, old girl?'

Dibbs, about twenty-five and not a natural blonde, rolled her eyes good-naturedly and smiled. She was beautiful. She should smile more often, Ena thought.

Ena tapped the door. No one answered. She tapped again, this time louder, but still no one came. She put her ear to the wood, but couldn't hear anything, so she walked along to the front of the building. From the outside, Hut 23 looked like all the other huts. It had a low brick wall around it. The green paint was blistering off the prefabricated panels, especially where the wooden frame nudged up to them. She looked through the dusty window. A net curtain hung over the bottom half. She stood on tiptoe but wasn't tall enough to see over the top of the net. She went back to the door and sat on the low wall.

Binkie had probably been called back to work, to do something vital for the war effort, and couldn't get away. Since she'd been coming to Bletchley, Ena had learned about much of the work that went on in the huts. The upper class girls did the important stuff. Some of them worked in the ordinance room, map plotting, calculating and charting where the Luftwaffe were in the skies over England, or where German battleships, like the ones Madge's Harry had scuttled, were in the sea. Working class girls like herself did more menial jobs at the Park. They worked as secretaries, cooks and waitresses, or cleaners. Jobs, Ena thought, that were just as important if places like Bletchley Park were to run smoothly.

Ena waited another five minutes and when Binkie still hadn't arrived, she turned the doorknob and gave the door a gentle push. It opened. Worried that by now Freda would have left the commander's office and, not finding Ena in the canteen, would come looking for her, Ena stepped into the hut, shutting the door behind her.

Looking into the room, Ena caught her breath. The other end of the building had been given over to what looked like a hairdressing salon. Against the far wall was a modern hairdryer on a stand. It had a big grey domed metal hood. Ena peered inside. There were holes at the top so the hot air could blow through and dry your hair. Next to the dryer, was a chest of drawers with a hand mirror and a metal hand-held hairdryer on the top. Ena picked up the hairdryer. At one end was a hollow tube, at the other a solid cylindrical black handle with what looked like a brass tap sticking out of the bottom. She pressed the red button on top of its barrel-body but nothing happened, the cable wasn't plugged in to the electric socket. Holding the hairdryer like a gun, Ena pointed it at an imaginary person and laughed.

Putting the hairdryer back where she had found it, Ena sat in a high-backed wooden chair in front of one of several mirrors that had been fixed to a long dressing table. Directly in front of her were Kirby grips, metal curlers, and metal wave grippers. No pipe cleaners or rags, which was what some of the girls at the factory used to curl their hair. She eyed the cosmetics with envy. There were half a dozen Cutex nail polishes in various shades of pink and red, a Yardley's hand cream and face powder, a Max Factor and a Goya lipstick. Ena twisted the outer case of one lipstick and pulled a bright red lipstick from it. Tempted, but not daring to try the colour, she slipped it back into its case. Whoever it belonged to had money. A lipstick like that would cost seven or eight shillings.

On the far wall were two hand-basins – a bar of Lux soap on one and Pears on the other. Above them shampoo and conditioning cream.

She looked at her watch. Freda would definitely be out of the interview with the commander now. Ena began to worry, but was quickly distracted by a clothes rail, the kind she saw in the smart dress shops in Coventry and Leicester. She jumped up to explore. The rack overflowed with elegant gowns for the evening, fashionable day clothes, and a selection of party dresses – high fashion and popular for occasions like the dance tomorrow night.

Next to the clothes rail was a table with a sewing machine, next to that an iron and ironing board. On the other side of the rail was a shoe rack packed with a dozen or more pairs of shoes. There were styles and colours for every occasion.

Ena jumped. 'Binkie? I didn't hear you. I hope it was all right for me to come in. The door was open.'

'It's fine.' Binkie sat at a mirror. 'I've just been called back to work. One of the girls has gone off sick and I'm covering the rest of her shift.' She looked at her watch. 'Better get cracking.'

Binkie's hair was clean, but a little too conditioned for the style Ena had planned. But with a card of Kirby grips to hold it in place, the result was better than Ena had hoped. Swept up into an off-centre parting with two rolls of hair on top, and two at the side, and a velvet ribbon tied at the back, like a highwayman's pony tail in the nape of her neck, Binkie's hair looked the height of fashion.

Binkie loved her new hairstyle. Ena thought it was as important that she saw it from the back, so gave Binkie the hand mirror, and held her breath. Binkie looked in the small mirror, turning her head this way and that to see her hair from every angle, and was delighted with it. Ena was too, and exhaled loudly.

Now all I have to do is get myself invited to the dance, she thought. She had enough money for the bus fare to Rugby and a return ticket to Bletchley – she would be given expenses to cover the transport costs eventually. And she had a room at the Station Hotel, courtesy of Commander Dalton. She doubted that the money for the hotel, and her expenses, came out of the commander's pocket, but she didn't care.

'Binkie, I don't want to keep you,' Ena said, as Binkie was putting on her coat. 'But is the dance tomorrow night only for people who work at Bletchley?'

'Yes, darling, so you're entitled.'

'But I don't actually work at the Park.'

'Technically you don't, but you're here so often that no one would question your eligibility. And you have a pass, so you'll be seen as just another worker bee among the thousands of bees who toil here for the greater good.' Binkie laughed. 'You'll be here anyway, making the girls look ravishing.' Ena pressed her lips together; she wasn't sure she dare just turn up. 'Bring something to change into, or borrow something.' Binkie pointed to the dresses on the clothes rail. 'If you are stopped and questioned, which I'm sure you won't be, let slip that you're a friend of the Honourable Lady Arabella Crofton-Dimbleby. Dibbs' Pa has a lot of clout around here, they wouldn't dare turn you away if they think you know Lord C-D.'

'I'm not sure, Lady... Dibbs is that keen on

me. Couldn't I give your name?'

'Sorry, darling, no can do. I shall be otherwise engaged with an extremely handsome cryptographer.'

Binkie talking about a cryptographer reminded Ena of Henry. 'Ah! I've just had a thought. I have a friend who works here. I might be able to persuade him to partner me.'

'I hope he's not my cryptographer,' Binkie said, taking a bright red lipstick from her handbag and applying it to taught lips. 'What's his name?'

'Henry Green.'

'Henry? Definitely not my cryptographer, thank goodness. How do you know old Highbrow Henry?'

'He's a family friend. My oldest sister Bess used to walk out with him.'

Binkie shot Ena a look of astonishment. 'What? Were they sweethearts?'

'Yes. There was even talk of them marrying. But my sister wasn't ready to settle down at the time. She went off to London, to teacher's training college, and Henry went to Oxford, but they stayed friends.'

'Well I never. Old Highbrow hasn't always batted for the other side, then? He certainly appears to now. I have never seen him with a girl and let me tell you that a chap as scrummy to look at as Henry Green would be fighting them off if he wasn't… Come to think of it,' she mused, 'in the three years that I've worked here, I have never seen him at a dance. Nice enough chap. And you'll be as safe as houses with him. Must dash,' she said, admiring herself in the full-length mirror as she passed it. 'I bet you ten bob you won't get Highbrow to the dance tomorrow night.'

'You're probably right. If he doesn't dance it wouldn't be much fun for him.' Ena was puzzled. 'Before you go, what did you mean when you said Henry hasn't always batted for the other side?'

'That he isn't sweetheart material, if you know what I mean.' Binkie winked conspiratorially, '*Ciao.*'

'Henry?' Ena shouted. He stopped walking, looked over his shoulder, and waited for Ena to catch him up. 'I've been all over the place looking for you,' she said, out of breath. 'Will you take me to the dance tomorrow night?' Henry's mouth fell open. He looked shocked, so before he had time to say no, Ena said, 'It's important. I wouldn't ask if it weren't. But I need an escort. Binkie's going to be with her chap, so I can't go with her. She said to let slip that I'm a friend of Lady Arabella Crofton-Dimbleby, which I'm not, and I'll look like a wallflower standing around on my own. Well? Will you take me?'

'I will if I can.'

'Henry Green, you're the best. I can't think why our Bess didn't marry you when she had the chance. I'm in two minds whether to snap you up myself right this minute.' Henry laughed the way Ena remembered him laughing when she was a teenager. 'Right! What time shall we meet? I shall be here all day. Did you know I've stepped in for some French hairdresser from Woburn Sands who's off with the flu? I styled Binkie Brinklow's hair earlier and she loved it. So I'm doing her pals tomorrow afternoon, for the dance at night.'

'Whoa! Slow down, Ena. I'm not sure whether I'm on the early shift or the late shift. If I'm on late, I'll have to swap with someone. Apart from that, I had promised a friend I'd go to the cinema if I was on earlies. I shall have to see him and tell him I can't make it.'

'So you will take me to the dance?'

'Y-e-s.' Henry said, drawing the word out. 'I expect I'll be able to swap shifts with someone if I need to. But now I really must go to work. I'll see you tomorrow.'

'Just one more thing, Henry?'

Henry turned with a sigh and pretended to stumble back to her. 'What?'

'If you see my friend Freda, don't say anything about the dance. I forgot to tell her about it you see. And now I'm coming down to do Binkie Brinklow's friends' hair, she might think I purposely didn't tell her because I'd rather spend my time with them, which I wouldn't of course, far from it--'

Henry put his hands up. 'My lips are sealed.' He looked at his wristwatch. 'I really do have to go.'

'Go!' Ena said, shooing him away. 'And thank you!' Henry lifted his arm above his head in a gesture of a wave, before disappearing into one of the huts.

Ena spotted Freda in the canteen, talking to a couple of ATS girls, and walked over. 'Good bye,' she heard Freda say, 'I'll see you tomorrow.' Tomorrow? Had the ATS girls told Freda about the dance? Stupid to think her friend wouldn't find out about it. 'Where have you been? I've been waiting ages,' Freda chided.

Ena opened her mouth to say she'd been talking to a friend, when Freda cut in. 'It doesn't matter,' she said, to Ena's relief. 'You'll never guess what these girls,' she pointed to the group of ATS women, 'have just told me.' Ena could guess, but again Freda didn't give her time to speak. 'There's a dance here tomorrow night.'

'I know,' Ena said, 'That's why I was late. I was talking to this woman named Binkie about it,' Ena said, smiling over Freda's shoulder at the ATS girls.

'So? Shall we come down and go to it? We haven't been to a dance for ages. It's time we had some fun, and the ATS girls said they'd sign us in.'

'Of course.'

'The thing is,' Freda explained, 'I promised my uncle I'd visit him this weekend, so I'll be going to Northampton after the dance, which means you'll be on your own for the remainder of the journey to Rugby.'

Ena wouldn't be on her own, because she wasn't going to Rugby after the dance, she was staying in the Station Hotel, not that she could tell Freda that. 'Don't worry about me,' she said, 'I'll catch an earlier train. It's only the last train that attracts the odd drunk. The nine o'clock, ten o'clock even, will be fine.'

'We can travel down together, though, can't we?'

'Sorry, I promised a couple of Binkie's friends

I'd come down early and do their hair. That's why I was late just now. I was chatting with them and lost track of time.'

## CHAPTER EIGHTEEN

After signing the hotel register, Ena was given her key. 'Room seven. Top of the stairs, turn right,' the receptionist said, pointing to a flight of stairs on the left. Ena thanked her, picked up her case and made her way up the narrow staircase. Passing room five on one side of the corridor and room six and the bathroom on the other, she opened the door of room seven.

The room smelled of stale tobacco, so dropping her overnight case by the side of the bed, Ena locked the door and ran over to the window. Reaching up, she turned the brass catch between the top and bottom windows. Seeing the edges of the bottom window had been painted over, she pulled down the top half.

Looking out, Ena watched a man walking a dog along a strip of grass that bordered roped-off plots of dry brown earth that men – and some women – were digging over to make allotments. To her right was the Coffee Tavern, the columned entrance to the station, and beyond that the Post Office. A faint smell of trains drifted in through the open window. Ena pushed it up, leaving an inch gap at the top.

She threw herself onto the bed. It was only a single but it was wider than her bed at home. She sank into it. It was soft and springy, and covered with a dusky pink candlewick bedspread and matching eiderdown. It had been turned down, showing clean white sheets and a plump pillow. Ena propped it up against the headboard, leaned back, and looked round the room. On one side of the window was a narrow chest of drawers and a man's wardrobe, which Ena thought was plenty big enough for one person's clothes. On the other side of the window was a dressing table, and hand-basin with a cream towel draped over it.

She wriggled down and made herself comfortable. She hadn't stayed in a hotel for years, not since before the war when she'd been a nanny to two children. Every summer, the family she'd worked for had taken her on holiday to the seaside to look after the children, but she'd not had a room of her own. She'd slept in the same room as her two charges.

A warm feeling washed over her, remembering those days, and she closed her eyes. What innocent times they'd been. She and the children in her care spent their days on the beach building sandcastles, collecting shells, and paddling in the sea. At least once during the week, Ena took her wards to the pleasure park or the fair. And at night, after washing them and putting them to bed, she would read to them before falling into her own bed, exhausted. Now she had a room to herself. And however small, it was all hers, until tomorrow.

Sensing the rumble of a train, Ena opened her eyes. Her heart almost stopped when she realised she had closed them for a second and fallen asleep. Looking at her watch, Ena swung her legs over the bed and stood up. She needed to get a move on if she didn't want to keep Binkie and her friends in Hut 23 waiting.

Flinging open her suitcase, Ena took out her

dress and hung it on the outside of the wardrobe. It was hardly creased. Anyway, there was an iron in Hut 23 that she could use if she needed to. Grabbing the skirt and blouse that she'd brought to go home in the next day, she hung them up in the wardrobe. Her clean underclothes she put in the top drawer of the small chest of drawers, and her night clothes she put under the pillow on the bed.

Leaving her evening shoes, handbag, washbag – with flannel and soap rolled up in a small towel – and her vanity case containing her makeup in the suitcase, Ena took down her dress, folded it, and put it back in the case. Before leaving, she pulled up the crumpled top sheet and straightened the bedspread and eiderdown. Why she wasted time doing that she didn't know, and sighed.

Putting on her coat, she picked up the small case and left. Before closing and locking the door, she glanced back into the room. It looked much the same as when she arrived. I'm staying in a hotel, she thought and laughed out loud. Whatever next?

As she approached Hut 23, Ena could hear Binkie laughing. She knocked on the door and went in to cheers of, 'She's here,' from Dibbs, and 'Hooray,' from Binkie. Binkie's hair, which Ena had dressed the day before, looked almost perfect. Dibbs however, was wearing a silk scarf tied round her head in the style of a turban. When she took the scarf off, Ena could see why she had worn it.

'I didn't think you'd have time to do more than set my hair before the dance tonight, so I got one of the girls in my digs to put a dab of peroxide on it earlier. Brighten it up, eh?'

A dab? Dibbs' hair looked as if she'd had the bottle poured over it. 'Yes, I'm sure it has,' Ena said, unable to hide the doubt in her voice. Dibbs sat down at the sink, her hair still damp from rinsing off the peroxide, looked across the room at Ena, and pulled a face.

'Don't worry,' Ena said. Stowing her case behind the clothes rail, she went over to Dibbs. 'It'll be fine if we wash it very carefully and put tons of conditioning cream on it.' She looked at Binkie. 'I saw some conditioner here yesterday.'

'Will this do?' Binkie said, passing Ena two bottles: one yellow and one pink. Ena whistled. 'Richard Hudnut? These look expensive.' She took the top off the yellow bottle and sniffed. 'Mm, smells lovely. Enriched Crème Shampoo with egg? With egg?' she repeated. 'I can't imagine why they'd put egg in it.' She read the label on the pink bottle. 'Crème Rinse, hair conditioner. These will do. Where on earth did you get them?'

'I didn't. A Yank who was sweet on Bertie had his sister send them over from the States.'

'Won't she mind if I use them on Dibbs' hair?'

'No, they're for everyone.' Binkie looked down at Dibbs's hair and grimaced. 'Use as much as you like, Ena.' Binkie bent down and spoke into her friend's ear. 'I think you left the peroxide on a little too long, Dibbs old girl.'

'Don't start, Binkie,' Dibbs mumbled, with her head in the basin.

Dibbs was sitting with the cream conditioner

on her hair when Bertie and Woody arrived. 'I'll wash Woody's hair,' Bertie said, 'while you set Dibbs' hair, Ena.'

'And I'll wash your hair, Bertie, while Ena sets Woody's. What fun. It's like a hairdressing production line.'

Fun it might be for Binkie, but for Ena it was hard work. Dibbs's hair was dry first. She had put her under the big dome hairdryer, on a low to medium heat. Ena daren't use the metal curlers that Dibbs had brought for fear that when she took them out, Dibbs' hair would stay round them. Instead she made barrel curls round her fingers, which were kept in place with Kirby grips and a hair net. At the front, she'd risked using metal wave grippers that had fairly big teeth, which, to Ena's relief, released Dibbs's hair from their grasp immediately without pulling out a single hair.

Woody and Bertie had simpler styles. Both had waves at the front, Woody's hair was longer and thicker with a natural curl that was easy to set in deep waves. At the bottom, however, it took real effort and patience for Ena to comb it around her fingers into a roll. Bertie's hair, although it had some natural curl, was shorter and finer. Sweeping it over to the right, Ena brushed it into soft waves turning the length at the neck into a small neat bun. After securing the bun, Ena placed a small diamante slide above her ear to hold a loose wave in place.

A quick comb through Binkie's hair to tidy it up, and the four friends were ready to go to the dance.

When the last of Binkie's pals had left, Binkie

told Ena to take anything she wanted from the clothes rail, the shoe rack too. Ena had brought her own dress, but thanked Binkie. Ena looked again through the dresses hanging on the portable clothes rail. She would have given anything to wear the green satin. It reminded her of the dress her sister Bess had worn on her twenty-first birthday. She took it from the rail, admired it, and put it back. The thought of spilling something on such an expensive dress petrified her.

Ena took her own dress from the case, ran the iron over it, and put it on. She stared in the mirror. She looked fine. Her own dress, royal blue flowers on a white background, fitted snugly over her small bust and hips. And the skirt, cut on the cross, was perfect for dancing.

She put on rouge and lipstick, and dabbed power on her cheeks to calm down the rouge. Giggling, Ena went over to the shelf where the perfumes were and picked up a bottle of L'Aimant by Coty. Dabbing it first on her wrists, she put a spot behind each ear and a little on her chest above the 'V' of the sweetheart neckline on her dress.

Going back to the mirror, Ena turned to the left and the right. She was happy with the way the dress looked on her. She liked the shape and the swing of the skirt, but it was more than that, she felt comfortable in it.

Ena met Henry as arranged, outside the dance hall at seven o'clock. She had never seen Henry dressed in anything other than corduroy trousers and a cable knit jumper, or slacks and a tweed jacket. Even when he and Bess had been walking out together, he always dressed casually. Tonight, in a dark suit and white shirt, with his hair slicked back with brilliantine, he looked very smart, and very handsome.

'What are you staring at?' he laughed.

'You. I haven't seen you dressed up before. You look...'

'Ridiculous?'

'No! Handsome.'

Red faced, Henry hooked his index and middle fingers behind the collar of his shirt and ran them around the inside. He loosened the knot of his tie. 'Not much call for clothes like this at the Park.'

'There should be.' Ena put her small case and handbag on the ground, and stretching up, straightened his tie. 'That better? Not too tight?' He shook his head and Ena looked to the sky. 'Come on, we don't want to miss the first dance,' she said, picking up her case and bag.

'I don't mind escorting you, Ena, but I'm no dancer.'

'So I've heard. Binkie thinks you'd be a catch if you weren't such a boffin. She calls you Highbrow Henry.' Henry clicked his tongue and threw back his head. 'She said she has never seen you dance, because you've never been to a dance. But we'll show her.' Ena linked her arm though Henry's and strode along to keep in step with him.

The band was warming up when they arrived. Ena checked her coat and small suitcase into the cloakroom. After scanning the room for Freda and not seeing her, Ena joined Henry who was queuing at the bar. 'What does young Ena drink these days?'

Ena grimaced. 'I'm warning you, if you treat me like a child, I shall behave like one and spill my drink down your suit,' she laughed.

'God no, don't do that. I hired it. It'll be going to a wedding next week and a funeral the week after.'

Ena laughed until she saw the serious look on his face. 'You are joking? Tell me you're joking,' she said, standing on tiptoe, looking into Henry's eyes for signs of a smile.

'I'm joking!'

Ena laughed again, loudly. 'You liar!' she said, slapping him on the shoulder. 'Gin and tonic, please.'

'It was dandelion and burdock the last time I took you out.'

Looking at Henry, quizzically, Ena leaned away from him. 'Now I know you're lying. If you had ever taken me out, I think I'd remember.'

'*Elephant Boy*, The Ritz Cinema, Lowarth, 1937. You were thirteen, or fourteen. Bess and I had to sit though it twice. You insisted on sitting in the middle of us. We couldn't even hold hands.'

'You're doing it again.'

Henry frowned, scrunched his shoulders, and held out his hands, palms up.

'I give up!' Ena said, 'I can't tell whether you're lying or telling the truth.'

'Claire had chicken pox, or some other child's ailment, and had to stay at home.'

'Oh my God. You're right. I remember now. It was a Rudyard Kipling story about an Indian boy.'

'Toomai.'

'He wanted to be a big game hunter when he grew up.'

'His father was an elephant driver--'

'And he had a pet elephant.' Ena hooted with laughter. 'Now I feel embarrassed.'

'And so you should, calling me a liar.'

The band began to play "I'm Playing With Fire". 'Come on,' Ena said, putting down her drink and dragging Henry to his feet. 'You've got to dance at least once.' Ena scanned the dance floor.

'Why? Who are you looking for?'

'Binkie. Or one of her friends.' Ena laughed. 'Binkie bet me ten shillings that I couldn't get you to dance tonight.' Ena watched the smile disappear from Henry's face. 'But that isn't why I'm dancing with you.' When the band finished playing, they walked back to their table.

'Honor Brinklow can be a bully, and her so-called friends are as bad. Be careful, Ena.'

'I will,' Ena said, hating herself for telling Henry about the bet. She'd done it again – said too much, let her mouth run away from her to make a stupid joke. She could have kicked herself. They were having fun and she'd spoiled it.

'Another drink?' Henry asked, and not giving her time to reply, set off for the bar.

'I'll get the next round,' Ena said, when Henry returned, 'I don't expect you to buy my drinks all night.' Henry was looking across the room. 'After all,' she said, following his gaze, 'it was me who invited you to the dance.' Henry didn't appear to have heard her. Damn, she had put her foot in it again.

'Come on, Ena,' Now it was Henry's turn to pull her to her feet. 'Honor Brinklow is over by the door watching us. I'll win you that ten shillings.'

'You don't have to, Henry.'

'Yes I do. Ten shillings is nothing to Honor Brinklow, but she hates to lose.' Henry held Ena close and looked dreamily into her eyes. Ena laughed. 'What is it now?'

'You,' Ena giggled. Unable to help herself, she laughed out loud. Henry swung her round several times, lifting her almost off her feet. They danced until the band announced they were taking a twenty-minute break, and then walked back to their seats laughing like a pair of teenagers.

Ena took her purse from her handbag. 'I'm going to buy you a drink.'

'No you're not,' someone said at her shoulder. 'At least not yet.' Ena looked up to see Binkie at her side with a bottle of champagne and two glasses. She put them on the table. 'Enjoy, children.'

'Champagne!' Ena exclaimed. 'Where on earth did you get champagne?'

'The Honourable Lady Dibbs, dear. But shush, don't tell everyone, or they'll all want a bottle,' Binkie whispered. 'Can't stop, darlings. *Ciao*.'

'Thank you,' Henry called to Binkie, as she turned to leave.

'Don't thank me, dear heart, thank Ena for stepping in at the last minute and making Dibbs and the rest of us look divine.' Binkie pretended to pat her hair into place as she danced across the room. She disappeared among her crowd who were shouting, 'Where have you been?' and 'Champagne for Binkie!'

Ena laughed and poured two glasses of champagne. Henry shook his head and pushed his glass into the middle of the table.

'I'll have that, if it's going begging,' Freda said, arriving almost immediately after Binkie had left. She fell into the nearest seat, reached across the table, and pulled the glass of pale bubbles towards her. 'Thought I'd never get here. Some friends took me to the local pub. Hello?' she purred, making a show of noticing Henry, 'I'm Ena's work colleague, Freda.'

'Yes, I know. How do you do, I'm Henry.'

'Henry? But--' Freda eyed Ena suspiciously and with a nod, tutted. 'Of course it is. Silly me. How do you do, Henry?' Freda shook Henry's hand, sat down, and picked up Henry's champagne. 'Cheers!'

Both women were content with champagne but Henry wanted beer and went to the bar, leaving them to chat. 'I thought you were walking out with an American named Ben?' Freda said.

'I am. Henry's an old friend from Lowarth. I told you that I'd seen him at the Park. It's because he works here that I asked him if he would accompany me tonight.'

'What about Ben?'

'Ben works in London. There wasn't time to write and tell him about the dance. I – we – didn't even know about it until yesterday.'

'I suppose.' Freda narrowed her eyes. 'So tell me. What does Henry do at Bletchley Park?'

'Something to do with communications. Beyond that, I have no idea.'

As Henry returned, the band started to play. He hadn't had time to sit down before Freda was on her feet and at his side. 'Would you like to dance, Henry? You don't mind do you, Ena?'

'Of course not,' Ena said, smiling up at Henry. He didn't look too happy about the prospect of dancing, but took a swig of his beer and allowed Freda to pull him onto the dance floor.

Ena enjoyed the music. She enjoyed watching the dancers too. Some were doing the modern Swing dance, others the Jive – both were new American dances. She watched Freda and Henry until they merged with the other dancers.

When they returned to the table, Henry sat down without waiting for Freda to sit first. Freda didn't seem to notice. Strange, Ena thought. She had never known Henry to be bad mannered, not when she was younger and he had walked out with Bess, nor during the time she had been coming to Bletchley.

'I'm going to the Ladies,' Ena said. Pushing back her chair, she got up and left the table. After using the toilet, she washed and dried her hands. Before refreshing her lipstick, she deliberated about the way Henry had behaved towards her friend. She wondered if he and Freda had disagreed about something while they were dancing.

It was obvious that Freda had been drinking, she'd said as much when she'd arrived. Ena had experienced her friend when she'd had too much to drink on several occasions. Her mood could change from bright and chatty to dark and morose in a very short space of time.

On her way back to the table, Ena encountered a group of people standing on the periphery of the dance floor, deep in conversation. She stopped behind them. She was only half interested in what they were talking about, her main reason for being there was to observe Henry and Freda. Swaying to the music, unnoticed by the group, and unseen by Freda and Henry, she watched the way her two friends behaved to one another.

By the frown on Freda's face, her mood had changed from friendly to angry. She looked at Henry. He picked up his glass of beer, took a long drink, and put the glass down heavily. Freda shot him a startled look. While she feigned interest in who was on the dance floor, Henry drummed his fingers on the table. Not to the beat of the music, Ena thought. Henry is as angry with Freda as she is with him – and it looks personal.

## CHAPTER NINETEEN

Returning to the table, smiling first at Freda and then at Henry, Ena said, 'Dance?' Henry jumped up straight away.

'I'll get some more drinks,' Freda said, and got up too.

Ena pulled Henry into the middle of the dance floor.

At the end of the first dance, she led him to an unlit corner of the room. There were drinks on a table and a handbag on one of the two chairs. She needed to get straight to the point in case the occupants of the table returned.

'What was that all about?' The lines on Henry's forehead deepened into a frown and he shrugged, as if he didn't know what she was talking about. 'Come on, Henry. When Freda first joined us the two of you pretended not to know each other. But you did, didn't you?' Henry didn't answer her. 'I know you did. The way you were arguing just now was not the way two people who have never met before argue. It was much more personal, intimate almost.' Henry looked at Ena, his eyes widening with surprise. 'So you do know her. Where from? Here?'

'Yes. Horace Dalton thought there was something about her that wasn't quite kosher. He got me to take her out to tea, as a friend, and find out what I could about her.'

Ena knew all about having to find out about people. She had done the same to Ben under Commander Dalton's instructions. 'And?'

'And we've had tea together twice when she's

been at Bletchley with Herbert Silcott.'

'Freda didn't say anything to me, nor did Mr Silcott.'

'He wouldn't have known. Both times were on Fridays when she was spending the weekend with her uncle in Northampton.' Ena looked over to where the three of them had been sitting. Freda had returned with the drinks and was placing them around the table. 'Perhaps she wants more from me than friendship.'

'And you?'

'No. I don't want more. I told you, Horace Dalton asked me to find out about her.'

'So?'

Henry looked at her as if he didn't know what she meant. 'Does the commander have any reason to be worried? Do I have reason to be worried? Could Freda be involved in sabotaging the work for Bletchley?'

'No,' Henry said with certainty. 'I'm positive she isn't involved in anything like that. I told you, I think it's just that she has read too much into me taking her out to tea. Which is why she was annoyed when she arrived tonight and saw me with you.'

'And why she asked me so bluntly about Ben. Now you've explained the situation, it makes sense. Sorry, I didn't mean to be angry with you, I'm just tired of suspecting everyone I meet of being a spy or a traitor.' Ena laughed. 'Except for you, of course. You couldn't be a spy *and* be as close as you are to Commander Dalton.' Ena put her hands up to her face and gasped. 'Perhaps it's the commander who's the spy. He could be sitting in his office now, plotting and planning the country's demise, laughing at us as we run round in circles accusing and falling out with each other. What do you think?'

'Horace Dalton a spymaster?' Henry shuddered and grimaced. 'That's much too frightening to contemplate.'

Ena looked over Henry's shoulder. 'Come on. Freda looks miserable on her own, let's join her.'

By the time they reached the table, Freda was sitting with her head in her hands.

Pretending to be out of breath from dancing, Ena picked up her gin and tonic. 'Thank you, Freda,' she said, taking a drink.

Freda lifted her head and nodded. 'Sorry, for being a misery.'

'Nothing to be sorry for.' Ena looked at her watch. She wished now that she hadn't lied to her friend. She should have told her about the dance, and that she was staying at the Station Hotel, as soon as Commander Dalton told her he'd booked the room. Ena sighed. Maybe if Henry had told her yesterday what he just said, she would have told her.

Ena wasn't a good liar, or good at getting out of situations by lying. Which was what she had to do now. 'It's time I left, or I'll miss my train.'

'I'll come with you,' Freda said. 'Well, as far as Northampton.'

'No! Honestly, Freda, there's no need. Besides, the dance doesn't end for ages, if we both leave poor Henry will be all on his own. No, you stay here and keep him company.'

'Are you sure?'

'Of course.' Ena turned to Henry. 'You don't want to leave yet, do you, Henry?'

Henry looked at Ena and shook his head very slowly. She could see in his eyes that he wasn't saying he didn't want to leave, but that he couldn't believe Ena's ploy to get away without Freda. He stood up as Ena stood. 'I'm going to get my coat and case, won't be a tick.'

Wearing her coat, and carrying her small case, Ena returned to the table and picked up her handbag. 'I'm off,' she said, kissing Freda on the cheek. 'Have a nice weekend with your uncle. See you at work on Monday.' She walked round the table, leant forward, and kissed the air next to Henry's cheek. He pushed back his chair to get up. 'Stay where you are!' Ena ordered. 'Thank you for accompanying me tonight, even if I did have to twist your arm up your back to get you to do it.' Henry began to protest, but Ena put up her hand and turned to Freda. 'Look after him, won't you. Make sure he doesn't spill beer down his suit. It goes back on Monday.'

Turning her back on Henry, Ena cut across the room to the door, yanked it open and left.

It was unseasonably cold outside. Ena stopped and buttoned her coat before setting off for the hotel. As she walked along the side of the building, she heard a girl call out. It made her jump and she stopped dead.

A second later, Ena heard a man's voice. It was deep and husky. She couldn't hear what he said, but whatever it was it made the girl giggle – so Ena resumed her journey.

In the distance, she saw the hooded headlights of a motorcar. It turned into the car park. Its lights extinguished, she heard someone, presumably the driver, open and shut the door. It was too dark to see where he was heading, the faint sound of his footfall disappeared in seconds.

As she neared the car park, Ena thought she heard other footsteps. She stopped and looked round. There was no one behind her, or to her left or right. She tutted loudly. With security guards on the gates around the clock, no one could get in or out of the Park without identification, a pass and a damn good reason to be there, which no stranger to the Park would have at this time of night.

She took a calming breath, told herself that Bletchley Park was the safest of places, and carried on walking. She hadn't gone more than a few yards when she heard the footsteps again. She stopped, and they stopped. Her nerves tightened at the top of her stomach and she could feel her heart pounding.

Approaching the entrance to the car park, she quickened her step. She was about equal distance from the mansion to the main gate when she heard the footsteps behind her speed up. She stayed close to the cars and when the footsteps grew louder, nearer, she sidestepped to her left and ducked down behind the first vehicle in a row of seven or eight.

She put her hand on the bonnet to steady herself. It was warm. It was the car she had seen parking a few minutes earlier. She held her breath and hoped the owner would return soon and help her. Her heart was pounding so loudly she feared whoever was following her would hear it.

Crouching, with one hand on the car's mudguard and the other on the bumper, Ena leaned to the left. Poking her head round the side of the car, she froze. The moon was on the wane, giving only a little light, but she saw clearly enough the silhouette of a man in an overcoat and trilby hat. She held her breath as she watched him walk towards her. If she didn't move he would be on top of her in seconds.

She slid her suitcase and handbag under the car and, on all fours, crawled as quickly and quietly as she was able along the ground until she was midway between the first and last car. She stopped and listened. The footsteps began again, slower, more of a shuffle, but nearer. She moved again, as she had the first time, until she arrived at the end of the row.

There was a footpath on her right. It ran along the front of several huts – and it was a mere six feet away. If she could only get to it, she could hide behind one of the low walls. She heard what sounded like someone exhale. She strained her ears, trying to work out where her stalker was. Not daring to look round the car, she bent down to look under it – and froze again. He was on one side of the car, Ena was on the other. With a few feet between them, Ena had no choice but to make a run for it now.

Easing herself up from a kneeling position to sitting on her haunches, ready to make her escape, Ena heard voices in the distance. Not allowing herself to be distracted, but hoping that her stalker was, Ena sprang up and fled from behind the car. Launching herself over the low wall, she landed between it and a door. With fear pounding in her ears, she waited for the footsteps to begin again. When they didn't, she reached up and tried the door. It was locked.

She was about to run to the next hut when she was grabbed from behind and pushed into the doorway. She opened her mouth to scream, but a mouth firmly covering hers, stifled any sound she attempted to make.

She tried to move, to wriggle free, but the man had her pinned against the door with his body and was gripping her arms at her side. She thought about kneeing him in the groin, but his legs were between hers. She couldn't move.

She heard footsteps again, but this time they walked past. The man who was kissing her had saved her from whoever had been following her. He loosened the grip on her arms and lifted his face from hers. 'Quiet,' he whispered.

'Henry?'

'Don't speak. He may be hanging about.' They stood in silence listening for the sound of footsteps. They didn't have to wait long. At first they seemed near, but they soon receded into the distance. Eventually they couldn't hear anything at all.

With his head bent down as if he were still kissing her, Henry said, 'I think he's gone, but he may be lying in wait. Look round me, see if you can see him.'

'I can't see anything, because I can't see past you.'

'Right. Hang on, I'm going to lift you up. When I do, moan a bit, or giggle. Pretend you're enjoying it and have a look around.' Ena didn't have time to say anything before Henry had lifted her up. With her legs round his waist, she began making similar noises to those she'd heard the girl make when she first left the dance. Embarrassed and feeling very stupid, Ena whispered, 'You can put me down now.'

'What?' Henry whispered.

'Put me down!' she hissed, boxing him on the shoulder.

Henry lowered her to the ground. 'Well?'

'I couldn't see him. I think he must have given up and gone into the dance.' She shivered. 'Do you think he knows me, was watching me in the dance, and waiting for me to leave?' she said, her voice trembling.

'No. He had no way of knowing you'd leave on your own. I'm sure he was just chancing his arm for a kiss and a cuddle.'

'Which reminds me. Thank you for, er…'

'Kissing you?'

'Almost suffocating me,' Ena retorted. 'But no, seriously--'

'It was my pleasure.' Henry's voice sounded hoarse. 'Not many men would disturb a couple canoodling in the shadows.'

'No.' Ena felt tearful. 'Oh God,' she cried, 'What would have happened if you hadn't left the dance when you did?'

'Don't think about that now. Come on, I'll walk you to the station.'

Before leaving the car park, Henry retrieved

Ena's suitcase and handbag from under the first car. Insisting on carrying the case, he handed Ena her bag. Her legs felt like jelly. She stumbled and went over on the side of her shoe. 'Hang onto me,' Henry said. Ena leant into him. She held him round the waist and he put his free arm round her.

At the entrance to the station, Ena stopped walking. 'I'm not catching the train.' Henry looked baffled. 'I'm booked in at the hotel,' she said, pointing to the Station Hotel a little further along the street. 'It was a last minute thing. I've been working all hours, most Saturdays and some Sundays. Anyway, Mr Silcott, insisted I stayed overnight on expenses,' she lied. 'I didn't tell you earlier because I thought it best not to say anything in front of Freda. She's been working long hours too, but he didn't offer to treat her to the hotel. Anyway, I didn't think it was fair to say anything.' Ena felt the colour creeping up her neck to her cheeks and laughed nervously. 'She'd probably have thought I'd planned it to--'

'To what?'

Ena laughed, again. 'Oh, I don't know... To get you back to my room and trap you in some way! But I didn't plan it, so she'd be wrong.'

Henry walked Ena to the hotel. 'I fancy a drink,' he said, opening the door. 'I promised Freda I would travel to Northampton with her, but I can't face going back to the dance. And I am not going to hang about the station for three quarters of an hour. Would you keep me company?'

'Yes. I could do with a drink, I'm still shaking.' Ena followed Henry through the lobby to reception and asked for the key to her room.

A minute later, they were in the hotel's lounge. At the bar, Henry smiled and raised his eyebrows. 'How about a brandy, calm your nerves?'

Ena wrinkled her nose. 'Gin and tonic will be fine. Better not mix them.'

Henry waited at the bar to order the drinks while Ena, taking her case, looked for somewhere to sit. There were no free tables. On the far wall, tucked away in an alcove, she spotted a leather Chesterfield and made for it. She sat down, putting her case on the floor and her handbag next to it by her feet. She gasped with shock. Her shoes were scuffed at the front where she had crawled around behind the cars in the car park, the heels were caked in mud, her knees were as dirty as her brother Tom's used to be after a game of football, and the hem of her dress was grass stained.

Taking her handkerchief from her handbag, she spat on it and rubbed her knees. The dirt came off quickly, so did the leg makeup that she had so carefully painted on her legs that morning. Exasperated, she dropped her hankie back into her bag. There wasn't time to go to the Ladies. Even if there had been, washing her knees would take more of the makeup off them and they'd look worse. She had a better idea and dragged the low table from in front of the Chesterfield nearer to her. With her feet under the table, her shoes couldn't be seen, but her knees could. Rubbing them with her handkerchief had made the liquid makeup patchy. They looked better dirty, but there was nothing she could do about it until she got to her room.

'The waiter's bringing the drinks over,' Henry

said, taking the edge of the table and pushing it away so he could sit down. Ena grabbed at the hem of her dress in an attempt to keep her knees covered.

'Oh dear,' he laughed, sitting down. 'Now you do look like Bess's kid sister.'

At that moment, the waiter appeared with the drinks. He put them on the table and, directing the question to Henry, asked if there was anything else. There wasn't.

Ena's face was red with embarrassment. She began to get up, but Henry caught her arm and she sat down. 'Stay and have your drink. No one can see you've got a bit of muck on your knees.' He picked up his drink and turned his head away.

Ena slapped him on the shoulder. 'I can see you're laughing. Oh, I give up.' She poured tonic into the gin, and took a drink.

'If the Station Hotel's patrons have nothing better to do than look at your knees,' Henry said, 'then they must have very sad lives. Having said that, they are very nice knees.' Ena tutted. She could feel her cheeks flushing.

They sat and sipped their drinks, watching the hotel's customers come and go for some time. It was Ena who broke the silence. 'What made you come looking for me tonight?'

'I was worried about you because you were angry when you left.' Ena opened her mouth to protest, but Henry put his hand up, the palm directly in front of her face. Her eyes sparkled with anger. 'Isn't nice is it, being shut up in that way?' Ena looked down. 'I knew you were upset, *angry*, by the comments you made about my suit, and by the friendly way you kissed Freda goodbye, but made a point of giving me the kind of kiss your friend Binkie Brinklow would have given to an unwelcome hanger-on.' It was Henry now whose eyes shone with anger. 'And all that stuff about having to twist my arm up my back to get me to take you to the dance. That was unnecessary and damn-well not true!' Henry caught his breath and took a swig of his beer.

'So far you've given me half a dozen reasons why you wouldn't come after me,' Ena said quietly.

'I know you were adamant that I didn't walk you to the station, but I had invited you to the dance, and I wasn't going to let you walk down on your own, especially at that time of night. So I grabbed my jacket, told Freda I'd see her at the station, and left. I could only have been a minute, two at the most, behind you but when I got outside you were nowhere to be seen. I saw a man in an overcoat and trilby walking down the drive. He stopped suddenly and then started walking again. I thought it strange when he turned into the car park. If you've got a car you go straight to it, not crouch down as if you're stalking a wild animal. He halted a couple of times, for no reason that I could see. But it was when he began looking between the cars that alarm bells rang.

'I walked along the drive to the edge of the car park. I thought if I could see him quite clearly, which I could, he would be able to see me, so keeping low to the ground I made my way across the lawn to the huts and crept down from there. When you ran from behind the cars, I was watching the man who was following you from the side of the building. You gave me quite a start. One step nearer and you'd have run into my arms.'

'I ended up in them anyway. Thank goodness you ignored me and came looking for me.'

'You twisted one arm to get me to take you to the dance, I thought I'd give you the opportunity to twist the other, and walk you home,' Henry laughed.

'Don't, it's not a laughing matter. I behaved badly. I am sorry.'

'Forget about it, unless you want to talk.'

'No thank you. I feel embarrassed enough about my behaviour without going over it again. I can't help wondering though, who the man was, and why he was following me.'

Just then, the lounge door burst open and a group of noisy people tumbled into the bar. Ena and Henry looked across the room at the same time. 'Oh no!' Ena said, 'It's Binkie and her friends. I hope they don't see us and come over.'

'So do I. Freda's with them.'

Ena scanned the group of Bletchley revellers and gasped. 'So is my American friend, Ben. He's with Freda. He must have been at the dance. I had no idea--' Feeling an assortment of emotions, and not understanding any of them, Ena grabbed her handbag. 'Sorry, Henry. I don't feel like explaining why I look as if I've been dragged through a hedge backwards. Do you mind if I sneak out?' She nodded towards a corridor and a sign with an arrow that said Hotel.

'No, you go. When they see me, I'll say I've

been sitting here having a quiet drink, while I waited for my train.'

'Thank you. I'd kiss you goodbye properly this time, but--'

'Next time.'

'Next time,' she agreed. 'And Henry?' Ena looked into his eyes, her own smarting with tears. 'Thank you.' Not wanting to leave but knowing she must, Ena edged along the Chesterfield, out of the alcove, and into the passage leading to the front of the hotel. She turned back to see Henry walking towards her carrying her suitcase.

'That would have given the game away, wouldn't it?' Ena went for the case's handle before Henry had let go, and her hand clasped his. Butterflies were flying around in her stomach and her pulse was racing. She stretched up and kissed him on the cheek. He didn't move, but bent down until his face was level with hers. Ena closed her eyes and Henry kissed her on the lips. Feeling dizzy, her heart beating like a drum, all Ena could say when Henry let go of her case was, 'Thank you.'

The sound of raucous laughter interrupted the moment and broke the spell. 'I had better go before they see me.'

'Leaving me to the mercy of that lot. Shall I ever be able to forgive you?'

Ena's stomach somersaulted and she pulled a face, pretending to frown. There was loud laughter again and she mouthed, 'Good night,' and walked away.

At the end of the passage, she looked back. Henry had gone.

## CHAPTER TWENTY

Ena kicked off her shoes, nudged the door shut with her elbow and crossed the room. Throwing her handbag onto the bed as she passed, she dropped her suitcase next to the wardrobe, and sat down on a small stool in front of the dressing table. Leaning forward, she peered into the mirror. Her hair was untidy and she had cried off most of her mascara, leaving dark smudges under her eyes. She yawned. At that moment she would have given anything to pull back the sheets and fall into bed. But not with half the car park at Bletchley Park on her feet and legs.

Turning the brass keyholes on her case, Ena took out her washbag, grabbed the towel that hung on the side of the hand basin, and went to the door. She had noticed when she arrived that morning that the bathroom was opposite her room. In a second she was out of her door and, locking it behind her, was across the narrow landing. Checking the small round disk next to the doorknob, and seeing it said vacant, she pushed open the door. Inside she slid the bolt into place to show the bathroom was occupied, put down her washbag, and turned on the hot water tap.

By the time she had been to the toilet, washed her face and cleaned her teeth, the bath was half full – and very hot. She dropped in a bath salt and turned on the cold tap, swishing the water about until the temperature felt right. Then, taking off her clothes and hanging them up on a peg behind the door, she stepped over the rim of the bath and lowered herself into a half-sitting, half-laying position.

Almost immediately, she felt a stinging sensation on her knees. She sat up and, bringing her knees up to her chest, saw cuts and grazes beneath the dirt – a consequence of crawling around on her hands and knees. She took her flannel and dabbed her knees in turn until the cuts looked clean.

Ena stretched out, her legs floating until her feet touched the smooth cast iron of the end of the bath. Relaxing back, slowly, so she didn't make the water swell, Ena lowered her body until her shoulders were under water and closed her eyes.

The water was cooling, Ena sat up and lathered the flannel. She washed herself all over, submerged her body again to rinse off the soap, and then climbed out of the bath. Aware that there were people in the corridor, other guests going to their rooms, Ena quickly dried herself. Pulling on her dress, she gathered her belongings in the wet towel, and opened the bathroom door. There was no one in the corridor, so she ran across to her room, unlocked her door, and was inside in a second. Locking the door behind her, she dropped the wet towel on the floor and threw herself onto the bed exhausted.

Ena had no idea how long she'd been asleep when a train rattled into the station and woke her. She stretched and opened her eyes. She felt lonely and a little disappointed that her friends Henry and Freda had left Bletchley. She looked at her watch. It was quarter past twelve. They'd have been gone more than an hour. Ena took off her filthy dress, which, being damp after her bath, felt cold against her skin.

Yawning several times, she put on her nightdress, switched off the light, and crawled into bed. She was bone-tired, but she was too keyed-up, too anxious, to sleep.

After tossing and turning for goodness knows how long, Ena got up, took her notebook and a pen from her case, and returned to bed. Tucking the bedclothes under her chin, but leaving her hands free, she wrote down everything that had happened after arriving at Bletchley that morning to getting back to the hotel at night, in chronological order. She wrote down what she had actually seen, followed by what she thought was suspicious.

At 3am, the events of the night blurring, Ena fell back onto the pillow. She wriggled down in the bed and pulled the blankets over her head. Five minutes later, or so it seemed, she heard a gong and groaned. Breakfast.

The journey back to Rugby was what the clerk in the ticket booth called Sunday service. 'Not only slower than usual, the train waits longer in each station, but the benefit,' the shiny cherubic-faced man beamed, 'is the time of day you're travelling. On a Sunday, at this time of day, you'll get a seat. They're all having their Sunday dinner, you see.'

The clerk was right. Ena found a seat in the first compartment. The only other occupants, two women, were both reading magazines. They looked up at Ena and smiled when she entered, quickly going back to their reading.

Putting her case on the overhead rack, Ena settled into her seat and took her notebook from her handbag. Reading it, Ena felt disloyal to Henry and Freda. She'd noted the way they behaved to one another, concluding with the observation that Henry had taken Freda to tea, which led to Freda hoping for more from the relationship than Henry was willing to give.

Mm... Ena still wondered why neither of her friends had mentioned going to tea. A thought crossed her mind and her heart took a dive. Was Henry 'H' who had been writing to Freda? What a ridiculous idea! Just because Henry's name began with H. Millions of people's names began with H – Herbert Silcott and Horace Dalton to name but two. Ena stifled a giggle, dismissing Horace Dalton, but Mr Silcott? The factory had once been rife with rumours about Freda and the boss. Perhaps they were true.

How long had she known Freda, and what did she really know about her? Ena cast her mind back. Freda had been working at Silcott Engineering for at least six months when Coventry was blitzed in November 1940. At a guess, she had begun working at the factory in May of that year, making it three years since they became work colleagues. But it wasn't until after Coventry, when they went to Bletchley together, that they became friendly.

Friendly? Freda appeared to be very friendly with the man on the train who, in 1942, poisoned Ena and stole her work. But being friendly – laughing with someone – doesn't necessarily mean you know them. Thinking about it, Freda couldn't have known the man. He later tried to strangle her.

Ena thought back to that terrible day, the day she had killed the man attacking Freda. Freda had shown herself to be a real friend, taking control of the situation, insisting Ena stay in their compartment while she went back to see if the man was alive or dead. Freda was convinced that if Ena hadn't stopped him, the man would have killed her, and then Ena. And when she told Commander Dalton, he agreed with Freda that Ena had acted in self-defence.

Freda kept Ena's shocking secret and they had become good friends. Freda had told Ena about her uncle in Northampton. Her brother Walter in the army. How she had lost her father in the First World War, and her mother dying... Thinking about it, Freda had confided in Ena much more than Ena had in her.

Ena hadn't told Freda much about herself at all. She had told her about meeting Henry, and that he was an old boyfriend of Bess's, and about meeting Ben. Not the circumstances in which she had met either of them, just that she had. Strange, she mused. Not that Freda had met Henry and Ben, but that she hadn't told Ena that she knew them.

Herbert Silcott: Ena had written NO next to his name. She skipped to Henry Green. She was positive Henry had nothing to do with spies or sabotage. Henry Green, involved with someone who was capable of poisoning her? Never. There was something he was keeping from her though, or why hadn't he told her that he knew Freda, and that Freda was fond of him?

Ena read what she'd written about Henry the first time she met him at Bletchley, the day her work was stolen. *Henry Green was in the hut. What a shock to see him. I thought I'd have an ally, but no. He didn't let on he knew me when I arrived with Commander Dalton. Think that was a bit fishy. He said later that if I was in some sort of trouble, he would be better placed to help me if no one knew we were friends.* Hum!

At the time, Ena had thought it a reasonable explanation, now she wasn't so sure. Henry lived in Northampton and so did Freda's uncle – and Freda visited her uncle regularly. Henry had moved there after leaving Oxford, so he'd been there a while. Ena scanned the next couple of pages, but couldn't find what she was looking for, or perhaps she hadn't written it down. There had been some sort of fuss when Henry had left University. If she knew what is was at the time, she had forgotten now. Bess would know. Ena made a note at the bottom of the page to ask her.

The next name she came to was, Ben F. Johnson. She felt foolish now, but when she first met him she had underlined his name and drawn a small heart by it, which she later rubbed out. Tilting the notebook so the sun shone on it, she could still see the imprint beneath the grey smudge.

Ena read through the endless notes she'd made on Ben. Smitten by his good looks and kindness, she wrote how caring he had been in the buffet on Euston station. Most men would have run a mile if they saw a girl crying, but Ben didn't. He gave her his handkerchief, fetched her a cup of tea – and listened to her. Ben cared. He went with her to buy her ticket, put her on the right train, even travelled with her to Bletchley to make sure she arrived safely. Ben had swept her off her feet. She went over what he had said when he told her he loved her, when he asked her to marry him and go to America with him. She had only seen Ben as a young man in love, until last night.

After Freda accused her of betraying Ben, and later seeing them arrive at the Station Hotel together, Ena had written a different profile on him. *On the day my work was stolen, Ben could easily have been the second figure on the train. He could have left the train after me and followed me into the buffet on Euston station. He could have befriended me to find out if I'd seen anything on the train that I shouldn't, or remembered anything that happened after I was drugged.* Ena remembered coming to for a few seconds and seeing two figures. She shut her eyes and squeezed them tight. It was no good. She couldn't even define whether the second person in the compartment was a man or a woman.

If Ben were a spy, he had done everything Commander Dalton warned her to look out for, which at the time she had largely ignored. He had approached her, befriended her, bought her gifts, swept her off her feet, and told her he loved her. And he had made her think she loved him.

Leaning back in the seat, Ena closed her eyes. They ached from straining to read her scribblings of the night before. The only notes left were those she had written about the girls who worked on the factory floor. Several manufactured parts for Bletchley and Beaumanor. Ena ran her eyes down the list. None knew what the work was for, nor did they care. She had long since crossed their names off the list.

Leaving the train at Rugby station, Ena headed for the telephone kiosk. Bess had taken her to Rugby station on Saturday morning, thinking she was going to Northampton to stay with Freda and her uncle, and would be going to a dance with Freda at night. Half the story was true... She put her money in the slot and dialled the telephone number for Foxden Hall. Bess had said she'd be happy to pick her up, but it was tea time. She wouldn't ask her sister to come to Rugby, she would suggest Lowarth – if anyone ever answered the telephone at Foxden. She heard the pips, pressed the 'A' button and listened to the money rattle through. 'Hello, could I speak to Bess, please?'

'Hang on, I'll fetch her,' a woman said.

Ena put another couple of pennies in the box. She didn't want the call to end before-- 'Bess, it's Ena.'

'Are you in Rugby?'

'Yes, but there's a bus any minute, so I'll catch it, and if you can, will you pick me up from Lowarth in half an hour?'

'Yes. See you in Church Street?'

'Thanks, Bess.' Ena heard the pips and put the phone on the cradle. She pressed button 'B' out of habit, but there wasn't any change.

Crossing from the telephone booth, Ena saw the bus was at the stop. She waved to the driver and ran for it. Stowing her suitcase in the luggage compartment, she found a seat and paid the conductor the fare.

The journey took less than half an hour, and when she got off the bus in Church Street, Bess was waiting for her in Lady Foxden's black Rover.

Opening the back passenger door, Ena threw her case and handbag onto the back seat, slammed the door, and joined her sister in the front of the car. 'It's good of you to pick me up,' Ena said, leaning back in the comfortable leather seat.

Bess pulled away from the kerb. 'No trouble at all, I'd have fetched you from Rugby station if you'd have wanted.'

Ena shook her head. 'I'd have had to wait in the cold waiting room. If the buffet had been open I'd have had something to eat, but it's closed at this time of day on Sundays.'

Bess laughed. 'Didn't Freda's uncle feed you before you left Northampton?'

'I had a big breakfast, but it seems like ages ago now. Bess?' Ena thought she'd ask her about Henry while they were on their own, which didn't happen often these days. Bess glanced sideways, and Ena carried on. 'Henry Green was at the dance. Well, I met him before when I was with Freda and arranged to see him there. Do you still hear from him?'

'I haven't heard from him recently. I think the last time was Christmas. Why?'

'Nothing really…'

Bess looked in the rear view mirror before steering the car left onto the Woodcote road. Ena could see she was smiling. 'Are you sweet on him?' her sister asked, as they cruised along the road to Mysterton.

'No!' Bess shot her a knowing look. 'I'm not sweet on him, but I like him.'

'And there's a difference?'

'Yes, there is. It's a bit... oh I don't know.' Ena floundered for the right words. She couldn't tell Bess where it had happened, but she could tell her when and what had happened. 'To cut a long story short, I went outside and a man followed me. Henry came out looking for me and, well, you could say he saved me.' Ena glanced at her sister. She looked worried. 'Nothing happened,' Ena said quickly, to put her sister's mind at rest. 'Anyway, I spent the rest of the evening with Henry, talking, and I got to know him. And I really do like him.'

'And you want to know what I think?' Ena nodded. 'He's quite a lot older than you and--'

'And what?' Before he sister had time to answer, Ena said, 'Does Henry... bat for the other side?'

'What? Where on earth did you hear that expression?'

'When I told Binkie, a friend, that you and Henry had walked out together when you were young, she said, '"Old Highbrow Henry hasn't always batted for the other side then."'

'Who is this *friend*? If I were you'd I'd steer clear of her. Sounds to me as if she's jealous.'

Ena laughed. 'Binkie Brinklow jealous of me? I don't think so! Binkie is very beautiful and very rich.'

'Then she's probably used to men falling at her feet, and when Henry didn't, she made something up to save face.' Bess threw her head back and tutted. 'Henry wouldn't fall for the likes of this Binkie character, she sounds too superficial for him.' Bess looked at Ena, her brow furrowed. 'Henry's lovely. He's a bit serious – and of course there's the age difference – but if you like him, I'm happy for you.'

As they pulled up outside their parents' cottage, Ena said, 'Don't say anything about Henry to Mam or Dad, will you. Henry might not feel the same about me. Even if he does, it's early days.'

'It's our secret.'

'And for goodness sake don't mention that I was followed,' Ena said, jumping out of the car. 'Dad would go mad.'

'I won't, but you must promise me that you won't go walking around a strange town on your own again – especially at night.'

'I promise. Thanks for the lift.' Ena closed the front door, opened the back, and hauled out her case and handbag. 'See you during the week.'

'Goodbye, love. And be careful.'

'I'm always careful.' As she said the words, a vision of the faceless man in the trilby hat who had followed her flashed into her mind. Pushing a strand of hair out of her eyes, Ena metaphorically brushed the man away.

Waving off her sister, Ena went up the path and into the house by the back door. 'Mm, something smells good,' she said, entering the kitchen.

'It's your dinner,' her mother said. 'We've had ours an hour since, yours is in the oven keeping warm.'

Ena's father got up from the table and kissed her on the cheek. 'Good to have you home, love. I'll put this in your bedroom,' he said, taking the case out of her hand. 'I've got to organise the ARP rotas. I'll be in the living room, at the table,' he said to Ena's mother and left the room.

'What's Freda's uncle like?' Ena's mother asked, placing her Sunday dinner on the kitchen table. 'Is his house posh? I expect it is.' She sat down to hear Ena's news. 'Well? What was it like?'

'Nice. A bit like our Margaret's in-laws house in Coventry. You know, semi-detached, three bedrooms, small front garden, long narrow back garden,' Ena lied.

'And her uncle?'

'Nice. He was out when we got there yesterday, and he went off early this morning, so I didn't see much of him, but he was very nice.' Ena's mother leaned forward, ready to hear more. 'I'm starving hungry, Mam. Can I eat my dinner while it's hot and tell you about the weekend later?'

Clearly unimpressed by the lack of information, Lily Dudley frowned. 'I'll put the kettle on then,' she said, getting up from the table and busying herself at the stove.

When Ena had finished eating, her mother brought the tea tray to the table, and asked Ena one question after another. 'Did you and Freda have a nice time at the dance?' 'Did you meet any nice young men?' 'I suppose that American was there?' What her mother had against Ben, Ena couldn't imagine. She had only ever said nice things about him. There were only nice things to say.

When she had answered her mother's questions, keeping what she told her simple, so she'd remember what she'd said if her mother asked her again, Ena yawned and pushed her chair away from the table. 'Thanks, Mam, that was lovely.' Getting up, she stacked the tea things on the tray and put them on the draining board. 'Don't you like to listen to the wireless at this time on a Sunday afternoon? Come on, let's go into Dad. He must have finished the ARP rotas by now.' Ena opened the kitchen door and waited for her mother.

## CHAPTER TWENTY-ONE

Ena arrived at work before Mr Silcott and Freda. Mr Silcott had no appointments in the diary and would probably arrive soon. Goodness knows what time Freda would get in, coming all the way from Northampton.

Ena put on the kettle to make a cup of tea and, while it boiled, sorted through the post. There were four letters. One for Freda and three for Mr Silcott, which she put on their respective desks.

Mr Silcott arrived as the kettle whistled. 'I timed that well.'

'You did,' Ena said. She poured their tea and took Mr Silcott his.

A despatch rider arrived with the usual large brown envelope from the Ministry of Defence. Ena took charge of it, and asked him if he would like a cup of tea. Checking his watch, he said, 'I'll have one in the canteen, if it's all right.'

Several couriers delivered work orders from the MoD, but this young chap, Ena remembered, had been talking to one of the girls on the factory floor the last time he was here. Ena had asked the girl afterwards if he'd asked her about the work she did. He hadn't. The courier looked at his watch again. Ena smiled. The cheeky monkey had purposely arrived at morning tea break, so he could talk to the girl he was sweet on. 'You know where it is.' Before she had time to thank him, he was gone.

Thinking about the young dispatch rider's lack of subtlety, Ena ran the paper knife along the top of the envelope, slicing through the words *Top Secret*. Every time she opened an envelope, or read a work order from the MoD, she was reminded that the work she and Freda did at Silcott Engineering was secret.

When the morning tea break was over, Ena discussed the work order, and what needed to be done, with her friend, Madge Taylor. Madge was the forewoman in charge of a hand-picked gang of women engineers. Some of the women were local, and some had worked for Williams Engineering in Coventry and relocated after the factory was bombed. The women worked hard, often on difficult and complicated jobs, and the hours were long and unsociable. But when they were working, Madge was working – and so was Ena.

Ena returned to the annexe. Freda still hadn't arrived. She picked up the letter Freda had received that morning, turned it over, and read the back. *The Lady of Liverpool Ferry Co*. A new customer, she thought. Well done, Freda. She hadn't been getting as much work of late. Ena dropped the envelope on the counter by Freda's desk. It landed with a thud. Heavy, she mused.

'Did Freda ring when I was on the factory floor, Mr Silcott?'

'No. Has she got anything that needs attending to today?' Wondering what was in the envelope, Ena was only half listening. 'Ena?'

'Sorry... Yes. The work for Beaumanor that she finished on Friday. She was going to deliver it today.'

Mr Silcott pushed his chair away from his

desk. 'I'd planned to go up there one day this week. So, as I have a full tank of petrol,' he said, grinning like a child with a new toy, 'I'll take the work up. You'll be all right on your own for a couple hours, won't you?'

'Of course. I'll get a sandwich from the canteen for my lunch, while you're here.' Ena took her purse and left her boss telephoning Beaumanor.

When she returned, Mr Silcott put the invoices in the top drawer of his desk and took out the key to the safe. 'Give me a hand, will you, Ena?'

Ena left the sandwich on the counter by Freda's desk and went over to the safe. Mr Silcott handed her the key.

When she had unlocked it, he lifted the heavy lid and Ena took out Freda's work. Placing the large box on Freda's desk, Ena helped Mr Silcott to put the lid back in place. The bunker was empty, but Ena locked it and returned the key to the top drawer of her boss's desk.

When Herbert Silcott left, Ena got on with her work. She took the chamois leather bundle of precision tools from her toolbox and marked up the first of several dials. She had been working for less than two hours when she heard the lunch bell ring, followed by enthusiastic chatter as the women went past the door of the annexe to the canteen.

Any other day, Ena would have joined them, but she wasn't in the mood today. She was hungry, and since she had put her tools down, decided to eat her sandwich. Where had she put it? She looked around and spotted the white paper bag containing the cheese and pickle sandwich on the side, where Freda worked. She got up and retrieved it, put the kettle on at the same time, and waiting for it to boil, ate half the sandwich. Refreshing the tea pot, Ena picked up Freda's letter. She weighed it in her hand and put it down. Something about it bothered her.

Finishing her sandwich, Ena tried to work, but she couldn't concentrate. There was only one thing for it. She would see what was in the envelope addressed to Freda.

Ena heard the women returning to work after lunch and waited. When it had been quiet outside the annexe for some minutes, she crossed the room and opened the door. There was no one in sight and the only sounds she could hear were the thumping and grinding of heavy machinery coming from the factory floor.

Satisfied that she wouldn't be disturbed, Ena closed the door and went over to the envelope. If she hadn't told Herbert Silcott there was a letter for Freda, she would have opened it in the usual way, pretending later that she hadn't realised it was a personal letter for Freda. She filled the kettle with the last of the water from the jug, lit the gas under it, and waited for it to boil.

It felt like an eternity, but eventually steam drifted out of the kettle's spout. Ena lifted the envelope and held it close to the increasing vapour. She watched the adhesive on the edge of the flap start to bubble and the ends of her fingers redden from the scalding steam. She was about to drop the envelope when the mist of minute water droplets moistened the bond fully and it gave up its tacky grip.

Laying the envelope down on the flat surface, Ena picked off rapidly drying gobbets of glue. One speck of dried glue, however small, and Freda would know the letter had been opened. With the flap of the envelope in near to pristine condition, Ena eased out its contents.

Ena caught her breath, unable to believe what she was seeing. She was holding three one-way tickets to Ireland on the *Lady of Liverpool* ferry for the week after next. Carefully she opened each of them. The first was in the name of Freda King, the second Walter King – Freda's brother – and the third Mr H. Villiers. Ena let out a sigh of relief. The 'H' who wrote to Freda was called Villiers.

After making a note of the ferry's name, the time and date of its departure from Liverpool and the arrival time in Ireland, Ena returned the tickets to the envelope. Taking a jar of paper glue from the stationery cupboard, she carefully brushed the adhesive along the top of the envelope. As if she were staying within the lines of a child's drawing, she took care not to go beyond the line where the previous glue had been.

When she had finished, she took a step back. There were no wrinkles, which meant she hadn't put on too much glue. The next part of the job was closing the envelope. There was no time for hesitation, indecision led to mistakes. In one confident movement, Ena folded the envelope, pressed on the seal, and walked away.

It would be five minutes before the glue set.

She looked at the door. If Freda came in now God knows what she'd do. Ena's hands were trembling. She walked up and down the room shaking them out, looking at her watch every few seconds. 'Five minutes,' she said at last, and went back to Freda's envelope. A nervous laugh escaped her lips and she blew out her cheeks. It looked perfect. She picked it up and turned it over. No one would know it had ever been tampered with.

Ena felt hot and her head ached. She put down the letter, left the annexe and went outside. She lapped the car park, as much to settle her nerves as to get some air, finally dropping onto the low wall by the factory's main entrance. She wondered what time Mr Silcott would return from Beaumanor. It took Freda three hours when she delivered work there. She guessed it would be the same for her boss.

Ena couldn't get the ferry tickets to Ireland out of her mind. Obviously Freda, her brother Walter, and this H. Villiers character, were going there together. But why? For a holiday? Freda always insisted she didn't need a holiday. People change their minds, Ena thought. Strange though, that Freda hadn't mentioned she was going to Ireland.

Ena stood up, arched her back and stretched out her arms. She felt better for the fresh air and went back to the annexe. She stood at Freda's desk. It had been a while since Ena had looked through Freda's personal letters. There may be more now. There might even be one that would shed light on why Freda was going to Ireland.

Without wasting more time, Ena opened the

top drawer of Freda's desk. It contained worksheets mostly. There were a few unpaid bills and a receipt held together by rubber bands, but nothing unusual. Making sure she left the papers in exactly the same order she had found them, Ena slid the drawer to and opened the next one down.

The second drawer held petrol vouchers – one or two a month going back to the beginning of the year. Closing it, Ena pulled on the bottom drawer. It didn't budge. Remembering it had stuck once before, because an envelope got jammed at the back, Ena pulled it again, harder. It not only didn't open, there was no give in it. It was locked. Ena's pulse began to quicken. Had Freda locked it as a precaution or because she knew someone had looked at her private correspondence before and was making sure they couldn't do it again?

Either scenario would mean trouble if she was caught. Ena weighed up the situation and decided that, after what she had learned about Freda today, anything she had hidden in a locked drawer was too important to ignore.

Keeping an eye on the door, Ena crossed to Mr Silcott's desk and took out his keys. She knew one of them opened the drawers in her desk, because the wages had been locked in there on the few occasions that Mrs Silcott had brought them to the factory early. Ena wondered if the same key would unlock Freda's drawer. It was worth a try.

On her knees, Ena slipped the key into the small keyhole. She turned it slowly and heard the locking bar click back. Her hands were shaking. She took out the key, pulled the drawer open, and looked inside. There were several letters.

Assuming the most recent would be on top of the pile, she took it and, getting to her feet, put it on the desk.

For fear Freda would arrive and accuse her of spying on her, which was exactly what she was doing, Ena ran to her desk, dragged it across the room, and pushed it up against the door. She then tipped the remainder of her tea on the floor. If anyone tried to come in the door would bang against the desk, giving Ena time to put the letters back where they belonged. And if they asked what she was doing, she would say she'd spilt her tea and had moved the desk out of the way to clean it up. Whether anyone would believe her was another matter. For the moment, it was all she could think of.

In an attempt to suppress the contradictory feelings of excitement and fear, Ena breathed deeply and slowly. Then, with the nerves on top of her stomach as tight as the skin on a drum, she opened the first of the letters. It was from Freda's brother Walter and began "My darling Frieda." There was something about the salutation that wasn't right. She read it again, "My darling Frieda." Darling was a little over-affectionate for brother and sister, but it wasn't that. After scrutinising the first three words, Ena saw that Walter had spelt his sister's name differently.

She read on. "I cannot wait until we are home." Ena looked at the envelope. The stamp was postmarked Northampton. So, home wasn't with their uncle... He went on to say, "I will be on the Liverpool train, as arranged," and he finished with "Wear the red beret I bought you in Paris, it reminds me of the happy times we shared when we were young."

Ena had never seen Freda in a red beret. Then it came to her. She had seen her wear a beret once. It was not long after she started working at Silcott Engineering. She wore it with a grey suit with matching gloves and-- Ena froze. She could hear voices outside the door. Quickly returning Walter's letter to its envelope, she put it in the drawer. She hadn't had time to look at the other letters, but after reading Walter's letter there was no need.

Bending down to make sure the grooves on the sides of the drawer were level with the ledges on the desk's frame, she noticed a strip of brown industrial tape across the back of the cabinet. Looking more closely she could see it was concealing something bulky.

Fearing that whoever was outside would come in and catch her, her heart thumped. She toyed with replacing the drawer and looking at what the tape held later, but once Freda had arrived, Ena wouldn't get the chance.

Besides, if Freda *was* planning to leave – and it looked like she was – she might take whatever it was behind the tape with her, and then Ena would never know. She ran to the door and put her ear against it. All she could hear was the throb of her own pulse. Satisfied that whoever had been talking outside had gone, she returned to the desk and dropped to her knees.

Reaching into the back of the wooden casing, Ena touched the bulk of what was hidden there. Then, walking her fingers to the end of the tape, she picked at it until it came loose. She took a calming breath and listened again for signs of life beyond the door. There were none. Now, fully focused on the job, Ena pulled the end of the tape and a key fell from its adhesive hold. Her worst fear had been confirmed.

Ena picked the key up and, holding it against the wood with one hand, drew the tape back across it with the other. She studied the tape for some seconds. She needed to be sure that the protrusion was in the same place as it had been when she first noticed it. It was.

After closing the drawer, Ena made two telephone calls: one to Mr Silcott at Beaumanor Hall, to ask him to bring back copies of the dates and times that Freda had booked in work at the facility. The second was to Commander Dalton, to tell him about finding the key to the safe, the ferry tickets and Walter's letter. When she had relayed every detail of Freda's forthcoming departure, she moved the desk away from the door and went to Maintenance.

Borrowing a mop and bucket, Ena cleaned the area where she had spilt tea and returned the desk to its original place. When the room was back to normal, she switched on the kettle. When it had boiled, she made a fresh pot of tea, and while it mashed, she returned the cleaning equipment.

## CHAPTER TWENTY-TWO

The continual hum filtering through from the machines on the factory floor, usually a comfort to Ena, irritated her as she tried to concentrate on her work. She looked at her wristwatch, it was four o'clock. Whoever took work to Beaumanor was usually back by now. She turned her attention back to the X-board she was working on. Sensitive to the slightest noise, she sat up with a jolt as the door clicked open.

'Mr Silcott!' Ena jumped up as her boss entered the room and she ran to meet him. Relieving him of his briefcase, she laid it on a side unit and helped him out of his coat. The telephone rang.

'Get that will you, Ena? And tell whoever it is, I'll ring them back.'

Desperate to see Freda's booking-in sheets from Beaumanor, Ena reluctantly crossed to the telephone. 'Silcott Engineering. May I help you?' she said, hoping whoever was on the other end of the telephone would ask for her boss, so she could end the call quickly.

'Hello, Ena, it's Freda,' her work colleague said, her voice a hoarse whisper.

'Freda?' In her head, Ena had thought of a dozen things to say when she saw Freda but she was so shocked to hear her voice she couldn't think of one. It didn't matter, Freda didn't give her time to speak.

'I'm still at my uncle's. I've had an upset stomach. Hopefully it's one of those twenty-four-hour things and I'll be all right tomorrow.'

'Wasn't anything you had to drink on Saturday night, I hope?' Ena said, her knuckles white from gripping the telephone receiver so tightly.

Freda laughed. 'You never know, we did have quite a night, didn't we?'

Ena forced herself to laugh. 'We did. It was certainly a night to remember.' And one that I won't forget in a hurry, she thought.

'Did Herbert take the work up to Beaumanor?'

'Yes.'

'Thank goodness. I was worried about it.'

'He's just got back. Would you like him to ring you--?'

'No need. Just tell him I'll be in tomorrow, late morning.'

'Don't come in unless you feel up to it,' Ena said. She was hoping Freda would ask about the letter. She didn't. 'You do sound poorly,' she continued, with as much concern in her voice as she could muster. 'I'm sure we could manage without you for another day.'

'Thank you, but honestly, I'm much better today. I'll be fine by tomorrow.'

'You know best. Goodbye then, see you tomorrow.'

'Oh, before you go?'

Here it comes, Ena thought, the question she had been waiting for. 'Yes?'

'Have I had any post today?'

'There's a pile of letters on the side, but with Mr Silcott going up to Beaumanor, I haven't had time to sort them out yet.'

'You wouldn't be a dear and have a quick look

to see if any are addressed to me?'

Got you! Ena punched the air. 'Of course, hang on a second.' Ena laid down the receiver and went over to Freda's desk. Ena counted to ten, picked up the letters and returned to the telephone. 'Now let me sort yours out.' Pretending to go through them, she said at last, 'Four addressed to Mr Silcott, and …. three addressed to you! Two are from suppliers – bills I expect.' Ena put them down on the desk, slowly, to make Freda wait. 'And one,' she said, turning it over in her hand to read the back of the envelope, 'is from a ferry company. I expect it's work. Do you want me to open it and see?'

'No!' Freda's rejection of Ena's offer of opening the letter was immediate and final.

'If you're sure?'

'Yes. I know what it is. It's a ticket for my uncle, for his birthday, which isn't until next month. I'll deal with it, and the other post, when I come in. Oh, Uncle has made me some soup, I'd better go. See you tomorrow.'

'Yes, see you tomorrow,' Ena said, through gritted teeth. She put the telephone receiver down and stood for some minutes, trying to calm her palpitating heart.

'Freda,' she said, when she eventually turned round and spoke to Herbert Silcott. 'She isn't well, but feels sure she'll be better by tomorrow. She said she was in Northampton, so don't expect her until late morning,' Ena said, unable to hide her anger.

Herbert Silcott acknowledged the information with a nod. 'Not like her,' he said. Ena didn't comment. 'Do you want to tell me what's going on, Ena?'

Suggesting her boss sit down, Ena ran through the events of Saturday night, finishing with how she was followed when she left the dance and had to hide behind the cars in the car park. 'I was frightened out of my wits. If it hadn't been for Henry Green leaving the dance a few seconds after me, noticing a man acting suspiciously, and coming to my aid, God only knows what would have happened.'

She chose not to tell Herbert Silcott that Henry had saved her life by kissing her in a dark doorway. She didn't think she could report that particular piece of information without embarrassing him as well as herself. Even now, just thinking about it, butterflies played havoc in the pit of her stomach.

A mixture of care and concern crossed Herbert Silcott's face. Rubbing his chin, he very slowly shook his head. With Freda's letters still in her hand, Ena showed her boss the address on the back of the largest envelope.

Reading the name of the ferry company aloud, he said, 'I don't understand. What is this?' Ena told him that, while he had been in Beaumanor that morning, she had steamed open the letter, and gave him the sheet of paper with the information that she had relayed to Commander Dalton over the telephone. 'And there's something else,' Ena said. Herbert Silcott lifted his head from Freda's travel details and raised his eyebrows. 'Freda's brother spelt her name with an 'i'. I expect it was a slip. He's never done it before, but he clearly wrote, F-r-i-e-d-a.'

Ena crossed the room to the kettle. Her throat was dry. She'd only had one hot drink since arriving at work that morning – the rest she'd let go cold. She also thought a cup of strong tea would be welcomed by her boss.

By the time Herbert Silcott had listened to every detail of Ena's expedition into the secret life of Freda King, if that was her name, the tea was made. Ena carried two cups to her boss's desk and handed him one. He accepted his cup with shaking hands.

They drank in silence.

When they had finished, Herbert Silcott took the delivery sheets that Ena had asked for from his briefcase. 'The one you'll be most interested in is at the bottom of the pile.' His mouth was turned down at the corners in disgust and his eyes flashed with anger. 'The first time Freda took work to Beaumanor on her own was the day I was set-upon by thugs, you were drugged, and your work stolen on the way to Bletchley.'

Ena took the delivery sheet from the bottom of the pile and read it. The time Freda had arrived at Beaumanor was 2:35pm.

The following morning, Ena arrived at work early. Meeting the postman by the front door, she took four letters from him. Two were addressed to H. Silcott, and two were addressed to Freda. One Ena knew was from a supplier because it was addressed to Miss F. King, had *Invoice* in brackets and had been written on a typewriter. The second was handwritten with *Personal* in the top left hand corner. She dropped that day's post on top of the previous day's, levelling the letters into a neat pile as she always did, and telephoned Commander Dalton for further instructions. There were none.

'I have passed on everything you told me yesterday to MI5,' he said. 'They are putting certain measures in place, which I will tell you about when I am told. For now, behave to Miss King as you would if you hadn't found the ferry tickets or the letter from her brother. Understood?'

'Yes, sir. Mr Silcott will be in soon. Shall I ask him to ring you?'

'No. I spoke to him last night.' There was a sudden silence. Sensing that the commander had more to say, Ena waited. 'Herbert is extremely angry. I told him that MI5 was involved and it was imperative that you and he treat Freda King as you always have – ordered him to do so – but he was still huffing and puffing when we said goodbye. I am relying on you to make sure he doesn't give the game away, Ena. Make him understand that he must behave normally towards her.'

'I will, sir. Is there anything else?'

'No. I'll let you know what MI5 plans to do, as soon as they tell me. Goodbye.' The commander put down the receiver without waiting for Ena to reply.

Herbert Silcott arrived within minutes of Ena speaking to Commander Dalton. He took off his coat and threw it over his chair. Ena said good morning and asked if he would like a cup of tea, to which he only grunted. Before lighting the gas jet under the kettle, she hung up his coat.

While she made the tea, Ena went through several scenarios as to how she was going to convey the importance of treating Freda normally to her boss. 'Commander Dalton phoned just before you arrived,' she said, handing her boss his cup.

'Does he want me to ring him back?' he asked, reaching for the telephone on his desk.

'No! He rang to make sure I understood the importance of treating Freda as I always have. I – we – mustn't act differently towards her.' Ena lowered her voice. 'He said MI5 was planning something, and it was imperative that we don't give her cause to suspect anything's wrong. You know.' Ena nodded at the stack of letters.

Her boss shrugged. 'I shan't say a word. I was angry. I am still angry. She has brought the Silcott name into disrepute. We may never be trusted to work for the MoD again. This business could be the end of Silcott Engineering.'

Ena put her hand on her boss's arm. He looked up at her. She could see he was fighting back the tears. 'Don't worry, my dear,' he said. 'I won't let Horace Dalton or damned MI5 down. I want the woman caught and thrown in jail. The last thing I want is for her to disappear back to Germany.'

'Quite right, sir. I told the commander not to worry, that we will both act normally for however long it takes. There is just one thing.' A puzzled frown appeared on Herbert Silcott's face. 'If Freda bats her eyes at you, you know the way she does sometimes for a joke, you mustn't react differently. Treat it as a joke, as you always do.

Every aspect of the working day must be normal. As you said, sir, if she gets an inkling we're on to her she'll disappear, and we don't want that.'

Herbert Silcott put up his hand. 'No, we do not! Trust me, Ena, if she does suspect we're on to her, it will not be because of anything I have said or done!' A sharp nod told Ena that, as far as he was concerned, the subject was closed.

The moment Ena dreaded came just after eleven o'clock. She heard the door open, the distinctive clip-clop of Freda's high-heels as she came into the annexe, and again when she turned and closed the door. Ena shot a look at Herbert Silcott and saw his back stiffen. She was annoyed that he hadn't acknowledged Freda's arrival, which he always did.

'Hello, Freda,' Ena whispered, 'shan't be a minute.' Pulling the last of the wires through the rotors on the X-board, she picked up the small drill and found the right bit. Usually used for boring holes in metal, Ena used it to engrave her initials on her work. Not as big in circumference as a knitting needle, the cutting tool created perfect cylindrical holes and … and was ideal for … piercing holes in pear drops!

Ena stared at the twist drill bit. Fingers of fear walked down her spine as the realisation of how the sleeping draught had been put into the pear drops, hit her. Her hands trembled. She made fists of them, clenched them beneath the desk and, leaning close to the work, pretended she was checking it. She needed time to calm down, put the poisoning of the pear drops and the theft of her work out of her mind. She needed to play the part of Freda's friend, as Freda had played the part of being her friend these past three years.

'That looks… fine!' she said, lifting her head from the work. She put down the drill and exhaled loudly. Not with relief, because she had finished the job, but because until then she hadn't realised she'd been holding her breath. 'Welcome back,' Ena said, beaming a smile at Freda, which she hoped looked natural.

Freda took off her coat and hung it up. Sighing heavily, she crossed the room to her desk and dropped onto her chair. 'I'm exhausted. I've hardly slept for forty-eight hours.'

'Tummy upsets are horrid,' Ena said, sympathetically. 'You open your post and--' Damn! She could have bitten off her tongue for mentioning the post so soon after Freda had arrived. It was too late now. 'You took your post, didn't you, Mr Silcott?' she said, her voice suddenly an octave higher.

He mumbled, 'No', but didn't turn round.

'What's he doing?' Freda mouthed, running the letter opener along the top of the first letter. Ena lifted her shoulders and shook her head.

Ena understood how her boss felt – she felt the same – but he needed to play along as she was doing. Freda was an intelligent woman. The slightest inkling that anything was wrong, and she'd be gone. Ena reckoned that knowing what he knew about Freda, Herbert Silcott would either pull out all the stops and treat Freda as he always had, or let fly at her. Ena couldn't let that happen.

'If there are any letters for Mr Silcott, take

them over to him, will you, Freda?'

Freda flicked through the pile. 'Only bills I'm afraid, Herbert,' she said, putting them on his desk.

'Thank you,' he mumbled, without looking at her.

Freda glanced over Herbert Silcott's shoulder at the sheet he was working on. She raised her eyebrows. Back in her own seat, she whispered, 'He's costing a job. Do you think we should buy him an abacus?'

'I heard that,' Herbert Silcott said. Turning round, he looked over the top of his glasses and winked at Ena. 'And what time do you call this, Miss King?' he said to Freda in an overly stern, theatrical, voice. Both women laughed. 'Good to have you back,' he said, and returned to his work.

Ena rolled her eyes with relief, and laughed. It wasn't until he made the joke about Freda's timekeeping that she dared to hope her boss would behave towards Freda as he had done before Ena had told him his assistant was a German spy.

Ena's cheeks ached from forcing herself to smile. She was bitterly disappointed by Freda's disloyalty to the company, devastated by her treasonous acts, and hurt that their friendship was a sham, but she would die before letting Freda King know she felt any of those things.

Work orders came in from Bletchley and Beaumanor as normal. The work was done and delivered on time as it always had been – Mr Silcott and Ena by train to Bletchley, Freda by car to Beaumanor.

The day-to-day production of discs and rotors, wires and X-boards, carried on as usual. It was important that nothing appeared to be different. To all intents and purposes, nothing had changed – and yet everything had changed. Freda was no longer the last person to check her work; that was done early on Friday morning by Ena, when she had finished reading Freda's correspondence.

At the beginning of Freda's second week back at work after she'd been ill, a letter arrived for her in the second post. 'It's from Walter,' she said. 'He's coming home on leave. After all this time fighting in France, he's coming home,' she said, her voice thick with emotion.

As she read on in silence, Ena watched the colour drain from her face. 'I need to take a day off next week. Do you think Herbert will agree to it? He must.' She leapt from her chair and went over to his desk to check the work diary.

Ena followed, and standing at Freda's shoulder, looked at the diary with her. 'I'm sure he will if you tell him how much it would mean to you to see your brother.'

Every nerve-end in Ena's body tightened. Was this what she and Commander Dalton had been waiting for? Did it mean Freda, her brother, and the Villiers character were on the move? 'What date will he be arriving, exactly?' Freda didn't reply. 'Be nice if you were there when he got home, wouldn't it?' Ena held her breath fearing that she had said too much, asked too many questions.

'Yes,' Freda said, 'it would be nice. I'll ask Herbert if I can have next Friday off.' Freda returned to her seat and put the letter in her handbag. 'I'll write and tell my uncle later. He'll be so pleased. Walter is his favourite.'

Before she went home that evening, Ena telephoned Commander Dalton. She told him about the letter from Freda's brother, relaying verbatim what Freda had told her. 'Which,' Ena said, 'I didn't believe was true. I think Freda only told me what she wanted me to know, so I'll help her to get next Friday off. She said she was going to write to her uncle in Northampton. If she does, and if she brings the letter in to post with the factory's mail, I'll get my friendly postie to let me have it. I'll say it's mine, and I need to amend something.' The commander didn't reply. 'I've done it before, sir.' There was a long pause. 'Are you there, Commander?'

'Yes.' There was another pause. 'Don't intercept the letter. I agree that she didn't tell you the truth about its contents. For a start, her brother isn't coming home on leave after fighting in France, or anywhere else, because he has never been in the armed forces. According to our intelligence, neither of them have crossed the Channel since arriving in England five years ago.'

'Perhaps the letter wasn't from her brother. If it had been, wouldn't she have put it in the drawer with his other letters?'

'Not necessarily. I'm sure it was from Walter King. She is too canny to leave it where you, or anyone else, could read it. And I don't believe she will write to her uncle. News as important as your long lost brother coming home from the war, you'd want to share more quickly; you'd telephone or send a telegram. No, all that was to make the story more feasible. Sounds to me as if she's feeding you misinformation.'

Ena suddenly felt very hot. 'Do you think she's on to me?' she asked, trying not to panic.

'No. She hasn't done or said anything to make me think that. Something in that letter has got her rattled. She'll be on her guard with everyone, so be careful what you ask her. I'm sure she still trusts you, she has no reason not to, but I expect she'll only tell you what she wants you to know; what she wants you to tell Herbert Silcott.'

'Like which day she wants off?'

'Exactly. Which makes me wonder if it really is this weekend that she plans to leave.'

'Are you sure you don't want me to look at the letter? If she does write to her uncle, she's bound to tell him the real date.' A thought hit Ena and she groaned loudly. 'How could I be so stupid?'

'What is it?'

'H. Villiers. He's Freda's uncle. Don't you see, sir? If I could see that letter--'

'No! And that's an order! It's too dangerous, Ena. You've done enough. Go about your business as normal. If she asks you to go to lunch, a dance, or to the damn cinema, go with her. You are her friend; someone she trusts. Don't do anything to make her think that has changed. And be careful. Freda King is a dangerous woman. Dangerous!' Commander Dalton, repeated. 'I'll telephone in a couple of days. By then I'll know what MI5 plans to do to catch these vermin.'

Vermin? Was Freda vermin? Ena supposed the

commander had every right to call her so, if she were a German spy. And dangerous? After being given drugs on the train, which could have killed her, Ena felt sick just thinking about what might happen if Freda found out she was spying on her and, through the commander, reporting back to MI5.

Ena put the telephone receiver on its cradle and went over to her chair. She sat down, put her elbows on the desk, and rested her chin on linked fingers. It was hard to think of Freda as a spy. She had led a double life for as long as Ena had known her, longer. And German? Everything about Freda was so English. She spoke perfect English. Her clothes and identity papers, even her engineering qualifications were English.

Ena looked across at Freda's empty chair with a heavy heart. They had been friends for almost as long as they had worked together – and their friendship had extended beyond the factory gates. Tears pricked the back of Ena's eyes as she brought to mind the times they had been shopping together, been to dances, to the pictures. And now it all counted for nothing, because everything about Freda was a lie.

Suddenly Ena's hands flew to her mouth. Freda had been with her when she killed the man on the train. She had dealt with the man's corpse, positioning it to look as if the man was asleep. She had been kind and understanding, helping her to come to terms with what she had done. Ena took a shuddering breath. Freda had kept her terrible secret, but under interrogation it was bound to come out.

Ena banished all thoughts of the man she had killed from her mind. She would face the consequences of her actions, of that fateful day, when the time came. Until then she must focus on the job she had to do, which was to expose Freda King, her brother Walter, and the man they called H. Villiers as spies.

Their friendship, if there had ever been any substance to it on Freda's part, was over and Ena was not going to let fear nor sentimentality stop her from playing her part in getting Freda King, her brother and uncle arrested for treason.

## CHAPTER TWENTY-THREE

Wondering if she could pull off the deception, Ena walked into Bletchley station amidst a gaggle of young women who, by their excited conversation, were going to London to celebrate one of their birthdays. Ena followed them along the southbound platform, hanging back as they neared the buffet. Two elderly women were leaving. Before the door closed behind them, Ena slipped inside.

Crossing the room, she saw a man look up from his newspaper. She glanced at him briefly. He gave a short nod. Ena didn't acknowledge him but opened the door leading to the northbound platform and made her exit.

Outside, she turned right, ignored the *Out of Order* sign on the door of the Ladies Toilet, entered, and was greeted by Commander Dalton and the two intelligence officers who had briefed her earlier. She let out a long shuddering breath, closed the door, and leant against it.

'Freda's clothes, or as good as,' one of them said, handing Ena a brown leather hanging suitcase, the kind used for transporting military uniforms. Ena took it and went into the nearest cubicle to change.

The grey suit was the same fabric and colour as one she had seen Freda wear but not quite the same style. The seamstress who had copied it had nipped the waistline in a little too much, making the bottom of the jacket flair more than was fashionable. Ena tugged gently on the lapels of the jacket. It fitted perfectly.

She took her feet from her own shoes one at a time and slipped them into a pair identical to Freda's. They were an inch higher than Ena was used to wearing, and narrower. She wiggled her toes. They were a snug fit but not uncomfortably tight. It didn't matter, she would be sitting down in them.

'Hat?' one of the security men said as Ena opened the toilet door, and handed her a red beret.

'She was wearing the beret then?' Ena asked. Putting on the hat, she pulled it slightly, so it tilted over her left eye, the way she remembered Freda wearing it.

'Yes. We brought a selection just in case, but she was wearing the one her brother asked her to wear.'

'We're not sure that they are brother and sister,' Commander Dalton said. 'There were only two bedrooms in the uncle's house – one not much bigger than a box room – and by look of the clothes in the small wardrobe, it was her uncle's bedroom. The other room, much bigger, had a double wardrobe with men's and women's clothes in it, and a double bed.'

'How do you know all this? More importantly, how do you know Freda won't be on the train?' The second she asked the question, Ena regretted it. 'Sorry, I shouldn't have asked.'

'Best you don't know,' the commander said with a wry smile. 'Right! Are you ready?'

'As I'll ever be,' Ena said. Pulling on a pair of pale grey gloves, she took a black handbag from the security officer. 'Don't forget these,' he said. He handed Ena an umbrella and laid a light grey coat over her arm.

When the officer stepped back, Commander Dalton stepped forward. He put his hands on Ena's shoulders and bent down until his face was level with hers. 'You're sure you want to do this?' Ena nodded. 'That's the ticket. You won't be on your own,' he assured her. 'Someone will be with you every step of the way. You may not see him or her but they'll be there.'

'And,' the security officer said, 'We are ninety-nine percent sure that the spies in Freda and Walter King's cell system would have gone to ground as soon as she told them her cover had been compromised. And she must have thought she'd been found out, or why would she leave so suddenly for Ireland?'

Ena looked from one to the other of the men standing before her. 'And the one percent? Freda bought three tickets for the ferry, so presumably she'd have bought three tickets for the train. Doesn't that mean someone, maybe two members of the spy ring, will be joining her at some point?'

Commander Dalton nodded. 'It looks that way. There was a lot of conflicting correspondence after you found the ferry tickets. We're not sure how much of it was real and how much was a smokescreen. MI5 intercepted what they think was Freda's last letter to Walter. She changed the travel arrangements, telling him that she wouldn't be on the train, she would see him in Liverpool.'

'He didn't receive that letter,' the security officer said. 'Whether she telephoned him…'

'But as far as we know,' Ena said, 'Walter thinks Freda will be on the train wearing the red beret he asked her to wear, the last time he wrote to her?' The three men nodded. 'And what about Villiers, the man the third ferry ticket to Ireland is for?'

The second intelligence officer looked at the commander who nodded. 'We're not concerned about him. If Freda King wrote to Walter telling him to meet her in Liverpool, chances are she'd have written to Villiers too. But we don't have his address, so we don't know.'

When the train pulled into the station, Ena shook hands with Commander Dalton and the intelligence officers. They wished her luck. 'From now on you are Freda King, looking forward to seeing your brother Walter,' the commander said.

'If you're ready, Miss King?' the officer said, to which Ena smiled and, holding the umbrella as Freda always did, she walked purposefully out of the Ladies toilet and along the platform. She wobbled once on Freda's high-heels, but recovered immediately.

In case she was being watched by any of Freda's co-conspirators, Ena kept her head down and boarded the train without looking back. If Freda's brother, lover, or anyone else was looking out of the train's window, Ena was not going to make it easy for them to see that the elegant woman in the charcoal grey suit and red beret was not Freda.

Squeezing past several soldiers in the crowded corridor, she finally arrived at the last compartment in the first class carriage. She pulled open the door. There was an empty seat on the right of the compartment, by the window, and two on the left. Ena took the seat nearest the window on the left.

Without acknowledging the other passengers, she stood her umbrella next to the window and put her coat and handbag on the seat next to her.

After a short time, Ena heard the hiss and clunk as the train's brakes released, and felt the locomotive jerk as it began its journey north. She watched the steam and smoke clear as the train left Bletchley for the Buckinghamshire countryside. She began to feel sick and opened the handbag. There were no pear drops, but there was a thin book that Freda had left at Silcott's, which Ena took from the bag.

Leaning sideways, so her back was to the door, Ena held the book towards the light from the window and pretended to read.

Some minutes later, she heard the compartment door slide open. Someone had entered. She couldn't tell if it was a man or a woman, and daren't lift her head to look. As the new passenger came further into the compartment, Ena glanced at the floor. Men's shoes. Giving the book her full attention, she heard him drop onto the seat opposite. She breathed a sigh of relief. The seat next to her was still empty. If he had been joining Freda, he would have sat next to her. She relaxed a little. The chances of anyone entering the compartment before the next station were slim.

The train slowed as it approached Northampton. Ena leant back in her seat. She didn't want anyone on the platform to see her if they looked into the carriage, in case they saw she wasn't Freda.

Ena's heart drummed with anticipation, but no one left the carriage and no one entered. Putting the book back into her handbag, Ena glanced at the man sitting opposite. *Ben?* Panic struck at her like a hammer. She couldn't breathe and felt sick.

'Excuse me, miss? I believe this is yours,' he said, holding a bookmark in his hand.

Ena took the narrow piece of card and whispered, 'It must have fallen from my book when I put it in my handbag. Thank you.'

'You're welcome,' Ben said politely.

With her heart pounding, Ena smiled fleetingly at the man she was walking out with, before turning her attention back to the window. As the train sped north and the fields and meadows of Warwickshire melted into the distance, Ena heard someone take a cigarette from a packet, light it, and inhale deeply. Someone else opened a newspaper and a third person left without closing the door.

Conscious that what happened in the compartment was not her concern unless someone took the seat next to her, Ena continued looking out of the window. Her eyes began to feel heavy and she closed them. Aware that she had slumped sideways and her forehead was touching the window, she began to drift off.

Somewhere between being awake and being asleep, Ena felt someone tap her on the shoulder. 'Hello, darling.'

Opening her eyes, Ena turned towards the voice and gasped with horror.

## CHAPTER TWENTY-FOUR

The man sitting next to Ena, looking at her with blue piercing eyes, was the man who had drugged her and stolen her work, who had attacked Freda, and who Ena had believed for more than two years she had killed.

The colour drained from the man's face. He was clearly as shocked to see her wearing Freda's clothes, as she was to see him alive.

'You look surprised to see me, *darling,*' he said. Then, lifting Ena's hair away from her neck, he put his mouth to her ear. 'Do you think you can make a fool of me, play me as if I were an imbecile? Where is my sister?'

'Walter?' Ena stared at Freda King's brother in in disbelief. Make a fool of him? Play him like an imbecile? It was him and Freda who had made a fool of her, setting her up to think she had killed someone. Ena clenched her fists. She was angrier than she had ever been, but she knew she had to stay calm. 'Let go of my arm or I will scream the place down.'

'Somehow I don't think you will,' he said, pulling a knife from his pocket and jerking it in Ben's direction. 'Because if you do, you won't have a heart to give your Yank lover.'

Ena shot Ben a look. He was miles away gazing out of the window. She glanced at the man sitting next to him, who she thought was military intelligence, he was still reading his newspaper, and the woman next to him had her head down looking for something in her handbag. Not one of them had noticed the man sitting next to her had a knife pressed against her ribs.

'Get up,' he whispered.

'What?' The muscles in Ena's body had seized. 'I can't...' Her voice was hardly audible. Then she saw the MI5 man lower his newspaper slightly and nod, once. She was to do as Walter King said.

'I said get up!' he hissed. 'If you do not do as I say, I shall stick this knife into your heart.' Then in a normal voice, 'You will not feel so sick if you walk around a little.'

Ena glanced down at the knife. He jabbed it towards her and her stomach churned. Pulling her roughly to her feet, Walter King pushed her towards the door and she stumbled. He put his hand on her shoulder, as if to steady her, and squeezed. The pain was excruciating. Without taking his eyes off her he said, 'Pick up your bag.'

Ena did as she was told and took another step. Her mind was racing, thinking of ways to escape. When they were sitting down, the knife was in Walter King's left hand, visible to Ena, but not to anyone else in the carriage. Now they were standing, surely the people opposite could see it. She looked down at King's left hand. It was in his coat pocket.

Smirking, he pushed her with his right hand. She didn't move. He pushed her again and, taking a couple of steps, Ena's foot caught the toe of the woman's shoe. She began to apologise, but the woman glanced up at her, smiled, and waved her hand as if to say it didn't matter.

Ena heard Walter King sigh loudly. He

squeezed her shoulder again, this time even harder. 'Open the door.' Ena hesitated and King reached round her. While he was bending forwards, and, Ena hoped, off balance, she spun round and, garnering all her strength, kneed him as hard as she could in the groin.

His face turned scarlet. His eyes, blazing with anger, bulged in their sockets. Cursing and holding his crotch, Walter King took a step back, but didn't fall down. Ben, the MI5 man, and the woman began to get up, but King recovered quickly and in an instant had the knife out of his pocket and at Ena's throat.

'Open it!' he shouted to the intelligence woman, who jumped up and did as she was told. 'Now sit down,' he ordered, and she returned to her seat. Pushing Ena out into the corridor, King closed the door.

With one arm around her neck, and the knife at her throat, he forced Ena along the corridor to the exit. 'I can't breathe,' she choked. 'Please, I think I'm going to faint...'

Ena's legs turned to jelly and as she slid to the floor, the world turned black. King put the knife in his pocket. 'Get up, you stupid bitch!' he shouted, slapping Ena's face to bring her round. He opened the window, hauled Ena to her feet, and propped her against the door.

Ena caught her breath and coughed. For a moment she didn't know where she was. Then she saw the *Welcome to Rugby* sign. The train had hardly stopped when King opened the door. 'We are going to leave the train and walk along the platform to the exit smiling as if we are sweethearts, understood?' Ena nodded. 'I shall put the knife in my pocket but if you so much as look at anyone it will be at your throat in a second. Got it?' Ena felt disorientated and her head ached. 'I said, got it?'

'Yes. I've got it,' Ena said, shaking.

'I don't want to kill you.' Ena hoped that was true. 'I take little pleasure in it, but if you do not do as I say, I will kill you in an instant.'

Ena nodded. 'I will do as you say.'

He slipped the knife into his pocket. 'When we are out of the station, and I am sure we have not been followed, I will let you go.' King nudged Ena down the train's steps and, gripping her arm, manoeuvred her along the platform. They walked quickly, overtaking passengers who had just left the train, until they were surrounded by people. Ena felt sick. In a few minutes they would be through the tunnel and out of the station, and then what? Would he let her go as he said? The alternative didn't bear thinking about.

Without warning, King pulled her to one side to allow a family – mum, dad, and two children, to go past. Then, with one hand clamped on Ena's arm and the other in the pocket where the knife was, he guided her towards the exit.

As if they were members of the family in front of them, Walter King laughed and chatted about their holiday. Ena, grim faced, looked over her shoulder. Two men appeared from the far side of the train. As they scrambled onto the southbound platform she recognised one as the MI5 officer, the other was Ben.

'You've got the tickets.' Startled, Ena brought

her attention back to Walter. 'Tickets!' he said, 'You should have two tickets.' King looked around, his eyes darting all over the place, not settling on anyone in particular. He obviously hasn't seen Ben or the MI5 man, Ena thought, and sighed with relief.

'They're in my handbag,' she said, as pleasantly as she was able. 'I can't open it and take out the tickets with one hand. If you let go of me, for a second...' He looked into her eyes, his own hard and cold. 'There's no one around,' Ena said, 'Even if there were, they wouldn't risk trouble in a crowd like this.'

'Tickets please!' the ticket collector said to the father of the family in front of them. He handed over his family's tickets and after the collector had torn the corner from each one, he waved the man and his family on. By the time King had let go of Ena's arm, to allow her to open her handbag, the family was through the barrier and nearing the exit. 'Tickets please!'

'Hurry!'

Ena raised her eyes. 'I can't find them.'

'You stupid--' As the few remaining passengers passed through the barrier, King snatched Ena's bag out of her hand and froze. Ena saw his Adam's-apple rise and fall as he backed away from her. 'You won't pull the trigger,' he goaded, his eyes fixed on the small revolver in Ena's hand. She tilted her head to one side and gave him a wry smile as if to say, "Try me". 'So,' he said, staring into her eyes and holding her gaze, 'I am going to walk out of here.' He continued to back away.

Looking past him, Ena saw a number of policemen, military men and civilians enter the station. Some stayed at the exit. Ben, the MI5 man, and several army officers were on the platform.

With a smirk on his face, sure that Ena wouldn't pull the trigger, Walter King's right arm shot up. 'Heil Hitler!' he shouted, turned, and charged through the cordon of officials.

Aiming blows at whoever came near, King downed a military policeman and a couple of security officers before Ben stopped him with a punch to the nose that sent him stumbling backwards, arms circling like a windmill, until he hit the ground.

King scrambled to his feet. With a bloody nose, he staggered forward like a drunk, and Ben knocked him down again. 'Enough!' he shouted, pushing himself up to a standing position. Suddenly, King doubled over in pain. Holding his left side with one hand, he raised his right hand in a gesture of surrender.

Something wasn't right, Ena thought. And as Walter King reached into his pocket, she shouted, 'Knife!' A second later Ben wrestled him to the ground and the MI5 man took the knife.

The female intelligence officer appeared at Ena's side, took the gun out of her hand, and bustled her along the platform. The last Ena saw of Walter King, who she thought she had killed several years before, and who would have killed her if she hadn't produced Commander Dalton's gun, was the back of his head as he lay face down on the platform of Rugby station.

Moving quickly, the two women crossed to the waiting room. There was a *Closed* sign on the door, which opened as they approached and closed immediately after they had entered.

'Commander Dalton?'

'Congratulations, Ena.' Dalton laid his hand on Ena's shoulder and gave it a squeeze. She winced from the pressure. He didn't appear to notice. 'Thanks to you, we've got them.' Them? Ena wondered if Freda had been on the train after all.

'Excuse me, sir, they're bringing the other one out,' an intelligence officer said.

Commander Dalton let go of Ena's shoulder and turned back to the window, where they watched police and military intelligence make their way to a carriage further along the train. An army officer alighted first, followed by a policeman handcuffed to the prisoner. A wave of panic went through Ena and she struggled for breath.

'Ena?' Commander Dalton called, walking away from the window. Ena didn't move. He called her again. 'Would you come away from the window? I need to speak to you.'

'One minute--'

'Now!' The commander ordered.

Ena left the window, not to join Commander Dalton, but to make a bolt for the door. 'Stop her!' Dalton shouted. As Ena reached the door, the female intelligence officer threw herself at it, blocking the door and knocking Ena out of the way.

'I'm sorry that was necessary,' the commander

said, stooping down to help Ena up.

Ena pushed him away and put her hands up as a warning. For what seemed like minutes, but could only have been seconds, they stared at each other. 'All right!' Ena said, at last. 'But can I speak to him?'

'Not possible,' Commander Dalton said, and took her by the arm. With the commander on one side and the intelligence officer on the other, Ena watched Henry Green, the man she was in love with, being dragged from the train in handcuffs. When he passed by the waiting room window, a few feet away from her, Ena lifted her arm and placed the palm of her hand on the glass, but Henry didn't look, didn't see it.

The door to the waiting room opened and a young army officer entered. 'Your car is here, sir. Yours too, Miss Dudley.'

Her head pounding, in a state of shock, Ena took a faltering step towards the door, stumbled, and reached for the intelligence officer's arm to stop herself from falling.

Commander Dalton took her other arm. Ena jerked it away. 'How could you, of all people, think Henry has anything to do with Freda and Walter King's spy ring?' she spat.

## CHAPTER TWENTY-FIVE

The day before Ena was due to go down to Bletchley Park to be debriefed by Commander Dalton, she went to RAF Grafton Underwood, near Kettering, to see Ben. The USAAF Eighth Air Force had been stationed at Grafton since 1942 – and it was where Ben and his boss were flying back to America from.

She arrived at the aerodrome late. Ben Johnson, she was told by a young airman who was part of Ben's party, was in a meeting. He suggested Ena wait for him in the NAFFI. 'I'll tell him you're here, miss.'

Ena was hungry, but couldn't face food so ordered a cup of coffee. She hadn't eaten properly since the day she had been part of MI5's mission to snare Freda and Walter King – and Henry. It had been almost a month and she still hadn't come to terms with Henry being a spy; she probably never would. Ena wondered who, if anyone, would tell his parents. He wasn't in the services, so they wouldn't get the dreaded telegram from the war office. Given the choice, killed in action was preferable to your son has been tried for treason and hanged as a spy. Tears blurred Ena's vision. She shook her head, defying them to fall.

Ena had gone over and over in her mind what she was going to say to Ben, but whatever she said she knew she'd be breaking his heart. Things had moved so fast. She liked him, had begun to love him, but he wanted too much from her, too soon. Getting married and moving to America was a huge step – one that Ena wasn't ready to take.

Jogging into the NAFFI, Ben pulled Ena to her feet and wrapped his arms around her. She winced. 'What is it?'

'My shoulder. It's still painful from the pressure Walter King applied when he forced me out of the train.'

Ben looked at her with concern. 'It's getting better, though, right?'

'Yes, every day it hurts less and the bruise has faded. It's mustard-yellow now, it was black at first.'

Ben dropped his arms to Ena's waist, pulled her close to him, and kissed her full on the lips. 'I have waited for this day for so long, honey.'

Ena put her hands on Ben's upper arms and gently eased herself away from him. He let go of her, and she took a step back. Looking around, Ben said, 'The guy who gave me your message said you didn't have any luggage with you.' Ena opened her mouth to speak. 'You've stowed your cases already, huh?' he cut in.

'You know I haven't.'

Ben ran his hands through his hair. He looked near to tears. 'So you're not coming to the States?'

Ena shook her head and whispered, 'I'm sorry.'

'But you're my girl. I want you to be my wife. I love you, Ena, I thought you loved me.'

'I do love you, Ben, but as a friend. I never said I'd marry you, or go to America to live.'

Ben looked downcast, his shoulders slumped. 'I guess I thought in time you'd grow to love me. I know,' he said with renewed optimism, 'don't make your mind up now. Give it a couple of months. I'll go over today, find us somewhere to live, and you can come over later.' Ben took hold of Ena's hands, his eyes pleading. 'What do you say?'

Ena hesitated. She didn't want to hurt Ben, but he wasn't listening to her. 'I don't love you, Ben. Not in the way you love me. Marrying you wouldn't be fair on you.'

'I don't care. I have enough love for the both of us. Hey?' he said, a new desperate thought lighting up his face. 'I'll show you America. I'll take you to see the Rockies and the Grand Canyon, and the Great Lakes.'

'Stop it! Even if I wanted to, I can't leave my family, my friends, my job, and move to the other side of the world. Not in the middle of a war.'

'But I need you, Ena.'

'So do my parents, Ben. I can't leave them while my brother is fighting on the front line in France, and my sister is goodness knows where in the world. And there's my job--'

'Okay! Don't come with me now.' Ben cuffed his tears. 'We'll write each other, and if you still don't want to live in the States when the war's over, I'll come back to England. We can get married here. We'll stay in England if that's what you want. We'll live in Oxford; you'll love it there. Or we could get a place near your folks. I'll get a job here in England and we'll go to the States on vacations.'

'Stop!' Ena cried. 'Please don't make this any harder than it already is.'

They stood in silence for some time. Then Ben said, 'Are you seeing another guy?'

'Not in the way you think, no.'

'What other way is there?' he shouted, his eyes narrowing.

'I love someone that I can never be with. Someone who I will never see again. And if I did see him, I would turn my back on him.' Now it was Ena's turn to cry. 'I'm sorry, Ben.'

'I'm sorry too!' Ben said. His voice had a bitter edge to it. 'Sorry that you're turning me down for that God-damn traitor, Henry Green?'

Shocked that Ben had guessed she loved Henry took Ena's breath. When she recovered she said, 'I am not turning you down for Henry. I'm turning you down because I don't love you. You know, Ben, it would be so easy to say yes, let's get away from everything that has happened during the last three years and start afresh, but it wouldn't be fair on you.'

Ena picked up her handbag and lifted the strap of her gasmask onto her shoulder. 'Good bye, Ben. Don't think too badly of me.' She wanted to hold him, tell him that one day he would find a girl that was worthy of his love, but that was the last thing he wanted to hear. Instead, she left him standing in the NAFFI and walked away. She didn't look back.

She had half an hour to wait until the base bus arrived to take the aerodrome's civilian workers into the town. She sat on the grass by the bus stop and burst into tears. She had cared for Ben, loved him. She might have fallen in love with him, eventually, if it hadn't been for Henry. Henry had put an end to her loving anyone after he'd kissed her on the night of the dance at Bletchley Park. Ena had never felt a surge of energy like it – not before, nor since. Her pulsed raced and her body ached for him then. It did now.

At the sound of an aeroplane's propellers whirring, Ena looked up. A big silver Douglas DC3 was lumbering down the runway. She watched the aircraft gather speed and cried for what might have been. Nearing the end of the runway, the nose of the huge silver aeroplane lifted. Seconds later, it was airborne.

Ena watched the plane climb high in the pale blue sky and disappear behind a patchwork of clouds. She wiped her face and whispered, 'Goodbye.' Goodbye to Ben and goodbye to love. She knew she would never see Henry Green again. She also knew that loving him had spoiled her for loving anyone else.

## CHAPTER TWENTY-SIX

There were three people in Commander Dalton's office for the meeting: Ena, Herbert Silcott, and the man who had sat next to Ben on the train, the day Walter King was captured, who Ena knew was from military intelligence.

Commander Dalton opened the meeting by welcoming everyone. He introduced Herbert Silcott and Ena to the man from MI5 calling him, Mr Robinson. 'Shall we get down to business?'

Mr Robinson nodded and read from his notes. 'Freda and Walter King's real names are Frieda and Walter Voight. Frieda has been on our files since arriving in England from Germany in 1938. Born and brought up in Berlin, she is the younger sister of Walter Voight. From an early age, they were members of the Hitler Youth movement and in their late teens were recruited by Abwehr, the German secret service, where they were trained as deep cover spies. They are both extremely intelligent – although it was Frieda who called the shots – and they are both ruthless, high-ranking Abwehr officers.'

Ena shivered. She hadn't known Freda at all.

'Thanks to your sterling work, Miss Dudley,' Mr Robinson said, 'Frieda Voight was apprehended in Liverpool trying to board the ferry to Ireland. Walter Voight, as you know, was captured in Rugby – again, thanks to you.'

Commander Dalton nodded. 'The relationship between Frieda and Walter is ambiguous. They are known to military intelligence as brother and sister but when the house in Northampton was raided it was obvious they shared a bed.' He glanced up at Commander Dalton who raised his eyebrows.

Mr Robinson returned to his notes, found his place, and continued, 'It was while Walter Voight was at University in Oxford in the mid-thirties that he met and befriended Henry Green.' Ena's heart was beating so loudly she thought everyone would hear it. She took a slow calming breath. 'During Voight's final year at Oxford, Frieda joined him. She found lodgings near the college, and together, she and Walter recruited Henry Green.'

Commander Dalton took over. 'Green and Voight shared a house in Northamptonshire after leaving Oxford, which Frieda put a stop to, saying that two men living together looked improper and would attract attention. So, in 1939, when we recruited Henry Green to Bletchley Park, he found lodgings in the town.'

'We have since learned the real reason for Frieda Voight getting rid of Henry Green was so she could spend weekends with her brother alone,' Mr Robinson cut in. 'To keep up appearances, Frieda flirted with men, appearing to enjoy the attention they gave her. In the early days, she even took one or two men back to the house in Northampton, but it was her brother who Frieda wanted, who she loved.'

When the man from MI5 had finished speaking, Commander Dalton gave a sharp nod. He looked from Ena to Herbert Silcott. 'Do you have any questions, or anything to add?'

'What happened to Frieda's uncle?' Mr Silcott asked. 'She was very fond of him. Was he also a spy?'

'There was no uncle. The spare room with its single bed and wardrobe full of an elderly man's clothes was part of their cover story.'

With the man from MI5 on one side of her and Commander Dalton on the other, Ena had felt out of her depth. But when she saw the commander close the file on Henry Green, she said, 'I have a question.' Knowing Henry would be tried and hung for treason, Ena had to say something on his behalf, however futile. The commander slowly lifted his head and sucked in a breath. He looked at Ena, a pained expression on his face. The other men followed his gaze. 'I do not believe Henry Green is a spy. He saved my life the night I was followed.'

The commander looked at the MI5 man, who raised his eyebrows. They don't believe me, she thought, and desperate to convince them, cried, 'I've known Henry since I was a child. And on the night he rescued me from who I now know was Walter Voight, we spent hours talking in the Station Hotel. He told me that he would have joined the services, except he was recruited to work at Bletchley.' The commander looked down at Henry's closed file. 'He didn't inveigle his way into Bletchley, Commander Dalton, *you* recruited him.' There was another look between the two men, but neither said anything, so Ena carried on. 'Sir,' she said to the man from MI5, 'I would like you to look into what you have on Henry Green. And when you do, you'll realise that a terrible mistake has been made – and that Henry is not a traitor.'

'I'm afraid he is, Miss Dudley,' the MI5 man said. 'When we searched the house in Northampton we found Nazi propaganda – printed leaflets and pamphlets. The originals were in Henry Green's handwriting. Ena's eyes filled with tears. 'I'm sorry, my dear.'

Standing up, Mr Robinson took Ena's hand and gently shook it. 'I must get back to London.' After shaking the hands of Commander Dalton and Herbert Silcott, he picked up his belongings and made for the door.

Ena started to go after him but was stopped by Mr Silcott who gripped her by the forearm and whispered, 'No!' She began to protest but quietened when the commander turned at the door and shot her a fierce look.

'Sit down, Ena,' Mr Silcott said.

'And calm down,' Commander Dalton barked, walking back to his desk.

Ena dropped into the nearest chair and put her head in her hands.

'We'd better go too, Horace. Come on, Ena.' Her boss put his hands on her shoulders and she lifted her head. 'You're exhausted. Let's go to the hotel and have something to eat. It's been a long and stressful day.'

Ena stood up, and with her head held high, looked into Commander Dalton's eyes. She braced herself to tell him again that Henry was not a spy, but her nerve failed and she offered him her hand. 'Goodbye.'

'Goodbye, Ena.' The commander took her

hand, but instead of shaking it, he held it. 'I understand how unhappy you are about Henry. I liked him too, very much. But in war it is necessary to sacrifice a few to save many. I want you to remember that. Remember too that your bravery in exposing Frieda and Walter Voight for spies has saved thousands of lives.

I can't say anymore, but with Walter's connections to the MoD and Frieda's here, if it hadn't been for you, God knows how much havoc they would have caused.' Ena smiled thinly through her tears. 'I'll get a car to take you to the hotel. And,' he said, picking up the telephone, 'I hope to see you in a couple of weeks.'

It was only five o'clock but it was already dusk. Standing in the doorway of the mansion, waiting for Herbert Silcott, Ena watched the commander's big black motorcar drive up from the direction of the motor pool. The car cruised to a halt a few feet from her and the driver got out and stood by the back door. Ena waved to him to let him know it was her that he was driving, and he touched his cap.

Arriving at her side, Herbert Silcott said, 'Right, let's get an early dinner. Horace Dalton has recommended somewhere just outside of Bletchley.'

'I'm not sure I'll be able to eat anything,' Ena sighed.

The driver opened the door nearest to Ena and she dropped onto the back seat. Herbert Silcott walked round to the other side of the car and got in. 'Drat!' he said, as the driver was about to close his door. 'Hang on a minute will you?' He opened his briefcase. 'I thought as much.'

'What is it?'

'I've left my portfolio case in Dalton's office.' Jumping out of the car he said to the driver, 'You know where you're going.' And to Ena, 'I'll see you there.'

'Can't you come back for it in the morning? There'll be time after breakfast, before--'

'There are documents I must look at tonight, in case I do need to return tomorrow.' Closing the car door, Herbert Silcott tapped the roof and the driver started the engine. Ena sank back into the soft leather seat and the car purred gracefully down the drive.

As they neared the main gate Ena took her identity card and Bletchley pass from her handbag, but the familiar vehicle was waved through.

The rhythmic hum of the big saloon made her sleepy and she closed her eyes. She felt the car pull to the left as it turned a corner, a slight jolt, and then the gentle throb as the engine laboured in neutral. Thinking they had arrived at the hotel, Ena opened her eyes.

'Why have we stopped?' she asked, looking out of the window into descending darkness. Leaning forward, Ena tapped the driver on the shoulder. 'Where are we?'

The driver half turned and started to answer her when the shrieking sound of an army transport train drowned his words. A second later, enveloped in smoke and steam, the car gently rocked. 'Railway crossing barrier,' the driver shouted when the train had passed.

'I gathered that! But why are we at a railway crossing?' She felt edgy. She had been anxious all day, but now she was panicked. In all the times she had been to Bletchley she had never noticed a railway crossing. 'Where are you taking me?'

'Don't worry, miss, you'll come to no harm.' The barrier rose and the car rumbled over the railway tracks to meet the road on the other side. Soon they were driving down country lanes made darker than night by overhanging trees.

Unable to see anything out of the side window, Ena leaned forward and craned her neck to look through the windscreen. From the small amount of illumination given off by the vehicle's shaded headlights, she could only see a few feet of road directly in front of them. 'I want to know where you're taking me!'

'My orders are to take you to the Goose Down Inn at Stoney Arden.'

'Where? It doesn't matter. Why are you taking me there?'

'I don't know, miss. Commander Dalton just said I was to take you there, and wait for you. When you're ready to leave, I'm to drive you back to Bletchley, to join Mr Silcott at the hotel.'

Ena relaxed a little. At least if she was being taken to an inn on orders from the commander she wasn't being kidnapped. She felt a slight jerk as the car accelerated.

For a while they travelled at a reasonable speed, then the car slowed and turned off the road.

'We're here, miss. The Goose Down Inn.'

Ena stepped out of the car, cautiously. 'Where am I to go?'

'The bar. By the back door.' The driver pointed across an expanse of ground, which Ena thought was a car park, to the corner of the building. 'Give the landlord your name. He's expecting you. More than that, miss, I wasn't told.'

'You will wait for me, won't you?'

The driver nodded.

Ena made for the corner of the building. Almost immediately, she saw a sliver of light radiating from a door that stood slightly ajar. She put her ear to it. She could hear the mumbling and chattering of people enjoying themselves. With caution, she pushed open the door, stepped inside, and closed it behind her.

From the dimly lit passageway, she saw elderly men sitting four to a table playing cards in a smog of pipe and cigarette smoke. She entered the room unnoticed. Ena had wondered how she'd know the landlord but there was only one man behind the bar. He wore an off-white cellarman's apron and stood at the end of the long counter, drying glasses. As she approached him, the man put down the glass and pushed the drying-up cloth into his belt. 'What can I get you, miss?'

'My name is Ena,' she whispered. And taking her purse from her handbag, said in a normal voice, 'Half of bitter please.'

The landlord pulled the beer but instead of passing it to her, said, 'I think you'd be more comfortable in the snug, miss. If you'd like to follow me?'

Ena dropped her purse back into her bag and with every nerve in her body tensed, her eyes alert, she allowed him to lead her out of the bar to a small entrance hall. The landlord crossed to a door, opened it, and entered. Ena followed. The room was dimly lit with tables and chairs along the walls. Behind her was a serving hatch with the word *Closed* on what looked like a blackout blind.

The landlord passed Ena her drink and nodded to the end of the room. A fire roared up a large chimney and there were armchairs on either side of it. Nervously Ena walked towards the vacant chairs. She was almost there when the snug door banged shut. Startled, she turned. The landlord had left.

Ena lowered herself onto the chair on the left. What had begun as nervousness had turned into fear. She kept telling herself that neither Commander Dalton nor Mr Silcott would put her in danger.

'Hello,' a familiar voice said from the darkness by the door.

Ena turned and peered in the direction of the voice, not daring to believe her ears. 'Henry?' As he walked towards her, the light from the fire lit up his face. Ena leapt to her feet and ran into his arms. 'I thought I'd never see you again!'

With his arms around her, Henry walked her back to her chair by the fire. Then he dragged the armchair from the other side of the hearth until it was next to Ena's, and sat down. Ena reached up, touched Henry's face, and smiled.

Henry took her hand, kissed it, and smiled back at her. It wasn't a happy smile. He looked tired, but it was more than that, much more. She was frightened of what the answer would be, but she had to ask. 'What is it, Henry? Now Walter and Freda have been caught it's over, isn't it?'

'No, Ena. It isn't over. It won't be over until the war is over.'

'But you're free. They must know you weren't involved, or you wouldn't be here.'

'Darling, you don't understand.'

'Then make me understand.'

Henry took a pack of Players and his lighter from his jacket pocket. He offered Ena a cigarette, which she drew from the pack with trembling hands. Henry lit hers before lighting his own.

She took a pull on the cigarette. She felt a little dizzy. She had inhaled too deeply. She leaned back in her chair, watched the man she loved smoke his cigarette, waiting for him to explain.

Henry looked into Ena's eyes. 'If I tell you, I could be putting your life in danger.'

'I don't care. I need to know. Just tell me, Henry.'

'Walter and I escaped. MI5 staged a breakout. Of course, Walter doesn't know they were involved, he thinks it was his idea, his resourcefulness. He has always been arrogant. But that's beside the point. I have to live and work with him until I know who the other members of the spy ring are.'

'Can't you tell him you've had enough? Say you've lost your nerve. Then he'd think you were a liability and be glad to see the back of you.'

'He would, but he'd never let me walk away, I know too much. He'd kill me rather than let me go.' Ena gasped in horror. 'Don't worry, darling, he won't hurt me. Without Frieda, he needs me.' Henry left his seat and pulled Ena into his arms. 'It's time you left,' he whispered.

'When shall I see you again?'

'You won't.' Ena tried to pull away from him, but he held her tightly. 'It's too dangerous for you, and for me.' Ena remembered the look of hate in Walter's eyes when he saw her in Frieda's seat on the train. She cast her eyes down. She understood. She didn't want to, but she did.

Henry lifted her chin and kissed her gently. 'Time to go.'

The feelings she had for him, the feelings that overwhelmed her on the night of the dance, came flooding back. She closed her eyes. 'I don't want to go. I love you, Henry, please don't send me away.' Ena stepped back. She looked into his face. 'Let me stay with you tonight.'

'There is nothing in the world that I would love more, but--'

'But what? Give me one good reason why two people who want to be together shouldn't be.'

'I can't think of one, I can think of several, and they're all dangerous.' Henry held her at arm's length. 'Are you sure?'

'Yes. I've never been more sure about anything. Can we get a room here?'

'I'm booked in for tonight. I'll check it's okay if you stay. If it is, I'll go out to Horace's driver and ask him to come back at nine in the morning. He won't like it that you're staying. Horace won't either, but since I don't work for him anymore, it will be you who will have to face his wrath the next time you see him.' Henry kissed Ena and left.

It felt like an age until Henry returned. 'I thought you'd run out on me,' Ena said.

'Never.' Holding Ena's hand, Henry led her out of the snug and along the corridor to a narrow staircase. 'The servants' stairs,' he whispered. 'Hope you don't mind, but you never know who's knocking about in the public area.'

They soon arrived at Henry's room. He took a key from his trousers pocket and unlocked the door. Turning to Ena, he put his finger to his lips and made the quietest shhhh sound before slowly pushing open the door and disappearing inside. Ena waited on the landing until Henry emerged some minutes later and beckoned her in. Closing the door quietly, he locked it behind her.

'Is this what it's going to be like for you from now on, Henry? Always on your guard. Checking every room, wherever you go?'

'Pretty much,' he said. Taking Ena by the hand, he sat her on the bed. 'I work for MI5,' he said, sitting next to her. 'I always have.'

'I thought you worked for Commander Dalton at Bletchley Park.'

'I did. The work they do at Bletchley Park is vital to us winning the war. I'm pleased I was able to contribute in a small way. But all the time I worked there, I answered to military intelligence. I was recruited by MI5 at university. The minute I realised Walter Voight was trying to turn me, I got in touch with them. Now, of course, Walter thinks he did turn me.'

Henry took Ena's hands in his. 'While I'm working undercover, on the run with Walter

Voight, I will be in constant danger.' Ena's eyes began to smart and she bit her lip. 'I'm not telling you this to frighten you, Ena, I'm telling you because for me to survive, I need to concentrate on the job a hundred percent. And I won't be able to do that if I'm worrying about you. So for my sake, as well as your own, when you leave here tomorrow you must forget about me.'

Ena looked into Henry's eyes, her own brimming with tears. 'That's tomorrow,' she said, and lifted her face to his. Henry kissed her tenderly on the lips. Ena responded by kissing him back, hungrily. 'I'm chilled to the bone,' she whispered. 'Take me to bed, Henry, and make love to me.'

Henry held Ena away from him, his handsome face full of concern. 'Are you sure?'

'Yes. It's what I've wanted since the first time I saw you at Bletchley, the day my work was stolen. I didn't know it then – my head was full of drugs. But when I was leaving and you called my name I felt something stir inside me that I have never felt before. At the time I confused it with the crush I had on you when I was a child. But I knew after the dance that what I felt for you was love. I feel it now. I'm in love with you, Henry.'

'But I can't be with you, Ena. Not tomorrow, or the next day, not even next year--'

'I know. I accept that. So why do you want to deny me your love tonight?'

'I don't,' he said, and without taking his eyes off her, Henry took off his clothes. Then he pulled her to her feet and undressed her. Together they threw back the bedclothes and climbed into the bed. Shivering – not from the cold, but from the excitement of being made love to for the first time – Ena snuggled up to Henry. He pulled the blankets up around her shoulders and held her until she relaxed. Then he made love to her slowly and gently, guiding her, and helping her to enjoy him as much as he was enjoying her.

Afterwards, glowing from their lovemaking, safe in Henry's arms, Ena said, 'I shall wait for you, Henry. The war can't go on forever. One day it will end and--'

'I don't want you to wait for me, Ena.' Henry eased himself up until he was half sitting and lent on his elbow. Looking into her face, he said, 'I want you to forget about me.'

'How can I forget about you? I love you, Henry. What am I supposed to do, forget tonight ever happened?'

'Yes. Because to survive the next however many years, I must forget about tonight. Damn it, Ena, if Walter Voight finds out I work for MI5, he'll go after anyone connected to me. He hates you already for exposing him and Frieda. God knows what he'd do if he knew I love you.' Henry reached for his cigarettes.

'Do you? Do you love me, Henry?'

'Yes. I do. But,' he said, after taking two cigarettes out of the pack, and lighting them, 'No one can know that I love you, or that we were here tonight. It has to be kept secret. There's too much at stake.'

As they lay together smoking, Ena said, 'I liked her, you know – Freda.'

Henry kissed the top of Ena's head. 'She liked you too.'

'Did she? Even though she made me think I'd killed a man. How could she do that if she liked me?'

'It was her way of getting you to trust her, making you beholden to her. She probably knew she couldn't turn you, so she needed something to hold over you. She'd have used it, too.'

'I still don't understand how she could have done such a wicked thing.'

'She did it for the Fatherland, the Führer, which is how she and Walter justify everything they do.'

'What will happen to her now? She'll go to prison, won't she?'

'Yes, but not for long. MI5 will interrogate her, then they'll try to turn her. They know she won't be turned, but it's part of the game.'

'Game?'

'Yes. A waiting game. They'll leave her to stew for a while, and then offer her a deal. Work for British Intelligence and you'll stay out of jail. Frieda will pretend to be outraged, but she'll do it because it's the only way she'll be free to look for Walter.'

'How will she justify spying for England to Walter, if she does find him?'

Henry laughed. 'She won't have to, because she won't stop working for Germany. She'll be a double agent. She'll work for both sides, or pretend to. We'll feed her what we want her to tell Germany, and they'll do the same. But let's not spend our last few hours together talking about

Frieda and Walter.'

'Let's not spend our last few hours talking,' Ena said. Giving Henry her cigarette to put out, she wriggled down in the bed, 'Brrrrr! It's cold out there. She pulled the covers over her head and snuggled into Henry's chest. When he had put out their cigarettes, he joined her under the covers and they made love again.

Ena didn't want to sleep. She wanted to spend every second until Henry had to leave looking at him, talking to him, making love. But her eyes grew tired and the more she tried to keep them open, the heavier they became. At last, spent in Henry's arms, Ena gave in and fell asleep.

When Ena woke the following morning, Henry had gone, as she knew he would have. She rolled over to his side of the bed and buried her head in his pillow. She felt tears stinging her eyes, but refused to cry.

She looked at her watch. It was ten to nine. When Henry sent Commander Dalton's driver away the night before, he had asked him to come back for her at nine. She had ten minutes to wash and dress.

In the cold, damp, room above the Goose Down Inn, Ena had given herself to the man she loved. As she closed the bedroom door, she knew in her heart – and in every fibre of her body – that she would see Henry again.

THE END

## Outline of the last book in The Dudley Saga

The fifth and final novel in the Dudley Sisters Saga, The Foxden Hotel, begins on New Year's Eve, ten years after the first novel, Foxden Acres. The Foxden Hotel brings the Dudley sisters, Bess, Margot, Claire, and Ena together with family and friends who feature in their individual stories.

On the night of the hotel's grand opening, an enemy from the war-years gatecrashes the celebrations. Recognised by the sisters and several of their guests, will the man get his comeuppance?

## ABOUT THE AUTHOR

Madalyn Morgan has been an actress for more than thirty years working in Repertory theatre, the West End, film and television. She is a radio presenter and journalist, writing articles for newspapers and magazines.

Madalyn was brought up in Lutterworth, at the Fox Inn. The pub was a great place for an aspiring actress and writer to live, as there were so many different characters to study and accents to learn. At twenty-four Madalyn gave up a successful hairdressing salon and wig-hire business for a place at E15 Drama College, and a career as an actress.

In 2000, with fewer parts available for older actresses, Madalyn taught herself to touch type, completed a two-year correspondence course with The Writer's Bureau, and started writing. After living in London for thirty-six years, she has returned to her home town of Lutterworth, swapping two window boxes and a mortgage, for a garden and the freedom to write.

Madalyn is currently writing her fifth novel, The Foxden Hotel. It is the last in a family saga of five books, about the lives of four very different sisters during The Second World War. The first four novels, Foxden Acres, Applause, China Blue, and The 9:45 To Bletchley are available on Amazon - e-Book and paperback.

Made in the USA
Charleston, SC
07 December 2016